Henry F. Brownson, Orestes A. Brownson

The Convert

Leaves from my experience

Henry F. Brownson, Orestes A. Brownson

The Convert
Leaves from my experience

ISBN/EAN: 9783337335458

Printed in Europe, USA, Canada, Australia, Japan

Cover: Foto ©Andreas Hilbeck / pixelio.de

More available books at **www.hansebooks.com**

THE CONVERT;

OR,

LEAVES FROM MY EXPERIENCE.

BY

O. A. BROWNSON.

A NEW EDITION EDITED BY
HENRY F. BROWNSON.

NEW YORK:
D. & J. SADLIER & CO., 31 BARCLAY STREET.
MONTREAL: 275 NOTRE DAME STREET.

TO THE

RIGHT REVEREND JOHN BERNARD FITZPATRICK, D. D.,

BISHOP OF BOSTON,

THIS UNPRETENDING VOLUME IS MOST RESPECTFULLY

DEDICATED AS A FEEBLE MARK OF THE VEN-

ERATION FOR HIS VIRTUES, AND THE

DEEP GRATITUDE FOR HIS SERVICES

TO THE CONVERT, CHERISHED

BY HIS SPIRITUAL

SON,

THE AUTHOR.

PREFACE

TO THE PRESENT EDITION.

It was the Author's intention in sending forth a new edition of "The Convert" to have added a new preface, wherein he would have shown the effect of eighteen additional years of Catholic life upon his views and his writings, and in which he would have made known the harmony of Catholic Theology with his more mature views of that Doctrine of Life which had led him to the threshold of the Catholic Church. He would have told those who, twenty and thirty years ago, were daily fore-telling his next change of faith, and who assumed that his was a restless mind that could never be made to work in subordination to the Catholic Church, that for thirty years no thought had ever entered his mind which could by any possibility be construed into a doubt of any doctrine of that Church, or a hesitation to obey her authority; that his mind was not restless, though ever active, and no more restricted in its freedom by the authoritative definitions of an infallible Church, than the cautious mariner by the charts and beacons that guide his course.

Reasonably believing the medical authority which promised him several years yet of useful work, he was about to revise such of his writings as he judged most deserving of republication, and had authorized this new edition of "The Convert;" but he had only corrected a few of the proof-sheets when his increasing infirmity forced him to lay aside the pen which his hand had wielded so powerfully for more than half a century. The revision and republication of his writings, as well as the editing of such unpublished works as were completed before his death, must, then, fall to the hands of one infinitely less able and experienced, although equally loyal to truth and to the Church.

The trials which the Author of "The Convert" had to pass through after his reception into the Church, were never such as could shake his faith in Catholic truth, or weaken his love for God and His Divine Spouse, the Church. Individuals could annoy him; and it was often a disappointment to find those who should have worked by his side with an eye single to the spread of truth and the enlightenment of the erring, turning aside at every impulse of jealousy or vanity, and giving reason to believe they cared less that the work should be done, than that it should be done by them or in their way. It is easy to conceive what must be the feelings of a man who has passed fifty years in the study of philosophy and theology, and acquired a world-wide reputation by his mastery of those sciences, when periodically assailed by a number of newspaper editors and correspondents gravely criticising, and, in a tone of authority, condemning doctrines, of the meaning of which they often had not the slightest conception. There was scarcely one of his critics who did not conceive himself more learned and profound than the writer whom he would put down with a "benign smile," or an assertion of superior knowledge. "In my country we dogs often attack lions."

As the Author became more familiar with the details of Catholic teaching and the writings of the Fathers and Doctors of the Church, the Doctrine of Life, which had prepared his mind for entering the Church, grew freely and expanded into a philosophical and theological system of amazing beauty and profound thought, as expressed in all his later writings. The grand harmony which he beheld between the natural and the supernatural orders, the analogy of the natural and the supernatural life, and the identity of that which is known and that which is, are the points on which he loved to insist. The reduction of the facts of the natural order to their principles, the fact of creation, was the object of his philosophy; and the reduction of all the facts of the supernatural order, articles, dogmas, and miracles, in turn, to their principles: the deification of the creature, the Incarnation,—was the aim of his theology. Such is, substantially, the last expression of his thought, that, as the Incarnation is impossible without the creation, so is creation impossible without the Incarnation. This denial of a natural end, or a natural beatitude for man, and the assertion that God created man for a supernatural end, although taught in the Catechism which the venerable Bishop of Boston put into his hands upon his conversion, was the first occasion of distrusting him by a learned body of Catholic teachers.

When the first news of the Syllabus of Pius IX reached this country, we had vague and inaccurate reports of its contents, and what errors were condemned by it. Many thought, in improbating ontologism, it affirmed psychologism, and enjoined the Scholastic processes and conclusions. The Author was startled at the news. It was hard for him to think the philosophy he had been insisting on was false, as he knew it must be if condemned by the Holy See; and he could hardly suspect that the Syllabus had been incorrectly reported. But when the full text was received, he found not a word in it to conflict with any doctrine he held in philosophy or Theology; nor does it condemn a single philosophical doctrine which the Author of "The Convert" had not, as he believed, already refuted.

It would be a most interesting study to examine in detail all the matters of difference which have existed between "The Convert" and the various schools, parties, and nationalities during the period which has elapsed since the publication of this book; but, on the other hand, it would revive many animosities, and might be the occasion of more harm than good at the present moment. The only object in now alluding to them at all is to repeat what he says of his earlier experience: that, whatever shortcomings he met with in himself or in others, though there was much to try him and to shake him, if he could have been shaken, there never entered his mind one doubt, one suspicion, of the truth of Catholicity.

On the other hand, during his Catholic life his most general experience was an enjoyment of sympathy and generous support from all ranks of Catholics, less noisy, indeed, than public opposition, but heartfelt, earnest, and encouraging. Nearly all of the Bishops and Clergy were his fast friends; and their friendship he esteemed as a rich reward for all his labors. As advancing years brought profounder knowledge of the truth, and clearer, deeper insight into the errors and vagaries of Protestantism and modern scientific infidelity, his love for the Church grew more and more fervent, and he blessed Almighty God daily more and more for the infinite goodness shown in rescuing him from his wanderings in the mazes of doubt and unbelief, and for bringing him to the clear light of truth in the bosom of the infallible Church.

H. F. BROWNSON.

Detroit, May 31st, 1876.

PREFACE.

THE volume here offered to the reading public is no work of fiction, and the person who gives an account of himself is no imaginary person around whom I have chosen to weave passages from my own experience. The person who tells his story is myself, and I have aimed to tell my story, so far as it bears on my religious convictions and experience, with simplicity, frankness, and truthfulness. The book, whatever else it may or may not be, is an honest book.

I have traced, with all the fidelity I am master of, my entire religious life from my earliest recollection down to my admission into the bosom of the Catholic Church. I have concealed none of my errors, disguised none of my changes, and sought to represent myself at no period as better or worse than I was. My aim has been, neither to vindicate nor to condemn myself, but simply to tell the truth.

Though I am the hero of my book, and speak in the first person, I trust the reader will not find me immoderately egotistic. I have not written to give myself importance in the eyes of the public, or from a feeling that my story, simply as mine, could have any great interest or value. Nearly all that is contained in the volume derives whatever value or importance it may have, from sources independent of my personality.

What is related as matter of fact, unless my memory has played me tricks, may be read with entire confidence.

The principles and reasonings set forth, and the judgments offered, speak for themselves, and must go for what they are worth. Truth is not mine, nor my reader's, and is the same whatever may be his or my opinions. It is above us both, and independent of us, and all that either of us should aim at is to ascertain and conform to it. I have no vocation to dogmatize or to teach. If what I say carries conviction, accept it ; if not, reject it, or suspend judgment till better informed.

The reader will at once perceive that my book is not designed to flatter one or another sect or party. I have expressed freely, frankly, unreservedly, my honest thought of persons and things that have come in my way, the results of my most careful observations and of my best judgment. I have not addressed my work especially to Catholics or to non-Catholics, but to the public at large. My purpose has been to render to all who may take an interest in the matter, an account of my conversion to Catholicity, and to enable the curious in such matters to discover the connecting link between my past and my present life, in order to enable them to discover the connecting link between nature and grace, the natural and the supernatural, and to perceive that, in becoming a Catholic, a man has no occasion to divest himself of his nature, or to forego the exercise of his reason.

In my reference to Catholic faith and doctrine, I believe I am orthodox; but in all such matters I recognize the Church, under God, as the only infallible teacher. I am a Catholic, and it would be in bad taste to seek to conceal or to disguise the fact. I have no wish to force my Catholic faith upon those who loathe its bare mention, but for myself I glory in it, and consider submission to the teaching of the Church the noblest exercise I can make of my reason and free-will.

My book, however, is the free production of my own mind, the free expression of my own honest convictions as formed by my experience, the inspiration of grace and the teachings of Catholic faith and theology, and may be taken by my readers as a specimen of that freedom which Catholicity secures to all her children.

The temper of the book, I hope, will be found acceptable to every class of readers,—free from all bitterness, harshness, or severity. It is not a controversial work, but a simple narrative, which may or may not carry with it a moral; and my aim has been to treat all of whom I have occasion to speak, with fairness and liberality, and to acknowledge cheerfully real worth wherever I find it. I may have erred in my judgments, but not from bigotry, prejudice, or an intolerant disposition.

I have aimed to tell my story simply, and to keep as clear as possible of all abstruse metaphysical or theological discussions; yet, as I had in some parts the profoundest problems of human life to deal with, and as my own path to the Church led through the field of philosophy, I have not been able wholly to avoid them, and there are parts of the work which will have little interest for those who read only for amusement. I have aimed to write an instructive, not an amusing, book.

The historian of the aberrations of human reason during the last half century will, if I am not much mistaken, find this volume not unworthy of his attention. The accounts I have given of the various sects, schools, and parties with which I came at different times in contact, together with the sketches I have ventured of their founders and chiefs, will be found, I think, devoid neither of interest nor value. These accounts and sketches might have been greatly extended, but I have made it a rule to confine myself to what served to illustrate my own story; and those contemporary movements and individuals that exerted little or no influence upon my own opinions or relations, I have passed over as foreign to my subject.

With these prefatory remarks, wholly unnecessary on my part, I commit my volume to the public to make or mar its fortune. It embodies no small portion of fifty years of an active, perhaps feverish, intellectual life, devoted to serious and earnest purposes; with what obstacles and with what results, it tells in a plain, unpretending style. In writing it, I have had occasion to review my whole past life, and to renew my thanks to Him who died that we might live, for having conducted me after so many wanderings, from the abyss of doubt and infidelity to the light and truth of His Gospel, in the bosom of His Church, where I find the peace and repose so long denied me.

THE AUTHOR.

New York, *September* 16, 1857.

CONTENTS.

CHAPTER IX.

CHAPTER X.

CHAPTER XI.

CHAPTER XII.

CHAPTER XIII.

CHAPTER XIV.

CHAPTER XV.

CHAPTER XVI.

CHAPTER XVII.

CHAPTER XVIII

CHAPTER XIX.

CHAPTER XX.

THE CONVERT.

CHAPTER I.

CHILDHOOD AND YOUTH.

I WAS born in the town of Stockbridge, Windsor County, Vermont, September 16, 1803. My father was a native of Hartford County, Connecticut; my mother of the beautiful village of Keene, New Hampshire. At the age of six years I was placed with an aged couple in the town of Royalton to be brought up. The man, when I went to live with him, was upwards of sixty; his wife was about fifty. They were plain country people, living on a small farm, and supporting themselves by their own industry. They had been brought up in New England Congregationalism, were honest, upright, strictly moral, and far more ready to suffer wrong than to do wrong, but had no particular religion, and seldom went to meeting.

I was treated with great kindness and affection, and as well brought up as could be expected from persons in their condition of life. They taught me to be honest, to owe no one anything but good-will, to be frugal and industrious, to speak the truth, never to tell a lie under any circumstances, or to take what was not my own, even to the value of a pin; to keep the Sabbath, and never to let the sun go down on my wrath. In addition they taught me the Shorter Catechism, the Apostles' Creed, the Lord's Prayer, and a short evening prayer in rhyme, which ran,

> "Now I lay me down to sleep,
> I pray the Lord my soul to keep;
> If I should die before I wake
> I pray the Lord my soul to take."

Properly speaking I had no childhood, and have more of the child in my feelings now than at eight or ten years of age. Brought up with old people, and debarred from all the sports, plays, and amusements of children, I had the manners, the tone, and tastes of an old man before I was a boy. A sad misfortune; for children form one another, and should always be suffered to be children as long as possible. Both childhood and youth are quite too short with us, and the morals and manners of the country suffer from it.

I early learnt to read, and was from my earliest recollection fond of reading; but we had few books, and our neighbors had fewer. Our family library consisted of a Protestant version of the Scriptures, a London edition; Watts's *Psalms* and *Divine Songs*, and *The Franklin Primer*, to which were subsequently added Edwards's *History of Redemption*;

Davies's *Sermons*; a History of the Indian Wars, by a Dr. Sanders, I believe, at one time President of the Vermont University at Burlington; a mutilated copy of *Philip Quarle*, a work of fiction, written in imitation of Defoe's *Robinson Crusoe*; and during the war of 1812 with Great Britain, a weekly newspaper, published in Windsor by Alden Spooner. My reading was confined to these works, and principally to the Scriptures, all of which I had read through before I was eight, and a great part of which I knew by heart before I was fourteen years old.

My thoughts from my earliest recollection took a religious turn, and my greatest pleasure was in conversing, or in hearing others converse, on the subject of religion. When about nine years old, I was permitted to accompany a much older boy to " the middle of the town," about four miles distant from our residence, to witness a muster, or general training of a brigade of militia. On returning home, I was asked what I had seen to interest me. I answered that I had seen two old men talking on religion. In fact, I was so much interested in their discussion that I quite forgot the soldiers, though I came of a military family, and almost forgot to eat my card of gingerbread. The discussion, I remember, was on free-will and election, and I actually took part in it, stoutly maintaining free-will against Edwards, who confounds volition with judgment, and maintains that the will is necessarily determined by the state of the affections and the motives presented to the understanding.

The simple history of the Passion of our Lord, as I read it in the Evangelists, affected me deeply. I hung with delight on the Mystery of Redemption, and my young heart often burned with love to our Blessed Lord, who had been so good as to come into the world, and to submit to the most cruel death of the cross that he might save us from our wicked dispositions, and make us happy forever in heaven. I wanted to know everything about him, and I used to think of him frequently in the day and the night. Sometimes I seemed to hold long familiar conversations with him, and was deeply pained when anything occurred to interrupt them. Sometimes, also, I seemed to hold a spiritual intercourse with the Blessed Mary, and with the holy Angel Gabriel, who had announced to her that she was to be the mother of the Redeemer. I was rarely less alone than when alone. I did not speculate on the matter. It all seemed real to me, and I enjoyed often an inexpressible happiness. I preferred to be alone, for then I could taste the sweets of silent meditation, and feel that I was in the presence of Jesus and Mary, and the holy angels; yet I had not been baptized, and had very little instruction except such as I had obtained from reading the Holy Scriptures.

The earliest wish I recollect to have formed with regard to my future life, was to be a minister of religion, and to devote myself to the work of bringing people to the knowledge and the love of God. For this, I longed to go to school, to get learning, to grow up, and to be a man. I early looked upon myself as one called and set apart to the service of religion. I had an irritable temper, and was subject to violent outbreaks of passion, but I tried hard to control myself, and neither to do nor to think anything wrong, and, till I was man grown, I do not believe I ever suffered the sun to go down upon my wrath. I had my faults as well as others, and did many things which were by no means right or excusable; but my conscience was active, and I always felt a deep remorse for them, and was ready always to do all in my power, to submit to any humiliation however great, to repair the faults I committed, or the wrongs I did. I always felt that the next best thing to never doing wrong, was to own the wrong done, and endeavor to undo it. So it was with me in my childhood, till I was fourteen years of age, when I left the kind old people, who had thus far brought me up, and went forth into the world alone, to make my way as best I could.

My youth was not as blameless as my childhood, and it was far less happy. Religion, however, never lost its place in my thoughts. But unhappily, while I had strong religious affections and the elements of Christian belief, I belonged to no Church, and had no definite creed. True, I had been taught the Shorter Catechism, but I was not taught it as something I must believe; and I soon learned that they who taught it to me did not themselves believe it. True, also, I was taught the Apostles' Creed, but I was not required to believe it, and received no instructions as to its sense. I probably did believe, however, the greater part of it. I believed in God the Father Almighty; that Jesus Christ was his only begotten Son; that he was conceived of the Holy Ghost, born of the Virgin Mary, was crucified by the wicked Jews, under Pontius Pilate, was dead, and buried; that he rose again from the dead on the third day; that he ascended into heaven; that he sitteth at the right hand of the Father Almighty, whence he shall come to judge the quick and the dead. I believed in the Holy Ghost; the forgiveness of sins for Christ's sake; the resurrection of the body, and the life everlasting. But to the articles of the Creed affirming the Holy Catholic Church, and the Communion of Saints, I attached no meaning; my attention was not called to them; and not till long years after, did it occur to me to ask whether they meant any thing or nothing.

There is no doubt that I was well disposed to believe, and that, if I had been properly instructed in the Christian faith, I should have heartily received it, and held as fast to it as an unbaptized person, as one who is only a catechumen, can do; but, as it was, I attached very little definite meaning to what I was taught, and was open to any kind of influences by which I was surrounded. Nobody, however, told me that baptism was necessary; and nobody told me any thing about the Church. The most I was told was, that I must "get religion," "experience religion," have "a change of heart," "be born again;" but how that was to be brought about, I could not understand. I took it for granted that I had not experienced religion, and I really wished I might be born again; but how I could be born again, or what I was to do in order to be born again, nobody explained to my understanding.

In the town in which I lived we had Congregationalists, called in my young days, "The Standing Order," Methodists, Baptists, Universalists, and Christians, or, as they insisted on the word being pronounced, *Christ-yans*. The Congregational meeting-house was four miles distant from our house, in the middle of the town, and we never attended it. The Methodists and *Christ*ians, a sect founded in New England by one Elias Smith, and one Abner Jones, in the year 1800, if I mistake not, held their meetings near by us, sometimes in a school-house, sometimes in private houses; and in the summer season, not unfrequently in a very pleasant grove. The Universalists were few, and so were the Baptists. The Methodists and Christians were the more numerous. I usually attended their meetings. They differed, I was told; but the only difference I could discover between them was, that the Methodist preachers appeared to have the stronger lungs; they preached in a louder tone, and when they preached, the people shouted more. I thought them the best, because they made the most noise, and gave the most vivid pictures of hell-fire, and the tortures of the damned. All I learned, however, from either was, that I must be born again or go to hell, get religion or be damned. The more I listened to them, the more I feared hell, and the less I loved God.

Love gave place to terror; and I became constantly afraid that the devil would come and carry me off bodily. I tried to get religion, and at times almost made up my mind to submit to the Methodists, and let them "bring me out."

One of our neighbors, an elderly woman, who had seen better days, had been well brought up and well educated, was a Congregationalist, a stanch adherent to the Standing Order. She was now very poor, and lived in a miserable log-hut on one corner of our farm, and was treated generally by our neighbors with great contempt, because she insisted on maintaining her self-respect and personal dignity, notwithstanding her poverty. I had a great affection for her, because I found her a woman of intelligence and refinement. I visited her one evening, when I was in great distress of mind, and told her my fears and my resolutions. She heard me with great patience, till I had concluded my story.

"My poor boy," she replied, "God has been good to you, and has no doubt gracious designs towards you. He means to use you for a purpose of his own, and you must be faithful to his inspirations. But go not with the Methodists or with any of the sects. They are New Lights, and not to be trusted. The Christian religion is not new, and Christians have existed from the time of Christ. These New Lights are of yesterday. You yourself know the founder of the *Christian* sect, and I myself knew personally both George Whitfield and John Wesley, the founders of Methodism. Neither can be right, for they come too late, and have broken off, separated from the body of Christians, which subsisted before them. When you join any body calling itself a Christian body, find out and join one that began with Christ and his apostles, and has continued to subsist the same without change of doctrine or worship down to our own times. You will find the true religion with that body, and nowhere else. Join it, obey it, and you will find rest and salvation. But beware of sects and New Lights: they will make you fair promises, but in the end will deceive you to your own destruction."

I was some twelve years old at the time, but the words made a deep impression upon my mind. They struck me as reasonable and just; and I think they prevented me from ever being a genuine, hearty Protestant, or a thorough-going radical even. She was not a Catholic, but her argument is one which, though I knew it not then, none save a Catholic can consistently urge. She was sincerely a Congregationalist, and held only the views which in my boyhood were generally insisted on by the old Standing Order of New England. However erroneous were the views of the New-England Puritans, they retained a conception of the Church of Christ, held that Christ had himself founded a Church, established its order, and given it its ordinances, and taught that it was necessary to belong to it in order to be saved. The loose notions of the Church, the humanism and transcendentalism, now so common among their descendants, were then unknown. They were as rigid and as consistent churchmen in their way as the Anglicans, and even more so.

But time went on, and after I was fourteen years of age, I was thrown upon a new world, into the midst of new and strange scenes, and exposed to new and corrupting influences. I fell in with new sectaries, universalists, deists, atheists and nothingarians, as they are called with us, who profess no particular religion. I still held fast to the belief in my need of religion, and there were times when my earlier feelings revived, and I enjoyed my silent meditations. But my young head became confused with the contradictory opinions I heard advanced, with the doubts and denials to which I listened, and for a time my mind was darkened, and I half persuaded myself that all religion was a delusion—the work of priestcraft or statecraft. I was in a labyrinth of doubt, with no Ariadne's thread to guide me out to the light of day. I was miserable, and knew not where to turn for relief. I felt that my own reason was insufficient to guide me; and the more I attempted by it alone to arrive at truth, the farther I went astray, and the more uncertain and perplexed I became.

One day, when I was about nineteen years of age, I was passing by a Presbyterian meeting-house. It was Sunday, and the people were gathering for the service. The thought struck me that I would go in and join with them. It was a beautiful September day, in Malta, Saratoga County, New York. The air was soft and balmy, the sky was clear and serene, and it seemed as if all nature was enjoying its sweet Sabbath-day repose. I went into the meeting-house: it was long since I had been in a place of worship. The singing was, perhaps, not very good, but it soothed me, while it affected me even to tears. I listened reverently to the reading of the Scriptures, to the prayer, and to the sermon. There was nothing in the sermon that I remember. It was a common-place affair. But I went out from that meeting-house much affected, and feeling that I had missed my way. As I pursued my journey, I could not help asking myself what I had gained by my speculations, and why it was that I must have no sympathy with my kind; why I must stand alone, and find no belief to sustain me, and have no worship to refresh me ?

I have, said I, in my self-communing, done my best to find the truth, to experience religion, and to lead a religious life, yet here I am without faith, without hope, without love. I know not what to believe. I know not what to do. I know not whence I came, why I am here, or whither I go. My life is a stream that flows out of darkness into darkness. The world is dark to me, and not a ray of light even for one instant relieves it. My heart is sad, and I see nothing to hope for, or to live for. For me heaven is dispeopled, and the earth is a desert, a barren waste. Why is this so ? Why does my heart rebel against the speculations of my mind ? If doubt is all there is for me, why cannot I discipline my feelings into submission to it ? Why this craving to believe, when there is nothing to be believed ? Why this longing for sympathy, when there is nothing to respond to my heart ? Why this thirst for an unbounded good, when there is no good, when all is a mere show, an illusion, and nothing is real ? Have I not mistaken my way ?

Was I not told in the outset that, if I followed my own reason, it would lead me astray, that I should lose all belief, and find myself involved in universal doubt and uncertainty ? Has it not been so ? In attempting to follow the light of reason alone, have I not lost faith, lost the light of revelation, and plunged myself into spiritual darkness ? I did not believe what these people said, and, yet, were they not right ? They were. They told me to submit my reason to revelation. I will do so. I am incapable of directing myself. I must have a guide. I will hear the Church. I will surrender, abnegate my own reason, which hitherto has only led me astray, and make myself a member of the Church, and do what she commands me.

In a few days I told my experience to the Presbyterian minister of the town where I was pursuing my academic studies, went the same day, at his request, and told it to the Session of his church, and the Sunday following was baptized and received into the Presbyterian communion. I did not ask whether the Presbyterian Church was the true Church or not, for the Church question had not yet been fairly raised in my mind ; and as it did not differ essentially from the Standing Order, and claimed to be the true

Church, and was counted respectable, I was satisfied. What it believed was of little consequence, since I had resolved to abnegate my own reason, and take the Church for my guide. My proceeding was precipitate, but after all was not rash, for it was logical, and justified by the resolution I had taken. So in October, 1822, I became a member of the Presbyterian church, Ballston, Saratoga County, New York.

CHAPTER II.

PRESBYTERIAN EXPERIENCE.

THE Monday following my reception into the Presbyterian communion we had a covenant meeting, or a meeting of all the members of the church. The Presbyterians, like most of the Protestant sects in this country, adopt the doctrine of the old Donatists, that the Church is composed of the elect, the just, or the saints only, and they therefore distinguish between the church and the congregation, or between those who are held to be saints, and those held to be sinners; that is, between those who profess to have been regenerated, and those who make no such pretension, although they may have been baptized. The church members, to the number of about six hundred, came together on Monday, and after being addressed by the pastor, and stirred up to greater zeal for the promotion of Presbyterianism, renewed their covenant obligations, and bound themselves to greater efforts for the conversion of sinners, the common name given to all not of the sect, even though members of the congregation, and born of Presbyterian parents. In this meeting we all solemnly pledged ourselves, not only to pray for the conversion of sinners, but to mark them wherever we met them, to avoid them, to have no intercourse with them that could be helped, and never to speak to them except to admonish them of their sins, or so far as it should be necessary on business.   There was to be no interchange of social or neighborly visits between us and them, and we were to have even business relations with them only when absolutely necessary. We were by our manner to show all, not members of the Presbyterian Church, that we regarded them as the enemies of God, and therefore as our enemies, as persons hated by God, and therefore hated by us; and we were, even in business relations, always to give the preference to church members, and, as far as possible, without sacrificing our own interests, to treat those not members as outcasts from society, as pariahs; and thus, by appeals to their business interests, their social feelings, and their desire to stand well in the community, to compel them to join the Presbyterian Church.   The meeting was animated by a singular mixture of bigotry, uncharitableness, apparent zeal for God's glory, and a shrewd regard to the interests of this world.

About the time I speak of, and for several years after, meetings of the sort I have described, were common in the Presbyterian churches; and a movement was made, in 1827, to induce all the members throughout the Union to pledge themselves to nonintercourse with the rest of the community, except for their conversion, and to refuse in the common business affairs of life to patronize any one not a member of the church.   How far it succeeded, I am not informed; but as, taking the country at large, the Presbyterians were but a small minority, and by no means able to control its business operations, I suppose it was only partially successful, and its abettors had to soften their rules a little so as to bring within the privileged the members of the other Evangelical sects.

It may readily be believed that the exhibition I saw was not over and above pleasing to me, and that it was only with a wry face that I took the pledges with the rest. I was in for it, and I would do as the others did. I saw at once that I had made a mistake, that I had no sympathy with the Presbyterian spirit, and should need a long and severe training to sour and elongate my visage sufficiently to enjoy the full confidence of my new brethren. Every day's experience proved it. In our covenant we had bound ourselves to watch over one another with fraternal affection. I was not long in discovering that this meant that we were each to be a spy upon the others, and to rebuke, admonish, or report them to the Session. My whole life became constrained. I dared not trust myself, in the presence of a church member, to a single spontaneous emotion; I dared not speak in my natural tone of voice, and if I smiled, I expected to be reported. The system of espionage in some European countries is bad enough, and it is no pleasant reflection that the man you are talking with may be a *mouchard*, and report your words to the *Préfet de Police;* but that is nothing to what one must endure as a Presbyterian, unless he has enough of malignity to find an indemnification for being spied in spying others. We were allowed no liberty, and dared enjoy ourselves only by stealth. The most rigid Catholic ascetic never imagined a discipline a thousandth part as rigid as the discipline to which I was subjected. The slightest deviation was a mortal sin, the slightest forgetfulness was enough to send me to hell. I must not talk with sinners; I must take no pleasure in social intercourse with persons, however moral, amiable, well-bred, or worthy, if not members of the Church; I was forbidden to read books written by others than Presbyterians, and commanded never to inquire into my belief as a Presbyterian, or to reason on it, or about it.

I tried for a year or two to stifle my discontent, to silence my reason, to repress my natural emotions, to extinguish my natural affections, and to submit patiently to the Calvinistic discipline. I spent much time in prayer and meditation, I read pious books, and finally plunged myself into my studies with a view of becoming a Presbyterian minister. But it would not do. I had joined the Church because I had despaired of myself, and because, despairing of reason, I had wished to submit to authority. If the Presbyterian Church had satisfied me that she had authority, was authorized by Almighty God to teach and direct me, I could have continued to submit; but while she exercised the most rigid authority over me, she disclaimed all authority to teach me, and remitted me to the Scriptures and private judgment. "We do not ask you to take this as your creed,"

said my pastor, on giving me a copy of the Presbyterian Confession of Faith ; " we do not give you this
as a summary of the doctrines you must hold, but as
an excellent summary of the doctrines which we believe the Scriptures teach. What you are to believe
is the Bible. You must take the Bible as your
creed, and read it with a prayerful mind, begging
the Holy Ghost to aid you to understand it aright."
But while the Church refused to take the responsibility of telling me what doctrines I must believe,
while she sent me to the Bible and private judgment,
she yet claimed authority to condemn and excom-
municate me as a heretic, if I departed from the
standard of doctrine contained in her Confession.

This I regarded as unfair treatment. It subjected
me to all the disadvantages of authority without any
of its advantages. The Church demanded that I
should treat her as a true mother, while she was free
to treat me only as a stepson, or even as a stranger.
Be one thing or another, said I ; either assume the
authority and the responsibility of teaching and
directing me, or leave me with the responsibility my
freedom. If you have authority from God, avow it,
and exercise it. I am all submission. I will hold
what you say, and do what you bid. If you
have not, then say so, and forbear to call me
to an account for differing from you, or disregarding
your teachings. Either bind me or loose me. Do
not mock me with a freedom which is no freedom,
or with an authority which is illusory. If you claim
authority over my faith, tell me what I must believe,

and do not throw upon me the labor and responsibility of forming a creed for myself; if you do not,
if you send me to the Bible and private judgment,
to find out the Christian faith the best way I can,
do not hold me obliged to conform to your standards,
or assume the right to anathematize me for departing
from them.

My position was a painful one, and I could not
endure it. I had gained nothing, but lost much, by
joining the Presbyterian Church. I had given up the
free exercise of my own reason for the sake of an
authoritative teacher, and had obtained no such
teacher. I had despaired of finding the truth by
my own reason, and had now nothing better, nor
so good, because I could not exercise it freely.
Certainly I had been too hasty, and reckoned without
my host. After all, what reason had I to regard this
Presbyterian Church as the true Church of Christ?
"Go not after the New Lights," said my old Congre-
ationalist friend. Are not these Presbyterians New
Lights, as much as the Methodists and the Christians?
If our Lord founded a Church and has a Church on
earth, it must reach back to his time, and come down
in unbroken succession from the apostles. But the
Presbyterian Church is a recently formed body, not
three hundred years old. It was founded in Scotland
by men who had been Roman Catholics, and who had
deserted the faith in which they had been reared; and
in England, by men who had belonged to the Church
of England, which itself had broken off from the
Catholic Church. Were these men authorized by

an express commission from God ? Did they act by
authority ? or did they follow their own private
judgment, and against the authority which they had
previously recognized ? The latter certainly. Then
what reason have I for regarding the church they
founded as the Church of Christ ?

I was answered that the Church of Christ had become corrupt, and been for a long series of ages perverted to a papistical and prelatical Church, and these
men were reformers, and simply labored to restore
the Church to its primitive purity and simplicity.
But had they a warrant from Christ to do that ? Or
did they act on their own responsibility, without
warrant ? If you say the former, where is the proof ?
If the latter, how can their acts bind me ? Am not I
a man, and as a man have I not as much right
to follow my private opinion as they had to follow
theirs ? But they follow the Bible. Be it so. But
was it the Bible as they understood it, or as it was
understood by their Catholic predecessors and contemporaries ?—You forget, the Catholic Church rejected the Bible, and did not follow it at all.—Yet
she preserved the Bible and taught that it was given
by inspiration of God, and it was from her that the
Reformers got it. She did not own that she rejected
the Scriptures, or that she taught, or allowed anything to be taught, inconsistent with them. How
know I that her understanding of the Bible was not
as good as the understanding of it by the Reformers ?
They thought differently from her, but were they
infallible? If they had a right to break from her and

set up their private understanding of Scripture, why have I not the right to break from them and from the Presbyterian Church, follow my private under standing, and set up a church of my own?

It was clear to me that the Presbyterian Church, though the church of one class of the Reformers, was not and could not be the Church of Christ, and therefore it could have no legitimate authority over me. If Christ had a church on earth which he had founded, and which had authority to teach in his name, it was evidently the Roman Catholic Church. But that Church, of course, was out of the question. It was everything that was vile, base, odious, and demoralizing. It had been condemned by the judgment of mankind, and the thought of becoming a Roman Catholic found and could find at that time no entrance into my mind. I should sooner have thought of turning Jew, Mahometan, Gentoo, or Buddhist. What, then, was I to do? There was no alternative. It was the Catholic Church or no Church. All the so-called Protestant churches were New Lights, were of yesterday, founded by fallible men, without any warrant from God, without any authority but their private interpretation of Scripture. I cannot accept any one of them as having any authority to teach or direct me. Being the work of men, honest men, learned men, pious men, if you will, they have no authority over my conscience, and no right to hold me amenable to them. Then, since I cannot be a Catholic, I must be a no-church man, and deny all churches, make war upon every sect claiming the slightest authority in matters of faith or conscience.

I was at this time about twenty-one years of age. The question with me was not what, but whom, I was to believe ; not what doctrines I must embrace, but what authority I was to obey, or on what authority I was to take my belief. As to particular doctrines, they did not trouble me. I paid very little attention to them. I regarded them of minor consideration, and never entered very deeply into their investigation. The important thing with me, from the first, was, to find out the rule of faith. I had not found it in my youthful and uninformed reason, and had submitted to the Presbyterian Church, hoping to find it in her authority. I failed to find it there, and, the Catholic Church being out of the question, I was forced, by the necessity of the case, to fall back on the Scriptures interpreted by my own private judgment for myself.

In becoming a Presbyterian on the ground I did, I committed a mistake, and placed myself in a false position, which it took me years to rectify. It was a capital blunder. Not that I was insincere, or governed by bad motives, but because, feeling the insufficiency of my own reason to guide me, I turned my back on reason, and took up with what I supposed to be authority without a rational motive for believing it divinely commissioned. As far as I could, I abnegated my own rational nature, denied reason to make way for revelation, rational conviction to make way for authority. Unhappily, the religious belief of my Protestant countrymen, as far as religious belief they have, is built on skepticism, and hence, if they think at all, they have a perpetual struggle in their minds between faith and reason. The two are presented, not each as the other's complement, but as antagonistical, the one to advance only over the dead body of the other. All those with whom I came into relation, either denied reason to make way for revelation, or revelation to make way for reason. At least such was their tendency. The one class declaimed against reason, used reason against reason, and sometimes assigned, apparently, a very good reason why reason ought not to be used. The other class either openly denied all supernatural revelation, or, admitting it in words, explained away all its supernaturalness, and brought it within the sphere of the natural order, and subjected it to the dominion of natural reason.

This was the natural result of Calvinism, which was the dominant doctrine of the American people; and, so far as they have any notions of Christianity at all as a revealed religion, the great majority of them, whether they accept or reject it, are even yet Calvinists. They apprehend Christianity always through Calvinistic spectacles, and under Calvinistic forms. The fundamental doctrine of Calvinism is, that man by his fall lost his natural spiritual faculties, and became totally depraved, incapable by nature of any thing but sin. Grace is conceived therefore as opposed to nature, and revelation as opposed to reason. A nature that is totally depraved cannot be redeemed, but must be supplanted or superseded by grace; a totally depraved reason is incapable of a rational act, and therefore revelation cannot be addressed to it to supply its weakness, or to place it in relation with truth lying in an order above its natural reach; but, if conceived at all, must be conceived as a substitute for reason, as discarding reason, and taking its place. Hence it is my countrymen, receiving their first notions of Christianity through Calvinism, are never able to reconcile faith and reason, or to harmonize nature and grace. They feel, against the dictates of common-sense, that they must either deny the one or the other. Some try to assert both, but find that their life is one of painful struggle precisely where peace and repose are promised by the Gospel.

In general, those Protestants commonly called Orthodox, when they are sincere and earnest, when their religion is not put on or retained for a sinister purpose, retain their belief only by refusing to examine its grounds. The eminent Dr. Payson, one of the most distinguished Calvinistic ministers of New England in the first half of the present century, records in his diary his temptations to doubt even the Divine existence, and says that the devil suggested to him arguments against the existence of God, which, if published, would shake the faith of more than one half of Christendom. I cite from memory, but believe his expression was much stronger. My own Presbyterian pastor told me, time and again, not to allow myself to read any book touching the grounds of my belief as a Presbyterian, or even to think on the subject. Large numbers of Calvinists, in their confidential intercourse with me, have assured me that the only way in which they could retain their faith, their belief even in revelation, was by refusing, even in their own minds, to reason on the subject. Their belief, as far as belief they have, is and must be a blind belief, an effort of the will alone, without any assent of the understanding; for they start with the assumption that reason is totally depraved, and therefore a false light, a deceptive guide. The gravest objection to Calvinism is its denunciation of reason, and its attempt to build up a system of theology on revelation made to an irrational subject.

God gave me reason, I said, in my self-communings. It is my distinguishing faculty, and to abnegate it is to surrender my essential character as a man, and to sink myself, theoretically, to the level of the brute creation. Revelation, if revelation there be, must be made to me as a man, as a rational subject. Take away my reason, and you can as well make a revelation to an ox or a horse, a pig or an ass, as to me. It demands reason to receive revelation, and the natural to receive the supernatural. If there is no natural, there can be no supernatural. If I am totally depraved, I am incapable of being redeemed; and if my reason is deceptive and never to be trusted, how am I to know that what I take to be revelation is revelation? It is God's word, you say, and God cannot lie. But how am I to know that it is God's word, or that there is any God at all, if my reason is totally depraved, and to be discarded as a false light? No, no, it will not do. We cannot build faith on skepticism; and just in proportion as we discredit reason, we must discredit revelation. Reason must at least be the preamble to faith, and nature must precede and be presupposed by grace.

I must then, I continued, revoke the act of surrender which I made of my reason to authority on entering the Presbyterian Church; for it was an irrational, an unmanly act. I offered in it no reasonable obedience or submission to God. It was a blind submission, and really no submission of my reason at all. It was a cowardly act, the act of an intellectual desperado, although the motive was good. I reclaim my reason, I reclaim my manhood, and henceforth I will, let come what may, be true to my reason, and preserve the rights and dignity of my human nature. This resolution, of course, separated me from Presbyterianism. The peculiar Presbyterian doctrines I had never believed or professed to believe, except on the authority of the Presbyterian Church. Grant her authority from God to teach, I was logician enough to understand that I must believe whatever she taught, whether I could or could not reconcile it with my own reason. That authority taken away, then I was not bound to believe her doctrines, unless I found reasons for doing so elsewhere.

The doctrine of unconditional election and reprobation, and the doctrine that God foreordains the wicked to sin necessarily, that he may damn them justly, I found difficult to swallow, and still more difficult to digest. My honest pastor told me that he regarded the doctrine as a hard doctrine, as revolting to human nature, and he had tried in the General Assembly of the Presbyterian Church, in 1821, to get it modified, or rescinded altogether, but failed by one or two votes. The doctrine was repugnant to my reason ; and having settled it, that revelation could never contain any thing repugnant to reason, I rejected it without taking the trouble to inquire whether it was Scriptural or not. It is unreasonable, it is unjust, and therefore cannot be taught in the Scriptures, if they are written by Divine inspiration. When a Presbyterian, I simply asked : What does the Presbyterian Church teach ? But having discovered that the Presbyterian Church was a self-created body, and without any authority from God, and having adopted reason as my test or criterion of truth, I asked simply : What is or is not contrary to reason ?

I felt, as every thinking man feels and always must feel, that reason is insufficient, and that, with no other guide, it is impossible to attain to all truth, or always to avoid all error; but it was the best guide I had, and all I could do was to exercise it freely and honestly upon all subjects,—to give it fair play, and abide the result. I did not absolutely reject the Scriptures, nor absolutely accept them. As the word of God, they were infallible; but they were and could be the word of God only in the sense intended by the Holy Ghost, and that sense I

had no infallible means of ascertaining. I could not,
then, feel myself bound by the strict letter of the
Scriptures, and felt that I had a right to interpret
them by my own understanding, and to explain
them in accordance with the dictates of natural
reason. I consequently, without rejecting them,
attenuated their practical authority, and made reason a rule for them, instead of taking them, as the
believer must, as a rule for reason. I thus passed
from so-called Orthodox Christianity to what is sometimes denominated Liberal Christianity. This was
my first notable change,—a change from a Super-
naturalist to a Rationalist. In fact, it should not be
regarded so much as a change as the commencement
of my intellectual life, for I was as yet only twenty-
one years of age.

CHAPTER III.

I DID not leave Presbyterianism because I had found another church, or another system of doctrine, perfectly satisfactory to my reason—one by which I felt I could be willing to live and die. I rejected Presbyterianism because I had no good reason for holding it, and because it could not meet the want I felt of an authoritative teacher. It did not even claim to be infallible, conceded that it might err, and could not give any proof that it had been instituted by Christ and his apostles, or that its founders acted under a divine commission. These were sufficient reasons for not continuing a Presbyterian, but not for embracing any other particular sect. Where, then, was I to go? What was I to believe?

I was unwilling to be an unbeliever, and felt deeply the need of having a religion of some sort. What should it be? Liberal Christianity was a vague term, and presented nothing definite or positive. Its chief characteristic was the denial of what was called Orthodoxy, and taking nature and reason for the rule of faith. The only definite form under which I was acquainted with it was that of Universalism, then far less generally diffused than it is now. Prior to becoming a Presbyterian, I had read several Universalist books, and been initiated into the mysteries of Universalism by a sister of my mother, who had in her youth listened to the preaching of Dr. Elhanan Winchester, one of the earliest Universalist preachers in America. Dr. Winchester had been a Calvinistic Baptist minister, and had, while a Baptist, acquired considerable reputation as a zealous, fervent, and eloquent preacher,—a reputation which recalled and almost rivalled that of the famous George Whitfield, one of the original Oxford Methodists. He preached in various parts of the United States and Great Britain, and stood very high with his sect. At the very height of his success as a Baptist, he began to doubt the doctrine of endless punishment. Inquiry led him to reject it, and to embrace the doctrine of the final salvation or restoration of all men, and even of the fallen angels, thus reviving the doctrine said to have been held by Origen in the third century, though probably so said without sufficient warrant. He preached and wrote much in defence of his favorite tenet, and, though preceded by that eccentric Irishman, John Murray, the first who avowedly preached universal salvation in the United States, he may be justly regarded as the founder of American Universalism. He had some pretensions to learning, but no philosophy, and very little theological science. He wrote several books in defence of Universal Restoration, among which his *Dialogues*, his *Lectures on the Prophecies*, borrowed in great part from a work on the same subject by Dr. Thomas Newton, an Anglican divine, I believe, and an Epic Poem, celebrating the Triumph of the Empire of Christ, were the more noticeable. I forget the exact title of the poem, but I remember that the author tells us in the preface that it was written in the course of three months, during his leisure moments, although it makes a good-sized duodecimo volume in close print, and that, if he had devoted all his time to it, he could have written it in a much briefer period. I recollect nothing in the poem to throw any doubt on this statement. The poem certainly was not equal to the Iliad, Paradise Lost, or the *Divina Commedia*, and not much superior to the Fredoniad or the Napolead, —two of our many American Epics known, I fear, to very few American readers.

My aunt had placed these works in my hands when I was between fourteen and fifteen years of age, and aided by her brilliant and enthusiastic commentaries, they had shaken my early belief in future rewards and punishments, and unsettled my mind on the most important points of Christian faith. Besides the works of Mr. Winchester, I had also read a work on Universal Salvation, by Dr. Chauncy, a learned and highly esteemed Congregationalist minister in the last century, in Boston, Massachusetts. Dr. Chauncy was the son of President Chauncy of Harvard College, and was born in Boston, January 1, 1705. He was ordained pastor of the First Congregational church in Boston, the church in Chauncy Place, 1727, and continued to be its pastor till his death, February 10, 1787, in the 83d year of his age.

He was strongly attached to the American cause in the struggle of the Colonies with the mother country, and rendered it important services. He was vehemently opposed to George Whitfield, the New Lights, and the religious enthusiasm which Whitfield's preaching excited, as also to Episcopacy, which he could in no manner tolerate. George Whitfield was an Englishman, a student of Oxford, and a presbyter of the Anglican Church. He was one of the original Methodists, and associated with John Wesley, from whom he subsequently separated on the question of unconditional election and reprobation. He visited the Colonies several times, and finally died and was buried in Newburyport, Massachusetts. In one of his numerous visits to this country, Dr. Chauncy met him as he was landing on the wharf in Boston, and taking him by the hand, said: "Mr. Whitfield, I am sorry you have come to this country. I am sorry to see you here." "No doubt of it," replied the missionary, "and so is the devil." The edition of Dr. Chauncy's book which I read was a moderate-sized octavo, printed in London, without the author's name, and I am not aware that it has ever been reprinted in this country. I do not recollect the work very distinctly, nor the precise ground on which the author defends the final salvation of all men; but my impression is that he urges it from the universality of the atonement, and the nature of punishment, which he holds is purgative or reformatory, not vindictive. The book was marked by a show of learning and some ability, but I thought it rather dull and heavily written.

About the same time I read another work, called *Calvinism Improved*, written by Dr. Joseph Huntington, pastor of the Congregational Church in Coventry, Connecticut. Dr. Huntington lived in the last century, and was of the same family with the Hon. Samuel Huntington, one of the signers of the Declaration of American Independence. His book was not published till after his death, and I am not aware that he was ever suspected during his lifetime of holding the doctrine of Universal Salvation. The work has not much method, but is written in a free, easy, flowing, and attractive style. The author starts with the Calvinistic premises of imputed righteousness and salvation by grace without works, and concludes the salvation of all men. He supposes two covenants: the covenant of works, made by Almighty God with Adam as federal head of mankind in the natural order; and the covenant of grace, made by the Father with the Son, the Federal Head of the human race in the spiritual order. The first covenant failed, and all mankind fell under the wrath of God, died in Adam, and were condemned to everlasting death; but the Son, becoming incarnate, fulfilled the covenant of works for men, expiated the guilt incurred by the human race, and under the covenant of grace redeems, restores, and saves them. Works have nothing to do with salvation, which is a work of pure grace. Under the covenant of works no man can be saved, and, if works entered into the covenant of grace, it would no longer be a covenant of grace. The sinner is saved by the covenant of grace alone, not in consideration of any good thing in him or done by him. He is saved solely by the free sovereign act of God imputing to him, or counting as his, the righteousness of Christ. This doctrine which Calvinism asserts, but confines to the elect only, Dr. Huntington extends to all men. He proves from the Scriptures that the atonement was made for all men, and was an ample and abundant satisfaction for the sins of the whole world. Hence, all men must be included in the covenant of grace, not a few only, and Christ must be regarded as the head of every man. In this covenant of grace God agrees to reckon the sins of all men as the sins of Christ, and to impute the righteousness of Christ to all who have transgressed. He transfers the sins to Christ, and punishes them in him; and then, finding his justice satisfied, pardons the sinner, transfers to him the righteousness of Christ, counts him just for Christ's sake, and receives him to his peace and love.

In the day of judgment, men will first be judged by the covenant of works, under which all will be condemned, for all have failed to keep that covenant; and the Judge, speaking in the name of the law of works, shall say to all the human family: "Depart from me, ye cursed, into everlasting fire, prepared for the devil and his angels." They shall then be judged under the covenant of grace; and the Judge, in consideration of the fact that the penalty incurred by the breach of the covenant of works has been borne and fully expiated by Christ in his own person, shall say, speaking in the name of free grace: "Come, yo blessed of my Father, enter into the kingdom of heaven, prepared for you from the foundation of the world." Thus the law is justified by the innocent suffering for the guilty, has its full and perfect vindication, and yet all men are saved,—yet, I might add, without personal sanctity,—a point, in the author's estimation, of no great importance. The good doctor does not shrink from making God the author of all our actions whether good or bad; and to the objection that sin is of a personal nature and its guilt is not transferable, he replies that sin is no more personal than justice, and that it is as easy for God to transfer our sins to Christ, as it is for him to transfer Christ's righteousness to us. Sin is, he says, God's property, God has the sovereign dominion over it, and may do with it what seems to him good, and transfer it to whom he pleases.

A neighbor put into my hands also a Treatise on the Atonement by ~~Hosea Ballou.~~ Mr. Ballou was a native of New Hampshire, originally a Calvinistic Baptist, but he became a Universalist through the influence of some members of his family, who had been converted directly or indirectly by the preaching and writings of Dr. Elhanan Winchester. He was, I think, of French descent, the son of a small New-England farmer, and obliged in his youth to assist his father and elder brothers in the cultivation of the farm, and in supporting the family. Nature was bountiful to him, both physically and intellectually. She gave him a tall athletic frame, symmetrical and finely moulded, handsome features, and an air of dignity and authority. His natural genius and ability fitted him to take rank with the most distinguished men the country has produced; but, unhappily, his education was very defective, and his acquired knowledge and information were even to he last very limited. But his intellect was naturally acute, active, fertile, and vigorous. He always struck me—and I knew him well in the later years of his life—as one who, if he chose, might excel in whatever he undertook. In his earlier years, he was regarded as harsh, bitter, and sarcastic in his temper; but when I knew him personally, he was witty indeed, fond of his joke, like most New-Eng landers, but an agreeable and kind-hearted old gentleman, very fond of children, and possessing great power to fascinate young men, and win their confidence and affection. In my boyhood he was settled in Barnard, Vermont, about five miles from the old people with whom I resided, and I often heard them speak of him, as some of their relatives belonged to his congregation. He was then a young man, but distinguished. From Barnard he removed to Portsmouth, New Hampshire, and after a short residence there he removed to Boston, where he continued to reside till his death, which occurred five or six years ago. He was the patriarch of American Universalism, and, at the time when I became a Universalist minister, was its oracle, very nearly its Pope.

It is many years since I have seen a copy of his Treatise on the Atonement, and I am not certain

that I have read it since my youth. It gave a new
phase to Universalism. Winchester, Chauncy, Hunt·
ington, Dan Foster, John Murray, and the Englishman, John Relly, the fathers of modern Universalism
in Great Britain, Ireland, and the United States,
had been what are called orthodox Protestants, and
retained their early views with the exception of the
single point of the endless punishment of the wicked.
They held the mysteries of the Trinity, the Incarna·
tion, the expiatory Atonement, and endeavored to
prove the final salvation of all men by Scriptural
exegesis, and arguments drawn from the love and
mercy of God. Mr. Ballou changes the whole
ground, and attacks the whole fabric of so-called
Orthodox Christianity. He adopts Arian views as
to the person of Christ, and labors throughout his
Treatise to demolish the doctrine of satisfaction, or
of an expiatory sacrifice. He is the first American
writer I am aware of, who combines the doctrines of
modern Unitarians with Universalism. He maintains that God demanded no expiation, that no expiatory sacrifice was needed, for God pardons the
sinner on simple repentance and reformation of life,
and an expiatory sacrifice, even if required, could
not have been made. He excludes grace, all transferable merit of the Head to the members, and
maintains that grace is nothing but the irrevocable
decrees of God irresistibly executing themselves in
the government of the world; he denies free-will,
denies accountability, denies a future judgment,
denies all rewards and punishments, denies virtue,

denies sin, in all except the name, and consequently the whole moral order. Sin, according to him, originates in the flesh, in the body, and does not affect the soul, the spirit, which remains pure, uncontaminated, whatever our fleshly defilements,—an old Gnostic and Manichæan heresy, which in early times was thought to open the door to gross disorders. Sin, pertaining only to the body, cannot survive its dissolution, but is deposited with it in the grave. Therefore, "he that is dead is freed from sin."

This was the ground on which Mr. Ballou placed his defence of universal salvation. Against the doctrine of endless punishment he uses the various Scriptural arguments used by his predecessors, apparently without perceiving their irrelevancy. He argues against it from the assumed injustice of all punishment not reformatory in its intention and nature, and also from the justice as well as from the love of God. God is the author of all our actions, and therefore of sin. He has no right to punish us eternally for sins which, when he made us, he not only foresaw, but foreordained, predetermined us to commit. It is clear that the conception of grace does not belong to his system, and that he demands the salvation of all men, not from the mercy, but from he justice of God, as a right, not as a favor. These views are set forth and defended with great freedom and boldness, with wonderful acuteness and power, in language, clear, simple, forcible, and at times beautiful, and even eloquent. A book fuller of heresies, and heresies of the most deadly character,

.iot excepting Theodore Parker's *Discourse of Matters pertaining to Religion,* has probably never issued from the American press, or. one better calculated to carry away a large class of young, ingenuous, and unformed minds. The heresies are indeed old, but they were nearly all original with the author. He had never read them, and there were no books within his reach, at the time when he wrote his Treatise, from which he could derive them. "My only aids in writing my Treatise on the Atonement," said he personally to me, in answer to a question I put to him, "were the Bible, Ethan Allen's *Oracles of Reason,*" a deistical work, " and my own reflections." n the circumstances under which it was written, it was certainly a most remarkable production; and if it did the author no credit as a sound thinker, it certainly entitled him to rank among the most original thinkers of our times. It is, however, an admirable commentary on the Protestant rule of faith—the Bible without note or comment, interpreted by every one for himself. The book made a deep impression on my young mind, although I was very far from accepting all its doctrines or all its arguments. It was subtle, yet even in my youth I detected some portion of its sophistry, and found it repugnant to my moral sentiments and convictions.

These works, together with some popular works openly warring against all revealed religion, indeed against all religion, whether revealed or natural, I had read before becoming a Presbyterian. They had a pernicious influence on my mind. They unsettled it, loosed it from its moorings, and filled me with doubt. I had in my despair gone to the Presbyterian Church, in order to get rid of the doubts they had excited, and to be taught the truth. Presbyterianism not being the true Church, being, in fact, only a self-constituted body, though she silenced these doubts for a brief time, could not solve or remove them. When I was forced to admit that Presbyterianism had no authority in the matter, I was necessarily forced back on the point whence it had taken me up, when I believed, so far as I believed anything, the doctrine of Universalism. The truth is, my mind was unsettled, and in reality had been from the time my well-meaning aunt had undertaken to initiate me into the doctrine of Universalism, and I had adhered to any fixed doctrines only by spasmodic efforts. In reality my mind continued unsettled for many years later than the period I am now treating of. I had no repose of mind, and found none till I got back to the Apostles' Creed, and found admission into the bosom of the Holy Catholic Church. But this by the way.

I could not, following my own reason, and without any divinely-commissioned teacher, have believed in the doctrine of the eternal punishment of the wicked. It seemed to me unjust. I could conceive it just, only on condition that God had given us an infallible means of knowing the truth, and sufficient power, naturally or supernaturally, of always obeying it, and resisting all temptation to evil. These I could not perceive had been given. The Protestant sophism could not deceive me. The Scriptures might, indeed, be infallible in themselves, but they were and could be to me only what I understood them to be. They were to me solely in my understanding of them, and my understanding of them was not infallible. I might err as to their sense, and entirely misinterpret them. Besides, only about one-twentieth of mankind can read, and to those who cannot read, the Bible is a sealed book; for them, it is as if it were not. What is to become of them? How are they to know the truth?—But all should know how to read. Be it so; yet they do not all know how to read, and we must deal with them as they are. They may die before they can learn to read the Bible.—But their natural light will suffice for them. Then the Scriptures are superfluous. Yet our natural light, even the best we have, is dim, our natural reason is weak, and to err is human. We have no infallible means of knowing the truth, of knowing what it is that God requires of us, the' belief and worship that will be acceptable to him.

Nor is this the worst. We are not only weak to know, but we are even weaker to perform. None of us do as well as we know. The spirit is willing, but the flesh is weak. I see the right, I approve it, and yet pursue the wrong. My will is weak, and my appetites and passions are strong. I am surrounded with temptations to which my firmest resolves succumb. I feel the want of a moral power that I find not. Now it cannot be that a just and good God has placed me in this world in the midst of

so many seductions, surrounded by so many enemies
to my virtue, where not to fail is a miracle—left me
in so much darkness, so frail and so morally weak in
myself, and yet attached the penalty of eternal death
even to my slightest transgressions. He knoweth
our frame, he considereth our weakness, and hath
compassion on us. These were reasons sufficient, I
thought, for rejecting endless punishment. Indeed,
the doctrine of endless punishment, as held by
Christians, pertains to the supernatural order, and
would not be just, if man had been left to the natural
order, and had not received supernatural gifts and
graces. It presupposes man to have been placed
under a supernatural Providence, and that he has
done more than abuse or misuse his natural powers.
It is inflicted for the abuse of supernatural graces,
which, if properly used, would have enabled us to
merit the beatitude of heaven. To deny the supernatural aids, and yet assert the endless punishment
of the wicked, is to outrage the natural sense of
justice common to all men.

As to the positive part of Universalism, I felt less
certain, both because I was not perfectly satisfied
that the Scriptures taught it, and because I had a
lurking doubt of the Divine inspiration and authority
of the Scriptures themselves. But having made up
my mind that the endless punishment of the wicked
was a thing not to be dreaded, I felt the less scruple
on the subject, as no grave consequences would or
could follow even an error on the subject. The
question of the authority of the Scriptures, I waived

as far as possible; and I honestly thought at the time that they might be and ought to be explained in the sense of the final salvation, or final happiness of all men. Taking reason for my guide and authority, I supposed that the Scriptures were to be explained in accordance with reason, so as to teach a rational doctrine; and certainly, I said, Universalism is a far more rational doctrine than its opposite. It may be that it is not proved by the strict letter of Scripture, but the letter killeth, it is the spirit that giveth life; and we must not be held to a strictly literal interpretation. We must allow ourselves great latitude of interpretation, and look at the general intent and scope of the whole, rather than at mere verbal statements.

I was the more ready to adopt these loose notions of Scriptural interpretation from the fact that, in falling back from Presbyterianism on my own reason, imperfect as I knew it to be, I necessarily excluded from revelation the revelation of anything supernatural or above reason. The revelation might be supernaturally made, and so far I could admit the supernatural; but it could be the revelation of no supernatural matter, or truth transcending the natural order. A revelation of supernatural truth, of an order of truth or of things whose nature could not be subjected to the judgment of natural reason, would demand a supernaturally endowed and assisted teacher and judge, to bring it within the reach of my natural understanding. I rejected, therefore, at once, all the mysteries of faith; treated them as *non avenues,* and reduced Christianity to a system of natural religion, or of moral and intellectual philosophy. If left to my natural reason, I could not accept what was beyond the reach of natural reason. Natural reason thus became the measure of revealed truth; and if so, I had the right to reject every interpretation of Scripture that deduced from it a doctrine which reason could not comprehend and approve. If I retained any respect for the Bible, I must give to its language a free and rational interpretation.

Moreover, the main thing could-not be to discover and know the exact truth. That could not be what God required of us, for, if it had been, he would have furnished us with facile and infallible means of doing it. What I should aim at was, not so much the truth, as the exercise of reason, its development and cultivation. So, even if Universalism should turn out to be not true, I need not disturb myself, if I developed my faculties, and conducted myself as a man. Consequently, as Universalism appeared to me the more reasonable of all doctrines known to me, I need not hesitate to profess and even to preach it. I accordingly professed myself a Universalist, and in the twenty-second year of my age became a Universalist minister.

CHAPTER IV.

AFTER leaving Presbyterianism, I devoted some
months to the reading of the Scriptures, and such
Universalist publications as were then extant, or at
least such as were within my reach. In the autumn
of 1825, I applied for and received a letter of fellow-
ship as a preacher from the General Convention of
Universalists, which met that year in Hartland, Vt.
I remained for a year in Vermont, continuing my
studies, part of the time with the Reverend Samuel
C. Loveland, a man of some learning, the compiler
of a Greek Lexicon of the New Testament, of no
great merit, and part of the time by myself alone,
and preaching on Sundays in various towns in the
State, chiefly in Windsor, Rutland, and Rockingham
counties. In the summer of 1826, I was ordained
an evangelist by a Universalist association, which
met that year at Jaffrey, N. H. The sermon was
preached, I think, by the Rev. Charles Hudson, the
ordaining prayer was made by the Rev. Paul Dean,
and the charge was given by the Rev. Edward
Turner.

Mr. Hudson was pastor of a Universalist society
in Westminster, Mass.. and professed himself a

Restorationist. He has since figured a good deal in politics, been several times a member of the General Court of Massachusetts, a member of the Governor's Council, and several years in Congress. Under the Taylor-Fillmore administration, he was naval officer of Boston and Charlestown, and after that connected with the *Boston Atlas;* but what or where he is now, I am not informed. He was then a young man, very industrious, very conceited, very- disputatious, with moderate learning, fair logical ability, and no fancy or imagination—a dry, hard man, and an exceedingly dull and uninteresting preacher. I enjoyed, however, a comfortable nap under his sermon. He could not endure Mr. Ballou's doctrine of no punishment after death, and pretended to be able to prove the final restoration of all men and devils from the Scriptures.

Mr. Dean was a native of Barnard, Vt., adjoining Royalton, and my eldest sister had been brought up in his father's family. He was at the time pastor of the Bulfinch Street Universalist Society in Boston, and regarded as the most popular preacher in the order, after Hosea Ballou, and many even preferred him. He was a handsome man, with a pleasing address, genial manners, and a most winning smile. He was a Restorationist, a Trinitarian, perhaps only a Sabellian, and by no means an admirer of Mr. Ballou, with whom he was on unfriendly terms. He ultimately, however, left the Universalist denomination, united with the Unitarians, and was preaching, when I last heard from him, for a Unitarian congregation somewhere in the Old Bay State. Mr. Turner was also a Restorationist, minister at the time to the Universalist Society in Portsmouth, N. H., though I am not certain but it was in Charlestown, Mass. He was a tall, majestic person, of grave and venerable aspect, a chaste and dignified speaker, and the best sermonizer I ever knew among Universalists. But he had too refined and cultivated a taste to be a popular Universalist preacher, and finally, I believe, followed my example, and associated with the Unitarians.

At the time of my ordination, those who believed in a future limited punishment, and those who denied all punishment after death, were associated together in one body, under the common name of Universalists. Subsequently, however, a division took place, and a portion of the former separated from the General Convention, as it was called, and took the name of Restorationists. This schism was formed mainly through the instrumentality of Adin Ballou, a distant relative of Hosea Ballou. He was a young convert from some evangelical sect—I forget what sect—and was full of zeal against the doctrine of no future punishment. He took with him Messrs. Dean, Turner, and Hudson, and several other ministers less known, and formed of them a distinct sect. But the majority even of those who held to a limited punishment after death, remained with the General Convention, and the Restorationist sect, after a few years of a fitful existence, became extinct. Its mem bers for the most part have coalesced, I believe, with the Unitarians.   I never went with the sect, though I was never one of those Universalists who restrict the consequences of our acts done in the body, whether good or bad, to this life.   On that subject I adopted a theory of my own, which I afterwards found to be very generally adopted by American Unitarians. Mr. Adin Ballou did not expire with his sect.   He became a socialist, and founded the community of Hopedale; and when I heard last from him, he was a spiritualist, spiritist, or devil-worshipper, conversing with spirits, and believing in Andrew Jackson Davis and the Fox girls.

In October, 1826, I returned to the State of New York, in which I had resided most of the time since I was fourteen years of age.   I stopped a short time in Fort Anne and Whitehall.   I resided for the greater part of a year in Litchfield, Herkimer County, then a year in Ithaca, a pleasant village at the head of Cayuga Lake, surrounded by varied and picturesque scenery, well worthy the visit of the tourist and the lover of nature.   I remained a few months at Genoa, Cayuga County, whence I removed to Auburn, in the same county, where I continued to reside till I ceased to be a Universalist minister.   At Auburn, I preached to the Universalist Society in that place, and edited *The Gospel Advocate and Impartial Investigator*, a semi-monthly periodical which, at the time of its coming under my control, was the most widely circulated and the most influential periodical, in this country, devoted to the interests of Universalism, though it had gained its circulation and influence less by its advocacy of Universalism, than by its opposition to the movements of the Presbyterian and other Evangelical sects to stop the Sunday mails, to control the politics, and to wield the social influence of the country,—what the same sects are still attempting by means of their Christian Young Men's Associations, and kindred societies. The periodical had been started at Buffalo by the Rev. Thomas Gross, who had been a Congregational minister in one of the Eastern States, but, being obliged to leave his parish, had turned Universalist, and by the Rev. Linus S. Everett, originally, I believe, a house and sign painter, a man of little learning, but a good deal of mother-wit. He had not a pleasant expression, but otherwise he was a fine-looking man, had a popular address, and engaging manners. He had little religious belief, and not much moral principle, but he was a philanthropist, and talked well.

The periodical had been removed by Mr. Everett to Auburn, and the proprietorship had been disposed of to Ulysses F. Doubleday, printer and bookseller, proprietor and editor of the Cayuga Patriot, and subsequently a member of Congress, a man of a strong mind, and an able writer. He was a Universalist when I knew him, but he afterwards became, I heard, a Calvinistic Baptist. I had written a good deal for the periodical while at Ithaca, had had charge of it during the absence of its editor, and had acquired through its pages considerable reputation as a writer, and, when Mr. Everett removed, its editorship was transferred to me. I conducted it for a year, but with more credit to my free, bold, and crude thinking, than to my piety or orthodoxy even as a Universalist. In it is a confused medley of thoughts, and the germs of nearly all I subsequently held or published till my conversion to the Catholic Church.

In the commencement of my career as a Universalist, I did my best to smother my doubts as to revelation, and to defend Universalism as a Scriptural doctrine. But I succeeded only indifferently. I had made up my mind that endless vindictive punishment was contrary to reason, and incompatible with the love and goodness of God; but when I became forced to study the Scriptures more attentively, in order to defend Universalism against the objections I had to meet, I became satisfied that they did not teach the final salvation of all men, if literally interpreted, and that I must either reject them as authority for reason, or else accept the doctrine of endless punishment. The answers we gave to the texts cited against us could not stand the test of honest criticism, and those we adduced in our favor were more specious than conclusive. Either, then, since the doctrine of endless punishment is contrary to reason, I must give up reason, and then have no reason for accepting the Scriptures at all, and no means of determining their sense; or I must make reason the judge not only of the meaning of Scripture, but of the truth or falsity of that meaning. I chose, as was reasonable in my position, the latter alternative, and rejected the authority of the Scriptures.

For a time, indeed, I tried to persuade myself that I could reject the Scriptures as authoritative, and yet concede their authenticity and divine inspiration. But it would not do. If the Bible is God's word, it is authoritative, not only because God has the right to command us as our sovereign Lord and proprietor, but because, since he can neither deceive nor be deceived, his word is the highest conceivable evidence of truth. God is the Supreme Reason; and if we have full evidence that what we take to be his word really is his word, it is final, and an infallible test of what is or is not reasonable. In cases of apparent conflict between it and the teachings of reason, I must conclude, not that it is wrong, but that I have misinterpreted reason, and assumed that reason teaches what in reality it does not. If I understood reason better, I should perceive no discrepancy, because God can never teach us one thing in his word, and a contradictory thing through our natural reason. What he tells us in his word may be above reason, but cannot be against it.

I saw this clearly enough. But my Protestant ism was in my way. Before I can thus surrender my reason to the Bible, and conclude the reasonableness of what it teaches, or its accordance with reason where I do not see that accordance or that reasonableness, I must have infallible authority for asserting that the Bible is the word of God, and for determining its true sense; for the Bible can bind me only inasmuch as it is the word of God, and it is the word of God only in its true sense,—the sense intended by the Holy Ghost. But I have not in either case this infallible authority. The Catholic Church, indeed, pretends to have received it, but that Church is out of the question.. I have only my reason with which to determine that the Bible is God's word, or with which to determine its true meaning. Here is my difficulty. Reason is no more in settling these two points,-than it is in settling the point as to what is or is not unreasonable; and as without reason I can neither determine that the Bible is inspired or what is its sense, I cannot surrender my reason to it in cases where it appears to me unreasonable. I may believe on competent authority that a doctrine is reasonable, although I do not perceive its reasonableness; but I cannot, if I try, believe what appears to me unreasonable, on the authority of reason alone. To say you believe a thing unreasonable, is to say that you do not believe it, and that you reject it. Belief always is and must be a reasonable act; in it reason assents, mediately or immediately, to the proposition that it is true. Where that assent is wanting, belief cannot be predicated. It is a contradiction in terms to say that you believe what you hold to be unreasonable. I cannot, on the authority of Scripture, established only by reason believe what appears to me unreasonable. Whoever knows anything of the operations of the mind knows that it is so. The Bible, then, without an infallible authority to assert it and deduce its sense, can never be authority sufficient for believing a doctrine to be reasonable, when that reasonableness is not apparent

to the understanding. By rejecting the authority of
the Church as the witness of revelation and judge
of its meaning, I found myself obliged, therefore, to
reject, in turn, the authority of the Scriptures.

But reason, I soon discovered, in order to be able
to judge by its own light of the truth or falsity of a
revealed doctrine, must know, independently of the
revelation, all that it can teach us. Revelation, then,
is superfluous. I can know without it all I can know
with it. God, then, cannot have made a revelation
to us, for he does nothing in vain, or without a purpose.
But, as the Scriptures evidently teach the unreasonable doctrine of endless punishment, they are, if
believed to be given by divine inspiration, worse than
useless ; they are calculated to mislead, to perpetuate
superstitious fear, and to prevent the world from rising
to just conceptions of the love and goodness of God,
and a just reliance on his providence. In the interests of truth and human happiness, then, I ought not
only to reject the Scriptures, but to do all in my power
to destroy belief in them as the word of God.

I had other difficulties with Universalism. The
ground on which I rejected endless punishment was,
that all punishment should be reformatory in its nature
and intention. All Universalists held that vengeance,
or vindictive punishment, designed to honor a broken
law, and vindicate an offended majesty, is incom
patible with the nature of a God who is love. Love
worketh no ill to his neighbor. The nature of love
is to make the object beloved happy as far as in its
power. God is love, his wisdom and power are

unlimited. He loves all his creatures; he can make them all happy, and therefore will. He can punish no one in his wrath; he can only chastise us for our profit, " that we may be made partakers of his holiness." Then, no vindictive punishment.

We all hold this doctrine. But this doctrine denies that sin is ever punished. If pain is inflicted upon a sinner, it is not to punish his sin, but to reform him. The quantity of pain must not then be measured by the quantity of sin committed. The infliction can have no reference to wrong done or guilt incurred, and its amount must be determined by the amount necessary to reform the wrong-doer. It then is not punishment at all. Its motive is not to punish, but to benefit him who suffers it, and may as well be inflicted on the innocent as on the guilty, if it will do him good, or will·redound to his advantage. From pain inflicted for one's benefit, it can be no advantage to save him. How, then, can I talk of a Saviour? Universalists say, Jesus Christ is the Saviour of all men. But from what does he save them? From punishment, from a penalty annexed to the Divine law? No, for God never annexed any penalty to the breach of his law, for he never punishes to vindicate his law. All the penalty, all the consequence of sin, is simply to be whipped till we sin no more, and from that whipping Christ saves no one. How, then, can I call him a Saviour?

He is a Saviour, we answered, in that he saves us from sinning. " Thou shalt call his name Jesus, for he shall save his people from their sins." Yet he does not save us from sinning, for we go on sinning every day. But how does or can he save us from sinning ? Not by infusing believing and sanctifying grace into our hearts, for the doctrine of infused grace is rejected by all Protestants, who, when they recognize grace at all as operating within us, recognize it only as a transient act of God, not as an infused habit of the soul. He can save us only by his doctrine and example. His example is for us only the example of a good man, better than that of any other, because more perfect, yet differing from that of others only in degree. His doctrine—who can say what it is ? Can I say honestly that I know what he taught ? Did he teach the endless punishment of the wicked ? If so, he does not save us by his doctrine from sinning, for Universalists are agreed that the doctrine of endless punishment has an immoral tendency, inasmuch as it denies the love and goodness of God, and represents him as partial, vindictive, and unjust. Did he teach Universalism, that all men are sure of heaven, and cannot possibly miss it ? Did he teach that vice has no punishment, virtue no reward; that Judas, Pilate, and Herod will receive a crown of life as well as Peter, James, and John, and a crown equally bright, unfading, eternal in the heavens ? How does that doctrine save us from sinning, or tend to make us virtuous ? What motive to virtue does it present ; what consideration to deter from vice ? Do my best, I cannot make my eternal felicity surer; do my worst, I cannot render it less sure. Why, then, shall I trouble myself about the matter ? Let me eat, drink, and be merry, for to-morrow I die, and go—to heaven. Here, then, I have lost the authority of the Church, the authority and inspiration of the Scriptures, even my Saviour himself, and with him the last vestige of revealed religion. Surely, I have a marvellous faculty in losing. Wonder what I have gained!

But, as the world looks upon Jesus as a Saviour, and gathers round him a multitude of superstitious notions which make men mental and moral slaves, and prevent them from asserting their freedom, their manhood, standing up and acting like men, he, so far from saving them from sinning, actually prevents them from being saved, and becomes the occasion of their moral degradation and misery. I ought, then, to war against him, and to do my best to deliver the world from its bondage to him. Thus I may myself become a saviour, and be entitled to the respect he usurps. Hence, my Universalism made me, so far as logic could go, not only a non-Christian, but an anti-Christian. This was my reasoning at the time, not merely my reasoning now.

But my troubles did not end here. In order to meet the objection that Universalism was of a licentious tendency, and opened the floodgates of iniquity, we laid particular stress on the certainty of punishment, and the impossibility of escaping it. We maintained that every one would receive according to the deeds done in the body, and even here in this world that God will by no means clear the guilty; that, as a man sows, so shall he reap, and that he must pay the debt he contracts, pay it in his own person, and "to the uttermost farthing." We were, after having said this, accustomed to turn upon our assailants, and to tell them that their doctrine of a punishment put off till after the day of judgment, and their doctrine of repentance and remission of sin, by which the vilest sinner, a hard-faced, grinding Presbyterian or Congregationalist deacon, by a simple act of faith, could escape his just deserts, and take his rank in heaven as a saint of the first water, might, with far more justice, be charged with an immoral and licentious tendency. But this doctrine, if it meant anything, denied all pardon, all forgiveness, all mercy, all compassion on the part of God, all interposition on his part in favor of the transgressor. God leaves the sinner to the mercy of the order he has established. He has made the world, adjusted its parts, impressed on it its laws, given it a jog, and bid it go ahead and take care of itself. Then I lose my Father in heaven, for God is only my creator, and is no more my father than he is the father of the reed or the oak. I lose Providence, and am reduced to an inflexible and inexorable nature. Prayer, repentance, devotion, entreaty, can avail me nothing. God has intrenched himself behind the natural laws, and cannot hear me, will not interpose to help me. With this went even natural religion.

But, as God inflicts pain only for the sake of reformation, as he never punishes sin or rewards virtue, all idea of moral accountability must be abandoned. God will never bring us into judgment for our conduct. Then there is no power above us to defend oppressed innocence, and to vindicate the majesty of right. Then, what is the criterion of right and wrong? Both must be alike pleasing to God; and if both are alike pleasing to him, if he regards with equal complacency the sinner and the saint, what is the radical difference between them? None that I can see. God wills our happiness: then what makes us happy must be regarded as good, and what makes us miserable must be regarded as evil. An action is virtuous, then, because it promotes our happiness, produces pleasurable emotions in ourselves or in others; and vice is that which does not promote our happiness, which causes painful emotions in us or in others. Virtue is virtue, because it promotes happiness; and vice is vice, because it brings misery. Then no objective distinction between virtue and vice, between good and evil. Here, said I, is the very foundation of morality undermined.

God governs the world, I said, only by general laws which he has impressed on it in creating it, and with the natural operation of these he never interferes. These laws admit the existence of evil. The world is full of suffering; man preys upon man, and the whole creation groaneth and travaileth in pain. What is to hinder it from being always so? What is to put an end to evil, to pain and suffering? What is to insure the triumph of good? No new law can be introduced, no new power can be developed. What, then, is to assure us that evil will ever be less? The goodness of God, you tell me. But how am I to

be assured that God is good?   I can prove his goodness only from nature, and in nature the evil seems
to surpass the good.   Here Universalism, said I, runs
itself out, and renders doubtful even its own premises.

It must not be supposed that I accepted all these
frightful conclusions.   They followed logically from
my premises, and logically I was obliged to accept
them; yet my good sense and my better feelings
rebelled against them.   My mind could neither reject nor accept them.   It was in doubt; it was
unsettled, uncertain, in a snarl, and I could see no
wiser course to pursue than to dismiss the whole
subject from my thoughts.   I know nothing, I said,
and can know nothing on the subject, and let me
not attempt to decide anything respecting it one way
or the other.   I may trust my senses, and believe
in the world of sensible phenomena.   I will henceforth confine myself to that, and leave alone all
metaphysical or theological speculations, and neither
assert nor deny the invisible and the spiritual.   Thus
I had, following reason, lost the Bible, lost my Saviour, lost Providence, lost reason itself, and had left
me only my five senses, and what could fall under
their observation: that is, reduced myself to a mere
animal.

But, with these doubts hanging over me, it was
clear that I could not, as an honest man, present
myself before the public as a Christian minister.   It
is true, I did not write or preach differently from
what I thought and felt: nobody could really be
deceived as to the state of my mind.   Many of my

brother ministers knew my doubts. They blamed me, it is true, not for entertaining them, but for not keeping them to myself. Some of them, I knew from their confidential communications, believed no more than I did; and my conviction at the time was, that Universalists generally had no belief in revelation, and were really deists or skeptics, and professed to be Christians only because they could combat all religion more successfully under a nominally Christian banner, than under the banner of open, avowed infidelity. In this I am inclined to believe I did them injustice. I gave them credit for being deeper thinkers and better logicians than they were. Few men ever reason out their own systems, or compare all the parts of the system they embrace with one another. I did not always do this myself. Universalists did not generally think beyond the few points brought into discussion between them and the so-called Orthodox, and never troubled themselves to inquire whether the ground on which they defended their Universalism could be assumed without involving a denial of Christianity, or not.

But, although I was beginning to acquire a prominent position in the denomination, I felt that I ought to leave it. I could not consent to profess what I did not honestly believe; and my irritation at myself for my want of manliness and strict honesty in continuing to preach after I had ceased to believe, increased my doubts, and made me think I doubted even more than I really did. The moment I broke off my connection with the Universalists,

and took my position openly and above-board, not as
a disbeliever, but as an unbeliever, I felt restored
to my manhood—I felt like a new man. My irritation ceased, and almost instantly the tone of my
feelings changed towards Christianity. I was no
longer obliged to profess, or to seem to profess, more
than I believed; and from that moment my mind
began to recover its balance, and the most anti-
Christian period of my life was the last two years
that I was a Universalist preacher.

CHAPTER V.

IT was never in my nature, any more than it is in that of the human race, to take up with a purely negative system. My craving to believe was always strong, and it never was my misfortune to be of a skeptical turn of mind. But, if I craved something to believe, it was never for the sake of believing. I wanted the truth, would labor for it, harder than most men perhaps, but never to stop with its mere apprehension or barren contemplation. My disposition was practical, rather than speculative, or even meditative, like that of the majority of my countrymen. I sought the truth in order to know what I ought to do, and as the means of realizing some moral or practical end. I wanted it that I might use it.

While my Universalism was escaping me, I had been engaged in acquiring a positive belief of another sort. My early religious belief, vague as it was, gave me an end to labor for,—that of getting religion, and preparing myself, with God's grace, for eternal happiness in heaven. Even the Assembly's Catechism had taught me that "the chief end of man is to glorify God, and enjoy him forever." I

) id in my childhood no difficulty as to the end; my difficulty was only as to the means of gaining it. Universalism deprived me of that end, as an end to live and labor for, by teaching me that it was just as certain without as with my personal exertions. It left my life here very nearly purposeless. The most I had to do was to combat Orthodoxy, and spread Universalism,—a very meagre work; for it effected nothing one way or another in relation to the fnal result. Why should I do it? And when I have done it, and got all the world to believe Universalism, what will remain for me or others to do? But some work I must have, something to do, to prevent my activity from recoiling upon itself; and as Universalism had made me doubt the utility of all labors for another world, I was forced to look for a work to be done for this world. I had made nothing of my religious speculations, nothing of my inquiries as to the invisible and the heavenly, and reason counselled me, obliged me to leave them, to drop from the clouds, take my stand on the solid earth, and devote myself to the material order, to the virtue and happiness of mankind in this earthly life. Certainly this did not perfectly satisfy me in the beginning; but it seemed the only alternative that was left me I had no choice in the matter. With the fear of hell, the hope of heaven had escaped; and, as the other world disappeared from my view, nothing but this world did or could remain.

About the time of my becoming a Universalist minister, Robert Owen, from New Lanark, Scotland, came to this country for the purpose of establishing a Community, and to commence the realization of his plans of World-Reform. Mr. Owen was a Welshman by birth, and bred a cotton-spinner. He was engaged, while still a young man, to take charge of the extensive cotton mills at New Lanark, in Scotland, owned by a Mr. Dale, whose daughter he subsequently married. Through this marriage he became part, and at length, if I am not mistaken, sole proprietor of the mills, which made him a rich man. While acting as manager, more especially as part or sole proprietor, he introduced several wise and judicious arrangements, which added much to the cleanliness, decorum, thrift, and physical comfort of the workmen. From the success of his experiments at New Lanark, and from the manifest improvement he had been able to introduce in the condition of the population employed in the mills, or under his care and supervision, he concluded that he had discovered the secret of so organizing mankind as to cure all individual and social evils, and to make all men rich, virtuous, and happy.

Mr. Owen was a man of much simplicity and benevolence of character. He knew little of Christianity, and believed less, but he was philanthropic, and was ready to make very heavy sacrifices for the happiness of mankind, or, rather, for realizing his plans for making them happy. He drew up an outline of his plan, and presented it to the principal crowned heads, ministers, statesmen, and literary and scientific men of Europe; but not meeting with the degree of encouragement he looked for, and doubting whether the Old World was the place for trying his experiment, he resolved on coming to the United States,—the best place in the world for visionaries to recover their wits, and to find their fanciful schemes explode. He came when John Quincy Adams was President, though I do not now recall the precise date, and laid his plans before Mr. Adams, the Congress, and the people of the United States. His respectability as a man, his sincerity, his apparent benevolence, and his practical sagacity in particulars, gained him respectful treatment and a candid hearing. Many listened with favor, and a few with enthusiasm. He soon succeeded in gaining a number of followers; and, elated, he purchased a settlement called Harmony, in Posey County, Indiana, named it New Harmony, and established there, with a band of enthusiasts and adventurers, some from Europe, some from the United States, a provisional community, preparatory to the complete introduction of his plan of community life, and universal World-Reform.

Mr. Owen's great principle or maxim was, that man is passive, not active in the formation of his character; that his character is formed not by him, but for him, by education, or the circumstances in which he is born, grows up, and lives. Since man is passive in the formation of his character, in the hands of circumstances like clay in the hands of the potter, it is practicable, by a skilful arrangement of circumstances, or by a proper arrangement of the external influences brought to bear on him, to mould his character into that of the most consummate wisdom and the most heroic virtue. Hitherto all had gone wrong; circumstances had been arranged t{ corrupt and debase man's character. Man has thus far been cursed with a trinity of evils: property, marriage, and religion. Abolish these, bring men and women to live together in communities of from one to two thousand in each, inure them to live in parallelograms, with all things in common, in perfect equality, with the circumstances bearing equally upon all and each, and you will form their characters to virtue, and provide for the proper education of their offspring. There will then be no poverty, no inequality, no want, no envy, no discontent, no disease, no vice, no crime, but all will be peace, love, mutual good-will, kindness, virtue, harmony, bliss. The dream was not without its charm. But the poor man was not destined to realize it. His Harmony after a few months proved to be no harmony at all, but harsh discord, rather. He had taken the precaution to keep the property he invested in his establishment in his own name. His disciples murmured at this, as an inconsistency on his part, though they were living at his expense, and thought he ought to carry out his principles and abolish private property at once, and bestow all he called his own on the community, to be held in common by its members. They succeeded, I believe, in cozening him out of a considerable sum, of involving him in pecuniary embarrassment, and forcing him to sell his New Lanark property. They

then separated, and several of them went through
the country abusing him for his want of consistency,
and his unwillingness to make greater sacrifices for
their benefit.

The plan was silly enough, and its success would
have made men only well-trained and well-fed animals, and I will say this for myself that I never fully
adopted it. I had some trouble in believing that
man was perfectly passive in the formation of his
character; and if he was, I could not see how the
circumstances were to be controlled by him, and be
brought to bear equally upon all and upon each. If
he was to have no want, I was puzzled to understand
what was to stimulate him to exertion; and if he
made no exertion, I could not understand how he
was to become intellectually great, or to produce the
wherewith to provide for his animal wants. But Mr.
Owen's discourses, publications, and movements drew
my attention to the social evils which exist in every
land, to the inequalities which obtain even in our
own country, where political equality is secured by
law, and to the question of reorganizing society and
creating a paradise on earth. My sympathies were
enlisted, I became what is now called a socialist,
and found for many years a vent for my activity in
devising, supporting, refuting, and rejecting theories
and plans of World-Reform.

Failing to find an authority competent to teach
me the true sense of a supernatural revelation, I had,
step by step, rejected all such revelation, and brought
myself back to simple nature, to the world of the

senses, and to this sublunary life. I neither asserted nor denied the existence of God. I neither believed nor disbelieved in a life after death. The position I took was : These are matters of which I know nothing, of which I can know nothing, and therefore are matters of which I will endeavor not to think. Of this world of the senses I do and may know something. Here is a work to be done, here is the scene of my labors, and here I will endeavor to love mankind and make them happy. I had, indeed, a very limited creed, but, nevertheless, I had one, which I firmly held. Half in mockery, but at bottom in sober earnest, I drew up and published it such as it was, just before leaving Universalism. I must be permitted to transcribe it.

MY CREED.

"Almost every man has a creed. There are few who do not worship their creed with more devotion than they do their God, and labor a thousand times harder to support it than they do the truth. Now, I do not like to be singular, and I know not why I may not have a creed as well as other folk. But, if I publish my creed, consistency may require me to defend it ; and when I have once enlisted self-love in its defence, I may become blind to the truth, and choose rather to abide by my first decision than to admit that I have once decided wrong. Yet a creed I must and will have, and my readers shall know what it is.

"My creed shall consist of FIVE points" (in allusion to the five points of Calvinism, defined by the Synod of Dort), "and shall embrace all the essentials of true religion. Furthermore, I wish to premise that my creed was not adopted merely to-day; it has been cordially embraced, and of its correctness I have had no doubts for at least nine months. . . . I would allege, in behalf of my creed, that it is plain, easy to be understood, and withal involves no mystery. The pious, however, from this circumstance may be led to doubt its *divine* origin, and infidels may like it so well that I shall be shut out from the Church. But I will state it, though I must still further allege that I believe it to be based on eternal truth, and it is calculated, if obeyed, to harmonize this world, and to enable the vast family of man to live forever under the smiles of fraternal affection. But for the creed:—

"ART. I. I believe that every individual of the human family should be HONEST.

"ART. II. I believe that every one should be benevolent and kind to all.

"ART. III. I believe that every one should use his best endeavors to procure food, clothing, and shelter for himself, and labor to enable all others to procure the same for themselves to the full extent of his ability.

"ART. IV. I believe every one should cultivate his mental powers, that he may open to himself new sources of enjoyment, and also be enabled to aid his brethren in their attempts to improve the condition of the human race, and to increase the sum of human happiness

"ART. V. I believe that, if all mankind act on these principles, they serve God all they can serve him; that he who has this faith and conforms the nearest unto what it enjoins, is the most acceptable unto God." *

It is easy to see from this creed, so called in mockery, that I rejected heaven for earth, and God for man, eternity for time, as the end for which I was to live and labor. The first article indicates my impression that people generally, whatever their pretences, did not seriously believe in a supernatural revelation. I had, too, been rendered impatient by the lectures I received from various quarters on my imprudence in not concealing my doubts. I disliked seeming to be what I was not, or professing to believe what I did not believe. I could see no merit in professing to be a Christian, when I knew I was no Christian. I wanted to appear fighting under my own colors, to speak out my honest thought, and let it go for what it was worth. Yet I was met with remonstrance. I was not blamed for my thought, but for telling it; and blamed for telling it, not on the ground that it was false, but on the ground that it was bad policy to tell it. I hated what is called policy then, and I have no great fondness for it even yet. A man's life-blood is frozen in its current, his intellect deadened, and his very soul annihilated by the everlasting dinging into his ears by the wise and prudent, more properly the timid and selfish, of the admonition to be politic, to take care not to

* *Gospel Advocate and Impartial Investigator*, June 27, 1829.

compromise one's cause or one's friends. My soul revolted, and revolts even to-day, at this admonition. Almost the only blunders I ever committed in my life were committed when I studied to be politic, and prided myself on my diplomacy.

Prudence is a virtue, and rashness is a sin, but my own reason and experience have taught me that truth is a far more trustworthy support than the best-devised scheme of human policy possible. Honesty is the best policy. Be honest with thyself, be honest with all the world, be true to thy convictions, be faithful to what truth thou hast, be it ever so little, and never dream of supplying its defect by thy astuteness or craft. Certainly be so, if thou believest in a God who is truth itself, and with whom to lie is impossible. Fear not for thy cause, if thou believest it his cause, for it must stand and prosper in his wisdom and power, not in thy human sagacity, thy human prudence, thy human policy. Throw thyself heart and soul on his truth, it will sustain thee; if not, be contented to fail. It is comparatively easy to know what is true, what is virtuous; but what, aside from fidelity to truth and virtue, is wise policy, or genuine prudence, surpasses the wit of men to say. Never yet has a great saint arisen without seeming, to even great and good men in Church or State as well as to the wise and prudent men of the world, terribly rash, shockingly imprudent. No one can be a man, and do a man's work, unless he is sincere, unless he is in earnest, terribly in earnest, throwing his whole heart and soul into his work; and whoever does so, may depend upon it that the chief men of his sect, his party, or his school, if not of his Church, will be alarmed at his conduct, will accuse him of being ultra, of going too far, of endangering everything by his rashness, his want of prudence, of policy. I am no saint, never was, and never shall be a saint. I am not, and never shall be, a great man; but I always had, and I trust I always shall have, the honor of being regarded by my friends and associates as impolitic, as rash, imprudent, and impracticable. I was and am, in my natural disposition, frank, truthful, straightforward, and earnest; and therefore have had, and, I doubt not, shall carry to the grave with me, the reputation of being reckless, ultra, a well-meaning man, perhaps an able man, but so fond of paradoxes and extremes, that he cannot be relied on, and is more likely to injure than serve the cause he espouses. So, wise and prudent men shake their heads when my name is mentioned, and disclaim all solidarity with me.

I must be pardoned this burst of indignation,—an indignation which dictated the first article of my creed of 1829, and which is stronger than I wish it in 1857. I have suffered so much from the *prudence* of associates, have received so many admonitions in relation to my alleged ultraisms and tendency to run to extremes, so many cautions to be moderate, to be prudent, to be politic, and the like, that I am a little sore on the point, and cannot keep as cool on the subject as becomes a man of my age, gravity, and experience.   Yet it is not wholly a personal matter with me.   I am past my prime of life, and shall soon be beyond the reach of any personal annoyance I may feel.   But I would leave my protest against this tendency on the part of the worshippers of rou tine to damp the courage and to stifle the energy ot young and ardent spirits who come forward to devote themselves to the cause of truth and virtue.   If what a man says is true, and is evidently said with an honest intention, do not decry him, do not disown him, do not beat the life out of him by lectures on prudence; stand by him, and bear with him the odium he may incur by telling the truth, encourage him by your respect for his honesty and candor, and shelter him, as far as in your power, from the reproaches of weak and timid brethren; for be assured we live in an age and country where honesty and candor, fidelity to one's honest convictions, and moral courage in avowing them, are not virtues likely to become excessive.   Fidelity to what one believes to be true, moral courage in adhering to our convictions before the world, is the greatest want of our times.   The age lacks above all things sincerity, earnestness. Give us back these, give us back the old-fashioned loyalty of heart, and we shall not need to labor long to bring the age to see, own, and obey the truth The subjective heresy of the age is a far greater obstacle to its conversion than its objective errors. What men most lack is principle—is the feeling that they should be true to the right; and that to be manly, is to be ready to follow the truth under what-

ever guise it may come, to whatever it may lead, to
the loss of reputation, to poverty, to beggary, to the
dungeon or the scaffold, to the stake or exile. I have
had my faults, great and grievous faults, as well as
others, but I have never had that of disloyalty to
principle, or of fearing to own my honest convictions, however unpopular they might be, or however
absurd or dangerous the public might regard them.
Give me rather the open, honest unbeliever, who
pretends to believe nothing more than he really does
believe, than your sleek, canting hypocrite, who rolls
up his eyes in holy horror of unbelief, and makes a
parade of his orthodoxy, when he believes not a
word in the Gospel, and has a heart which is a cage
of unclean beasts, out of which more devils need
to be cast than were cast out of the Magdalen.
The former may never see God, but the latter
deserves the lowest place in hell. There is hope of
the conversion of a nation of unbelievers; of the
conversion of a nation of hypocrites, none. Sincerity in error is respectable; insincerity in the truth
is of all things the most reprehensible, for it proves
the heart is wholly false, a mass of corruption, in
which even divine grace can find, I was about to say,
nothing to work upon, certainly nothing likely to
concur with it.

If my conscience would have let me pretend to be
a Christian, after it became clear I was no Christian
believer; if I could, without suffering its reproaches,
have continued to profess myself a Universalist, after
I had ceased to believe in revelation, though writing

or preaching nothing which I did not really believe, I doubt if the grace of God would ever have
rescued me from my errors; and I must think it was
his grace that would not suffer me to do so. My honest
avowal of unbelief was, under the circumstances, a
step that brought me nearer the kingdom of God. I
believe that the mass of my countrymen will make
little advance towards the Gospel till they come back
to honest nature, and consent to own to themselves
and to the world what they really are. It is necessary, first of all, to make away with all shams, to
use one of Carlyle's terms, to get rid of all illusions,
and to believe a lie is a lie, and that no lie shall
stand. We live in an age of shams, of illusions;
and the saddest thing of all is, that, while we have
no faith in reality, we believe in shams, we trust
illusions, and say, These be thy gods, O Israel! that
have brought thee up out of the land of Egypt. If
we have not advanced to faith in the Gospel, let
us return to simple nature, and have at least the
natural order, which, after all, is real, on which to
plant our feet.

The end of man, as disclosed by "my creed" of
1829, is obviously an earthly end, to be attained in
this life. Man was not made for God, and destined
to find his beatitude in the possession of God, his
supreme good, the Supreme Good itself. His end
was happiness, not happiness in God, but in the
possession of the good things of this world. Our
Lord had said: "Be not anxious as to what ye shall
eat, or what ye shall drink, or wherewithal ye shall

be clothed, for after all these things do the heathen seek." I gave him a flat denial, and said: Be anxious, labor especially for these things, first for yourselves, then for others. Enlarging, however, my views a little, I said: Man's end for which he is to labor, is the well-being and happiness of mankind in this world—is to develop man's whole nature, and so to organize society and government as to secure all men a paradise on the earth. This view of the end to labor for, I held steadily and without wavering from 1828 till 1842, when I began to find myself tending unconsciously towards the Catholic Church. The various systems I embraced or defended, whether social or political, ethical or æsthetical, philosophical or theological, were all subordinated to this end, as means by which man's earthly condition was to be meliorated. I sought truth, I sought knowledge, I sought virtue for no other end, and it was, not in seeking to save my soul, to please God, or to have the true religion, that I was led to the Catholic Church, but to obtain the means of gaining the earthly happiness of mankind. My end was man's earthly happiness, and my creed was progress. In regard to neither did I change or swerve in the least, till the truth of the Catholic Church was forced upon my mind and my heart. During the period of fourteen years, the greater part of which I was accused of changing at least once every three months, I never changed once in my principles or my purposes, and all I did change were my tools, my instruments, or my modes of operation.

In renouncing Universalism, which with me was only a stage in my transition from the religion of my childhood to socialism, I had renounced all fear and all hope in regard to another world; and though subsequently, as a Unitarian, I held to a future existence, it was merely a continuation of our natural life, a natural immortality, which did not include the resurrection of the flesh, or rewards and punishments in a Christian sense. I felt easy in regard to the future, and was in the habit of maintaining that the best way to secure a heaven hereafter is to create a heaven for mankind in this world. For years I held this maxim, and never troubled myself at all in regard to what might be my fate or that of others after death. I had a firm belief in progress, full confidence in philosophy, and a strong desire to contribute to the welfare of my fellow-men, to reform the world, and create an earthly paradise for the human race; but I had very little thought or sense of my duty to God, and no serious care for anything beyond the service of my neighbor in relation to this life. I recognized God, but only in man, and I held that he exists for us only in human nature.

For years I went no farther in my thoughts, and thirsted for nothing higher or broader. I had schooled my feelings and my imagination to my narrow carnal Judaism, and experienced nothing of that craving for an unseen and spiritual good, that secret longing for God and religion, of which so much use is made in our arguments against unbelievers. I felt none of that trouble which I felt formerly

when I found my childhood's belief escaping me. I
am convinced by my own experience that our philanthropists and world-reformers may become so
engrossed in their plans that they do not experienc
that aching void within, that emptiness of all created
things, which we sometimes imagine. Their phil-
anthropy is a religion unto them. Even failures do
not at once discourage them, for they find their relief
in their doctrine of progress. It is idle to tell them
that the good they seek is bounded, and that the
soul craves an unbounded good; for, holding to progress, to the indefinite perfectibility of man, they
are unable to assign any limits to the good to which
they are wedded; and as progress implies imperfec-
tion, they have a ready excuse for their failures. We
have failed to-day, but we shall succeed to-morrow.
I was mistaken, my experiment was not successful,
but I will do better next time. Or, if I die without
succeeding, the human race is progressive, each new
generation is wiser than the last, and the generation
coming after me will succeed, and my labors, my
experiments, my failures even, will perhaps contribute to its success. So they will not be in vain.
Individuals die, but the race survives, is immortal.
Thus hope revives from failure; and the individua
consoles himself with the belief that what he cannot
accomplish, the race in its march through the ages
will effect, and his labors meet their reward in the
increased virtue and happiness of mankind.

We cannot reach the socialist, who has made a
religion of his socialism, by appeals to his love of

happiness, or to the failures of his undertakings. I would that I could feel the fervor, the enthusiasm, in the cause of the truth, which at one period I felt in the cause of socialism. The fact is, the socialist is not all wrong. You may declaim against him as much as you please, but it will be none the less true that he is often governed by noble instincts, by generous sentiments, which Christianity does not disown, but accepts and consecrates. He has also certain aspects even of Christian truth, or aspects of truth which, without the Christian revelation and the operations of Christian charity, he never would have beheld. In those aspects of truth which he has, and to which he is devoted, we must take our point of departure in leading him to renounce his errors.

CHAPTER VI.

METHODS OF WORLD-REFORM.

I HAD fixed the end for which I was to labor,—the creation of an earthly paradise; but the means of gaining it were not well determined. My own mind was very nearly balanced between two contradictory theories: the theory of individualism, and that of communism. I had read, had, in fact, studied with great assiduity, one of the most remarkable works in our language, *An Enquiry concerning the Principles of Political Justice*, if I recollect the title aright, by William Godwin, originally a Calvinistic dissenting minister, at Stowmarket, England, whence, in 1787, he removed to London, where he devoted himself to literature. He was the author of "Caleb Williams," "St. Leon," "Fleetwood," "Mandeville," "Cloudsley," a work on "Population," in reply to Malthus, "A History of the Commonwealth of England," "The Life and Times of Chaucer," and several other works, the titles of which I forget. He married, in 1797, Mary Wollstonecraft, a writer of some distinction, best known as the author of a work entitled, "Rights of Woman," a pendant to Paine's "Rights of Man," and which may be regarded as the Bible of our Women's Rights party. She was the mother of Mary Godwin, who wrote Frankenstein, a most fearful story, fitted to give one the nightmare for three weeks after reading it; and who, after his divorce from his wife, was regarded as married to the poet Shelley. Godwin's novels were much read in their day, and it is easy to trace their influence in the productions of Charles Brockden Brown, one of our earliest American novelists, who merits a higher rank in American literature than has been commonly assigned him. Sir Edward Bulwer Lytton owes, in his earlier novels, much to those of Godwin, and *Caleb Williams* and *St. Leon* are still read. As a writer, for calmness and strength, for repose and energy combined, Godwin has scarcely a rival in the English language; and his style deserves to be studied by every one who would master the purity, elegance, and force of our mother-tongue. I know no other English writer who, unmoved himself, so powerfully moves his readers; and he is almost the only English writer, since Burke's unhappy influence on the language, who has written truly classical English, or our language according to its real genius.

The work on Political Justice was first published in 1792, and was republished in a second edition, much modified from the first, in 1794. My edition was the second. I have it not now, and have not seen it these twenty years, but I remember its contents very distinctly. It was inspired by the enthusiasm created by the French Revolution of 1789 in a large class of the civilized world, and contains nearly all the false and dangerous principles of that

Revolution, systematically arranged, developed, and pushed to their last consequences with a merciless logic, and a chasteness, vigor, grace, and elegance of language, which I have never seen surpassed. I had read this book when quite a lad, but without understanding it; and I had read it again as a Universalist, and appropriated many of its ideas. I now read it still again as a Socialist, and I think it has had more influence on my mind than any other book, except the Scriptures, I have ever read. There is scarcely a modern error that it does not contain; and he who has mastered it, may regard himself as in possession of nearly every error the human mind is capable of inventing. It denies as unjust all punishment, except restraint from actual violence, and consequently all capital punishment, and all penitentiaries. The author contends that the only law is justice, and justice requires us to treat every man according to his intrinsic worth, although he forgets to tell us how we are to discover it; and therefore, that if my neighbor has more intrinsic worth than I, I am to love him more, if less, I am to love him less, than myself. If his father, mother, sister, brother, wife, or child, is more worthy than mine, then am I to love them more than mine; if mine are the more worthy, then am I to love mine the most. If a rude man attacks me and threatens my life, I am to consider whether his life or mine, upon the whole, is the more worthy; if mine, then I am to defend my life at the expense of his, if necessary; if his, then I am to offer him no resistance, but let him kill me, if he chooses. Marriage, by which two persons pledge themselves to love each other exclusively until death separates them, is repugnant to justice, for it may happen that neither is the most worthy ; or if, at the time of marriage, they be so, one or the other, or both, may cease to be so, long before the death of either. There is no magic in that pronoun *my*, by which I am justified in loving *my* wife, because she is mine. If my neighbor's wife is more worthy than mine, I am bound to love her the most. I am to love the most worthy, and all are bound in like manner to love her most who is really the most worthy of all. It would happen, then, that all would be bound to love the most one and the same woman. But might not this create rivalries, jealousies, etc. ? No, for we could all enjoy her conversation, and anything more could be easily enough arranged. The author forgot, and it did not occur to me to ask, how all the men of the world were to find out what particular woman among all living women is the most worthy, or how, in case she is found out, she is to entertain them all with her conversation. Women have great facility in the use of the tongue, but it would be somewhat difficult for one woman to converse with a hundred millions of men.

Godwin did not propose precisely to abolish property, but he laid down the principle, that justice declares the property belongs to him who most needs it. Justice is reciprocal. What it is just for me to give another, he has a right to demand. If my neighbor needs what is in my possession, or some portion of it, more than I do, he has the right to take it without asking my leave. This doctrine rather pleased me, for I had less than my share, and therefore more to gain than to lose by it. In the name of justice the author denied all schools, especially public schools, for they all impose, in some form, the opinions of the masters, or, through them, of the parents and guardians, on their pupils. This is contrary to justice. What right have I to impose my opinion on another, or to take measures to bring up my child or another's in my opinions, religious, political, or moral? Thought is that which is most essentially the man, and therefore that in him which should be freest. We may urge the man or the child to think, but must never tell either what he ought to think. This seemed to me so reasonable and just,—if the rule of private judgment be adopted,—that so long as I remained a Protestant, I took good care never to give my own children any religious instruction. Parents, Godwin maintained, have no more right to control the thoughts or the opinions of their own children, than they have the children of others. How he managed with his own daughter Mary, I know not. He was not married when he wrote his book.

On the same principle that he destroys the family, and all family affections as such, Godwin destroys patriotism and the nation. Why should I love my country more than another? Why am I to love anything because it is mine? Why am I to prefer my countryman to a foreigner? What right have I to regard any man as a foreigner ? If my country is in the right, I may indeed support her, not because she is mine, but because she is in the right. But if in the wrong, I may neither defend her, nor wish her defended. Justice requires me to wish her defeat. On this doctrine, distinct nations cannot exist, and the author contends that they ought not to exist. Justice breaks down and obliterates all national distinctions; and thus at once abolishes all national rivalries and jealousies, and all international wars, by removing their causes. The author, also, rejects all government. All men are equal before the law of justice, and no man has the right to govern another. For the same reason no number of men, not even the majority, have any right to make their will or their reason prevail as law. Each man has the sovereignty of himself. All government, therefore, whether monarchical, aristocratical, democratical, or mixed, is founded in injustice, is a usurpation, a tyranny, and without authority.

These principles involve complete individualism, and leave every man free to do what seems right in his own eyes. The plain, old-fashioned reader, unacquainted with world-reforms, naturally wonders how it is that a man of the ability and education of William Godwin, a man of a sharp intellect, and some knowledge of human nature, could ever have fancied that mankind could attempt to carry such principles into practice, without falling into anarchy and a worse than the savage state. It is because he does not know all the resources of world-reformers

He takes their plan as something to be adopted by mankind as they are, as a piece of new cloth to be sewn on to an old garment, and sees at once that they would take from the old, and the rent be made worse. But they propose an entire new garment, in fact, a recasting of the essential nature of man, and they intend to introduce all the changes necessary to the successful working of their schemes. According to Godwin, man has no innate instincts, or natural tendencies in the way of the reformer, no stubborn natural character that persists through all the modifications introduced by education or moral and intellectual culture. All the vices of individual character, and all the evils of society, whence man has become the greatest plague and tormentor of his kind, come from without, not from within, and are due to civil government. Abolish civil government, recognize natural justice as the only law of the race, and leave the law to execute itself, and you will remove all evils, individual and social. Leave men to reason, confide in reason, and never attempt to give reason the aid of physical force, or think of correcting the mind by inflicting pain on the body. Men, freed from all unjust restraint, from all vexatious interference of authority, finding their reason respected and their just rights allowed, will have no temptation to rebel, no provocation to encroach on any one's rights, and will of themselves fall into their proper places, and observe with fidelity all the laws of justice. As the experiment has never been tried, it is not easy to prove the contrary; and if you adopt the doctrine of the inherent integrity of nature, and the indefinite perfectibility of man, you cannot deny that the scheme has, on one side at least, a certain degree of plausibility. There is no doubt that the author is right in denying the justice of all government resting on purely human authority; and I have never been able to understand how they who deny that, though governments are constituted by men, they derive their authority to govern immediately from God, can deny Godwin's doctrine, that all governments are founded in injustice. There is just as little doubt that many of the depravities of individual character, and many of the evils of society, originate in the effort to govern men by brute force. Princes should be shepherds of the people, not dominators.

Even the absurdest and most mischievous ot Godwin's principles have a certain reflection of Christian truth. His doctrine, that we should love the most worthy, irrespective of their personal relation to us, is true in the abstract; and hence we are to forsake father and mother, wife and children, houses and lands, and even give up our own life for our Lord, for God, the infinitely worthy. In a certain sense, the proprietor is only a steward, and the surplus of his property belongs to the poor; but Christianity makes its distribution an act of charity, not of justice. Marriage, in the Christian sense, is really practicable with the majority of the non-laboring classes only by the grace of the sacrament. For men and women in easy circumstances, who are not Christians, but abandoned to simple unassisted nature, it is a burden too great to be borne, as the experience of all ages sufficiently proves. Almighty God, under the old law, dispensed the Jews from many of its rigors; and the Protestant Reformers, denying marriage to be a sacrament, authorized divorce from the bond of matrimony, and, in certain cases, permitted polygamy. Christian marriage is above the strength of human nature in our present fallen state, and needs Christian grace. It need not surprise us, then, that honest and enlightened men and women, far enough themselves from being of a licentious turn, yet ignorant of the Christian faith, and with no knowledge of, or belief in, the Christian sacraments, should revolt at Catholic marriage, and labor not only to render it dissoluble, but easily dissoluble, and for slight, even trivial, causes.

But, though Godwin had a powerful influence on my mind, he did not absolutely master it. I would retain my own individuality, but I could not bring my mind to believe that all social organization, all associated action, must be condemned as repugnant to justice. Man is social by nature, and he has wants which can be met only by the provisions of society. Grant that the depravities of individual character originate in government,—kingcraft and priestcraft; but in what have these originated? If they are unjust, as you maintain, there must be a source of injustice prior to them, and independent of them. Then their simple removal will not necessarily secure the reign of justice. Then how are we to remove them by simple individual action? By simple appeals to reason, by simply enlightening the understanding? But is it not a well-known fact that prejudice is a bar to enlightenment, and also that men are very far from acting always in accordance with their convictions of right? Men know what is just, and yet do it not. I find, when I would do good, evil is present with me, and the good I would, I do not. No: to remove corrupt and corrupting governments, to overthrow kingcraft, to abolish priestcraft, to free men from superstition, from vain hopes and idle terrors, from the effects of false education, unfavorable circumstances, evil influences, the prejudices accumulating through long ages of ignorance and barbarism, and to render man the free, the noble, majestic being I would have him, I need something more than simple individual intelligence, and something more than the simple strength of individual will. I want and must have a greater than simple individual power. For the present, at least, I must avail myself of the principle of association, and, instead of sweeping away all organization, must endeavor to perfect social organization, and use it as a means of gaining the end I propose.

Here I found myself coöperating with the well-known Frances Wright, who seemed to me to have hit upon a just medium between the individualism of Godwin, and the communism of Owen. Frances Wright was born in Scotland near the end of the last century, and inherited a considerable property. She had been highly educated, and was a woman of rare original powers, and extensive and varied information. She was brought up in the utilitarian principles of Jeremy Bentham, was often an inmate of the family of General Lafayette at La Grange, and in the general's suite she visited this country in 1824. Returning to England in 1825, she published a book on the United States, in a strain of almost unbounded eulogy of the American people and their institutions. She saw only one stain upon our character, one thing in our condition to censure or to deplore : that was negro-slavery, which struck her as it does most Europeans, as an anomaly, and wholly incompatible with our theory of human rights.

When in the next year Mr. Owen came, with his friends, to commence his experiment of creating a new moral world at New Harmony, Frances Wright came with him, not as a full believer in his crotchets, but to try an experiment, devised with Jefferson, Lafayette, and others, for the emancipation of the negro slaves. The plan was to make the slaves work out the price of their own emancipation, and to prepare them, while they were doing it, by a peculiar system of training, for freedom. She believed it possible to make the labor of the slaves sufficiently profitable to support themselves, and to remunerate her for the price she must pay their owners for them ; and while they were doing this, by subjecting them to the moral and intellectual discipline of her philosophical principles, or the system of education she proposed to adopt, to render them moral and intelligent, free and independent in character, in every respect the equals of the whites. She accordingly purchased a plantation and some negroes at Nashoba in the State of Tennessee, about fifteen miles from Memphis, and commenced her experiment, which failed in less than two years, as she alleged, in consequence of her own illness for several months, and her inability to find persons to manage it, who combined the several qualities requisite, on the one hand, for its economical management, and, on the other, for carrying out her educational system, or her moral and philosophical ideas. Yet it should be mentioned to her honor that she gave her slaves their freedom, and settled them in Hayti, which was then a republic under President Boyer.

The negro experiment having failed, Fanny enlarged her views, and discovered that the people of the United States were not as yet prepared to engage in earnest for the abolition of slavery, that the whites were as much slaves as the blacks, and that negro slavery was only a branch of the huge tree of evil, which overshadowed the whole land. There was little wisdom in wasting one's time and resources in the attempt to lop it off while the tree itself was left standing. The axe must be laid at the root of the tree, and slavery must be abolished only as the result of a general emancipation, and a radical reform of the American people themselves.

The first step to be taken was to rouse the American mind to a sense of its rights and dignity, to emancipate it from superstition, from its subjection to the clergy, and its fear of unseen powers; to withdraw it from the contemplation of the stars or an imaginary heaven after death, and fix it on the great and glorious work of promoting man's earthly well-being. The second step was, by political action, to get adopted, at the earliest practicable moment, a system of state schools, in which all the children from two years old and upward should be fed, clothed, in a word, maintained, instructed, and educated at the public expense. In furtherance of the first object, Fanny prepared a course of lectures on *Knowledge,* which she proposed to deliver in the principal cities and towns of the Union. She had acquired a high literary reputation, and had still property enough left to permit her to go through the country and deliver her lectures at her own expense. She thought she possessed advantages in the fact that she was a woman, for there would for that reason be a greater curiosity to hear her, and she would be permitted to speak with greater boldness and directness against the clergy and superstition, than would be one of the other sex.

She commenced delivering her lectures in the autumn of 1828, at Cincinnati, and soon produced no little excitement. She gave them subsequently in New York, Boston, Philadelphia, Albany, Utica, Auburn, Buffalo, and various other places. Her lectures were eminently popular. Her free, flowing, and ornate style,—French rather than English,—her fine, rich, musical voice, highly cultivated and possessing great power, her graceful manner, her tall, commanding figure, her wit and sarcasm, her apparent honesty of purpose, and deep and glowing enthusiasm, made her one of the most pleasing and effective orators, man or woman, that I have ever heard. The Evangelicals, of course, were hostile to her, and said all manner of things against her, for the most part untrue, and did all in their power, not, of course, to disprove her doctrine, but to render her personally odious. This was particularly the case in Auburn, Cayuga Co., N. Y. Auburn was then a village containing between three and four thousand inhabitants, divided, as usual in all our villages, into a large number of sects. The hard things that were said of Fanny came to her ears, and at the close of one of her lectures, she quietly, and in the sweetest manner imaginable, remarked:

"We have here this evening considered the subject of Religion. To-morrow evening, at half past seven o'clock, we will meet again at this place to discuss the subject of Morals. I observed, in driving through your beautiful village to-day, the spires of six meeting-houses, belonging to as many different religious denominations, and I was told that there were two or three other denominations that have not as yet erected meeting-houses for themselves. It is evident that religion must have been well discussed among you, and that you are eminently a religious people. I have travelled much and visited many countries, and in no place have I been so uncourteously received, or been the subject of so much personal insult, as in your most religious village.

Perhaps it will not be inappropriate for us to spend one evening in discussing the subject of Morals."

About the time that she commenced her brief career as a public lecturer on *Knowledge*, Fanny, in connection with Robert Dale Owen, the eldest son of Robert Owen, and Robert L. Jennings, a Scotchman, started a weekly journal in New York, called *The Free Enquirer*, converted an old meeting-house into a "Hall of Science," and put in operation all the machinery of a most vigorous propagandism. In 1830 she revisited France, where she became the wife of M. Darusmont, who, as William Phiquepal, had been her travelling companion and man of business during her lecturing tours. She was present in Paris during the Revolution of July, and remained abroad for several years. She returned, indeed, to this country, finally took up her residence in Cincinnati, the wreck of what she was in the days when I knew and admired her, and where, not long since, deserted by all her former friends, and in poverty, if not destitution, she died. The only person, as far as I can learn, who did not desert her, but did all she could to lighten her afflictions, to soothe her last moments, and to direct her mind to the only source of help and comfort, was a most estimable lady, a convert from Quakerism to Catholicity.

Poor Fanny! I have always regretted her fate. Her husband treated her, I have understood, with great unkindness and brutality. And certain it is, that after her marriage her charm was broken, and her strength departed from her. Yet few who knew

her as I did, when she was about thirty years of age,
still fresh and blooming, with her feminine sweetness
and grace, and her masculine intellect, however
they may regard her principles, will fail to remember
her with much personal kindness. She followed out
with logical consistency the principle of private
judgment in faith and morals; and none who recognize that principle, and deny all infallible teaching,
have any right to reproach her. She did great
harm, and the morals of the American people feel
even to-day the injury she did them; but she acted
according to her lights, and was at least no hypocrite.
Many who condemn her have been and are greater
sinners than she.

CHAPTER VII.

THE great measure on which Fanny and her friends relied for ultimate success was the system of public schools, which, as I have said, were to include the maintenance, as well as the instruction and education, of all the children of the State. These schools were intended to deprive, as well as to relieve, parents of all care and responsibility of their children after a year or two years of age. It was assumed that parents were in general incompetent to train up their children in the way they should go, to form them with the right sort of characters, tempers, and aims; and therefore it was proposed that the State should take the whole charge of the children, provide proper establishments, and teachers and governors for them, till they should reach the age of majority. This would liberate the parents, and secure the principal advantages of a community of goods.

The aim was, on the one hand, to relieve marriage of its burdens, and to remove the principal reasons for making it indissoluble; and, on the other, to provide for bringing up all children in a rational manner to be reasonable men and women, that is, free from superstition, all belief in God and immortality, or regard for the invisible, and make them look upon this life as their only life, this earth as their only home, and the promotion of their earthly interests and enjoyments as their only end. The three great enemies to worldly happiness were held to be religion, marriage or family, and private property. Once get rid of these three institutions, and we may hope soon to realize our earthly paradise. For religion we were to substitute science, that is, science of the world of the five senses only; for private property, a community of goods; and for private families, a community of wives. No, not a community of wives, for in our new moral world there were to be no wives or husbands; there were to be only men and women, who would be free to cohabit together, according to their mutual likings, and for as long a time as they found it mutually agreeable, and no longer. Marriage as a sacrament, as a sacred thing, as a mystery, making of the twain one flesh, was denied as a superstition, or an invention of the priests, to render their own office so much the more necessary and profitable; but marriage, as the expression of mutual love between a man and a woman, was to be recognized. Yet, as the end of all marriage is mutual happiness, and as that results only from mutual love, it follows that where the love is wanting the marriage is illegitimate, is immoral, and should never take place, or should cease.

The great defect of this theory is in the assumption that the mutual love which is demanded by marriage is not within the power of free-will, and therefore does not depend on the parties themselves. The love promised in the marriage contract is not love as an uncontrollable sentiment, but love as a free, voluntary affection,—love in the sense in which we are free to love or not to love as we choose. Marriage, in the Christian sense, is certainly indefensible, if we accept the modern theory that love is necessary, *fatal*, independent of free-will. Taking this theory, a theory which follows logically from Calvinistic and infidel philosophy, and is assumed as undeniable by all our modern novelists and romancers, the doctrine of Mary Wollstonecraft, William Godwin, the poet Shelley, Robert Owen, Frances Wright, and the advocates of Free Love, is reasonable and just. Christian marriage, if that theory be true, is immoral, because no one has a right to promise to do what it does not depend on his free-will to perform. Christian marriage proceeds on the assumption that man, with the grace of God, is free to love, and can love, and faithfully perform, if he chooses, all that is implied in the marriage contract. But Calvinism and infidelity alike denying free-will in fact, even when they do not in name, are obliged to reject marriage in the Christian sense, and, to be consistent, should assert what is called Free Love.

There is no question that the views of matrimony taken by Fanny Wright and her school are abominable, but it does not necessarily follow that they were adopted from loose or licentious passions, or from really immoral motives. They were and are justified by the theory of love adopted by very nearly the whole non-Catholic world. It must not, moreover, be assumed that they appeared to us in the gross and shocking light that they do to the public, or even to myself at the present time. Things do not always appear to us at twenty-six as they do at fifty-four. We saw clearly enough that they were not views to be carried into practice in the present state of society, and we proposed them to be adopted only by a future generation, trained and prepared in our system of schools founded and sustained by the public, to adopt without abusing them. In our minds, the wonder-working effects of these schools were to precede their practical realization.

Our illusion, after our misapprehension of the nature of the love promised in marriage, was the undue estimate we placed on education. Our theory was, that the child is passive in the hands of the educator, and may be moulded as clay in the hands of the potter. Yet, in this we did but follow the popular philosophy of Locke and Condillac, and draw the conclusions warranted by the premises supplied us by the age and country. The sensism of Locke and the utilitarian morals of Paley were then taught in nearly all our colleges and universities. Most of the generation to which I belong have been brought up to believe that the mind has no inherent character, and is in the beginning a mere *tabula rasa*, a blank sheet, with simply the capacity of receiving the characters which may be written on it. It is only recently that Locke and Paley have been dethroned in our universities, and they are not yet expelled from our popular literature. Thirty years ago the whole non-Catholic world believed in the power of education to redeem society, and to secure the reign of truth and justice; and that belief has still many a stalworth champion, not precisely of the Fanny-Wright school.

Be all this as it may, our dependence was placed on education in a system of public schools managed after a plan of our own, or rather of William Phiquepal, a Frenchman, subsequently the husband of Fanny Wright, and who I see has not long since been cast in a suit for damages for the neglect and abuse of some of the pupils he brought with him from France to this country, and whom he pretended to educate. I know something of his mode of managing with these boys; I knew it from his own lips, and him I never trusted. But the more immediate work was to get our system of schools adopted. To this end it was proposed to organize the whole Union secretly, very much on the plan of the Carbonari of Europe, of whom at that time I knew nothing. The members of this secret society were to avail themselves of all the means in their power, each in his own locality, to form public opinion in favor of education by the State at the public expense, and t get such men elected to the legislatures as would be likely to favor our purposes. How far the secret organization extended, I do not know; but I do know that a considerable portion of the State of New York was organized, for I was myself one of the agents for organizing it. I, however, became tired of the work, and abandoned it after a few months. Whether the organization still exists, or whether it has ever exerted any influence or not, is more than I am able to say, or have taken the pains to ascertain.

Our next step, and in connection with this, was the formation of what was known as the Working Men's Party, started in Philadelphia in 1828, and in New York in the year following. This party was devised and started principally by Robert Dale Owen, Robert L. Jennings, George H. Evans, and a few others, without exception Europeans by birth. The purpose in the formation of this party was to get control of the political power of the State, so as to be able to use it for establishing our system of schools. We hoped, by linking our cause with the ultra-democratic sentiment of the country, which had had, from the time of Jefferson and Tom Paine, something of an anti-Christian character; by professing ourselves the bold and uncompromising champions of equality, by expressing a great love for the people, and a deep sympathy with the laborer, whom we represented as defrauded and oppressed by his employer, by denouncing all proprietors as aristocrats, and by keeping the more unpopular features of our plan as far in the background as possible, to enlist the majority of the American people under the banner of the Working Men's Party; nothing doubting that, if we could once raise that party to power, we could use it to secure the adoption of our educational system.

Into this party I entered with enthusiasm. I established in Western New York a journal in its support, and coöperated with *The Daily Sentinel*, conducted by my friends in the city. But I soon tired of the party, and gave my influence and that of my journal, in the autumn of 1830, to the Jackson candidate, E. T. Throop, against Frank Granger, the candidate of the Anti-masons, for Governor. This defection ruined my journal as a party journal, and a few days after the election, I disposed of it to my partner, and ceased to be its editor. The truth is, I never was and never could be a party man, or work in the traces of a party. I abandoned, indeed, after a year's devotion to it, the Working Men's Party, but not the working-men's cause, and to that cause I have ever been faithful according to my light and ability.

I was not naturally a radical, or even inclined to radicalism; but I had a deep sympathy with the poorer and more numerous classes. This sympathy I still have, and trust I shall have as long as I live. I believed, and still believe, that the rights of labor are not sufficiently protected, and that the modern system of large industries, which requires for its prosecution heavy outlays of capital, or credit makes the great mass of operatives virtually slaves,— slaves, in all except the name, as much so as are the negroes on one of our Southern plantations. It is a system which places the laborer under all the disadvantages, without securing him the advantages, of 'reedom. I looked, and still look, upon democracy, as it is called, which has its expression in universal suffrage and eligibility, as affording no adequate protection to the laboring classes, as in fact no better than a mockery. The British system, the mercantile system, the credit system, the banking system, the system which gives the supremacy to trade and manufactures, inaugurated by the Peace of Utrecht in 1713, I regarded, and still regard, as worse than the serfdom of the middle ages, and worse even than slavery as it has existed or can exist in any Christian country. It cannot last forever; but it is too powerful to be successfully combated at present. The industrial and commercial supremacy of Great Britain must be annihilated before we can get rid of it, and that supremacy is not easily shaken; for Russia is the only modern nation that is in a condition to offer it the slightest resistance, and Russia is preparing to adopt it.

My few months' experience as the editor of a working-man's journal satisfied me that it was idle to attempt to carry out our plans by means of a working-man's party, or, so to speak, a proletarian party. The working-men, except in the cities and manufacturing villages, do not, in our own country, constitute, as a distinct class, the majority. They are neither numerous nor strong enough to get or to wield the political power of the State. They cannot afford to engage in the struggle to obtain it Capital or credit, in its various forms and ramifications, is too strong for them. The movement we commenced could only excite a war of man against money; and all history and all reasoning in the case prove that in such a war money carries it over man. Money commands the supplies, and can hold out longer than they who have nothing but their manhood. It can starve them into submission. I wished sincerely and earnestly to benefit the working-men, but I saw, as soon as I directed my attention to the point, that I could effect nothing by appealing to them as a separate class. My policy must be, not a working-men's party, but to induce all classes of society to coöperate in efforts for the working-men's cause. The rich and poor, the learned and unlearned, the producers and consumers, the head workers and the handworkers, must unite, work together, or no reforms were practicable, no amelioration of the condition of any class was to be hoped for.

No doubt I was for a moment fascinated by the visionary schemes of my friends, but my motive for supporting the Working Men's Party was never precisely theirs. I did not do it merely for the sake of the proposed system of education, but with the hope of benefiting the working-men themselves. I acquiesced in that system of education for a moment, but never really approved it. I was a husband and a father, and did not altogether relish the idea of breaking up the family, and regarding my children as belonging to the State rather than to me. Parents might not be in all cases well qualified to bring up their children properly, but where was the State to get its army of nurses, teachers, governors, etc., better qualified? What certainty was there that these public schools would be better conducted, or be more favorable to the morals and intelligence of children, than the family itself? After all, what could these schools do for our children? They would bring them up to be rational, it was said; that is, free from superstition, free from all religious prejudices, ignorant of all morality resting for its foundation on belief in God, in immortality, in moral accountability, and restricted in all their thoughts and affections to their five senses and the material world, therefore, to purely material goods and sensual pleasures. Suppose the schools to fulfil these expectations, they will turn out our children only well-trained animals—a sort of learned pigs. After all, is this desirable?

I cannot carry out my reforms without love, disinterestedness, sacrifice. If man is a mere animal, born to propagate his species, and to die and be no more, why shall I love him, and sacrifice myself for him? Where is his moral worth, his dignity, the greatness and majesty of his nature? What matters it, whether, during his existence of a day, he is happy or miserable, since to-morrow he dies, and it is all the same? For a being so worthless, wherefore devote myself? What is there in him to inspire me with heroism, and enable me in his behalf to dare poverty, reproach, exile, the rack, the dungeon, the scaffold, or the stake?

No longer irritated against religion by being obliged by my profession to seem to profess what I did not believe, I found myself almost instantly reverting with regret to my early religious principles and affections. The moment I avowedly threw off all religion and began to work without it, I found myself impotent. I did not need religion to pull down or destroy society; but the moment I wished to build up, to effect something positive, I found I could not proceed a single step without it. I was compelled to make brick without straw. Philosophers had told me, and I had believed, that self-interest would suffice as a motive power, that all one has to do is to show men what is really for their interest, and they will do it. Nothing more false. Men are selfish enough, no doubt of that; but nothing in the world is harder than to get them to labor for their own best interest. They act from habit, from routine, from appetite and passion, and will sacrifice their highest and best good to their momentary lusts. It is an old complaint, that men do not act as well as they know. They see the right, approve it, and yet pursue the wrong. It is not enough to show them their interest, to convince their understandings. I must have some power by which I can overcome what religious people call the flesh,—a power which will strengthen the will, and enable men to subdue their passions and control their lusts. Where am I to find this power except in religious ideas and principles, in the belief in God and immortality, in duty, moral accountability?

I need, then, religion of some sort as the agent to induce men to make the sacrifices required in the adoption of my plans for working out the reform of society, and securing to man his earthly felicity. Certainly, I was far enough from the Christian thought; but this conviction, real and sincere, was a step in my ascent from the abyss into which I had fallen. Certainly, it does not follow that religion is true because it is needed to secure man his earthly well-being; but the conviction that it is necessary for that purpose, if not rudely treated, may, in an ingenuous mind, lead to something more. I had fixed it in my mind that the creation of an earthly paradise, a heaven on earth for my race, was the end for which I should labor; and I saw that I could not gain that end without the agency of religion. Therefore I accepted religion once more, and, on quitting my journal, resumed my old profession of a preacher, though of what particular Gospel it would be difficult to say.

CHAPTER VIII.

I RESUMED preaching, but on my own hook, as an independent preacher, responsible to no church, sect, or denomination. Do you say I was wrong, that I acted precipitately, and should have waited till my beard had grown? Perhaps you are right. But perhaps I was not in a condition in which I could wait. A man may often be placed in a situation in which he must act, although perfectly aware that to act is premature. I was still young, only just entering my twenty-eighth year, and knew perfectly well that I had made no thorough examination of the great questions which had been raised in my mind; but I must do something, not indeed what I would, but what I could. The question with me was simply, what in my condition was practicable, and whether what to me was practicable was honest, such as involved the violation of no principle of natural morality. Satisfied on this point, I could resume my profession with a good conscience, provided I pretended to believe no more than I really did believe, and did not attempt to dogmatize in matters of opinion, or give myself out for what I was not.

"But you ran without being sent." Certainly I

did; but that was my privilege as a Protestant? No Protestant had or has a right to upbraid me, for all Protestant ministers run without being sent. None of them have received, in the ecclesiastical sense, a mission. I stood on the same footing with Luther, Calvin, and all the Reformers. They were all preachers on their own hook, self-commissioned ministers. I could be no more bound by them than they were by the Pope; or by any Protestant sect, than that sect itself was bound by the Catholic Church, from which it had separated.

Do you allege that my creed was unorthodox? What standard of orthodoxy had I as a Protestant? The Bible? The Bible as each one understands it for himself, or as it is interpreted by a divinely-commissioned authority? The essence of Protestant-ism is, in denying all such authority, and in asserting the right of private interpretation. On Protestant principles, orthodoxy is *my* doxy, heterodoxy is *your* doxy. For the Protestant, each man's private judgment is the only admissible standard of ortho-doxy. Leave me then to follow what seems right in my own eyes, or else go back yourselves to Mother Church; prove to me that your private judgment is more worthy to be followed than mine, before you arraign me as heterodox because I do not follow it. You differ from me as much as I do from you; and why is it heterodoxy for me to differ from you, any more than it is for you to differ from me?

My creed, no doubt, was very short, but no Protestant had any right to snub me because it was not longer. In resuming my profession, I acted as a consistent Protestant; and as I had already been set apart to the work of the ministry by the laying on of the hands of a Protestant presbytery, I stood as legitimately in the pulpit as any Protestant minister does or can. So far, I was irreproachable on Protestant principles. I will say this much for myself, that never did I, after reascending the pulpit, profess to be what I was not. I never claimed to be an authorized preacher, or to have authority to dogmatize on any subject. I never pretended to be a doctor. I professed to be only an humble inquirer after truth; and all I professed to do was to stimulate my hearers also to inquire after it for themselves. I warned them that I was a fallible man, and that they must believe nothing, simply because I believed or asserted it.   There is, my brethren, I said to them, more truth than we have yet found. Even what truth we really do hold, may be modified as we discover more truth. As yet we are learners and inquirers; and we must inquire earnestly for the truth, and hold ourselves ready to embrace it, let it come in what shape it may, and follow it, let it lead whithersoever it will.

I have never reproached myself for the position I assumed after my connection with Fanny-Wrightism. I followed the best light I had, honestly, sincerely, unflinchingly. God gave me this grace, and he finally led me, without my foreseeing whither he was leading me, into the bosom of his Church. Yet when I recommenced preaching, I had hardly the simplest elements of natural religion. My great aim was, not to serve God, but to serve man; the love of my race, not the love of my Maker, moved me. I was still bent on social reform, and regarded religion and all things else solely in relation to that end. I found in me certain religious sentiments that I could not efface; certain religious beliefs or tendencies, of which I could not divest myself. I regarded them as a law of my ntaure, as natural to man, as the noblest part of our nature, and as such I cherished them; but as the expression in me of an objective world, I seldom pondered them. I found them universal, manifesting themselves, in some form, wherever man is found; but I received them, or supposed I received them, on the authority of humanity or human nature, and professed to hold no religion except that of humanity. I had become a believer in humanity, and put humanity in the place of God. The only God I recognized was the Divine in man, the divinity of humanity, one alike with God and with man, which I supposed to be the real meaning of the Christian doctrine of the Incarnation, the mystery of Emmanuel, or God with us,—God manifest in the flesh. There may be an unmanifested God, and certainly is; but the only God who exists for us is the God in man, the active and living principle of human nature.

I regarded Jesus Christ as divine in the sense in which all men are divine, and human in the sense in which all men are human. I took him as my model man, and regarded him as a moral and social reformer, who sought, by teaching the truth under a religious envelope, and practising the highest and purest morality, to meliorate the earthly condition of mankind; but I saw nothing miraculous in his conception or birth, nothing supernatural in his person and character, in his life or his doctrine. He came to redeem the world, as does every great and good man, and deserved to be held in universal honor and esteem as one who remained firm to the truth amid every trial, and finally died on the cross, a martyr to his love of mankind. As a social reformer, as one devoted to the progress and well-being of man in this world, I thought I might liken myself to him, and call myself by his name. I called myself a *Christian*, not because I took him for my master, not because I believed all he believed or taught, but because, like him, I was laboring to introduce a new order of things, and to promote the happiness of my kind. I used the Bible as a good Protestant, took what could be accommodated to my purpose, and passed over·the rest, as belonging to an age now happily outgrown. I followed the example of the carnal Jews, and gave an earthly sense to all the promises and prophecies of the Messias, and looked for my reward in this world.

For several months I went on preaching, very much as I had lectured during the time of my avowed unbelief. Very little was changed except my tone and temper. I was willing to agree with the Christian world as far as I could, and no longer wished to fight it. But I found myself gradually, I hardly know how or wherefore, cherishing views and feelings more and more in accordance, I will not say with Christianity, but with natural religion. I began to approximate to a belief in God as a creator and moral governor, not so much from any reasoning on the subject, as from the silent operations of my natural religious sentiments. I fell in with a sermon by the celebrated Dr. Channing on the Dignity of Human Nature. Its eloquence, its noble sentiments, and its elevated thoughts, affected me powerfully, and made me almost a worshipper of man. It made me think so highly of man, of his deathless energies and glorious affinities, that I felt contented to believe that his soul could not die, but must live forever. I saw in man, more clearly and more vividly than I had before, something worth living for, something one could love, and, if need be, die for; I found myself almost instantly abandoning my old doctrine of interested for disinterested affection. There was something higher and nobler in man than I had hitherto admitted; something which could serve as a basis to that love of mankind necessary as the agent for introducing the social changes and organizations through which I hoped to obtain my earthly paradise.

Dr. Channing's writings drew my attention to the Unitarians, a denomination with which I had previously had no acquaintance. I found that they were liberal, that they eschewed all creeds and confessions, allowed the unrestrained exercise of reason, and left their ministers each to stand on his own private convictions, and to arrange matters each as best he could with his own congregation. The few members I met were educated, cultivated, intelligent, respectable, and I felt that among them I should find my home, and my natural associates. I offered my self to a Unitarian congregation in the summer of 1832, and was accepted and settled as their minister. Then, almost for the first time, I began to study philosophy and theology with a little method and earnestness. I was thrown into a society new to me, and had access to a whole literature to which I had hitherto been a stranger. I learned French and a little German, and began the study of the rationalistic literatures of France and Germany, more especially of France. A new world, or rather many new worlds, seemed to open to me, and I almost forgot my socialistic dreams.

The first work I read in French, and which held me enchained quite too long, was a work, forgotten now, of Benjamin Constant on Religion, considered in its Origin, its Forms, and its Developments. It chimed in with my modes of thinking at the time, and seemed to be just the book I wanted to enable me to clear up, develop, systematize, and confirm with the requisite historical proofs my own convictions. Benjamin Constant is a historical character. He was born in Switzerland of a French Huguenot family, and educated in Geneva, Scotland, and Germany. He was recognized as a French citizen under the Directory, and for several years played a prominent part as a French politician. Accompanying Madame Staël when the First Consul exiled her from Paris, travelling with her in Italy, Germany, and

England, and residing with her for some time at Coppet, he devoted himself to literature, till the fall of Napoleon in 1814. He was admitted to the council of the emperor during the Hundred Days, and after the second Restoration, became a distinguished member of the Chamber of Deputies, on the Liberal side, and took an active part in French politics till his death in 1830.

Benjamin Constant had been brought up a Protestant, and became, like so many others of his generation, an unbeliever in revelation, perhaps even in God, and is said not to have lived a very edifying life. He commenced his work with the intention of directing it against religion; but he was forced by his inquiries and discoveries to write, as he believed, in its favor. His theory, not peculiar to himself, and held by men far profounder and more erudite than he, is, that religion has its origin in a sentiment natural to man, which may be termed a law of his nature. This sentiment is vague and not easily defined. It is that in man which places him in relation with the unseen, makes him tremble before the invisible with fear, or thrill with delight, and leads him to open some means of communication with supernal powers.

This sentiment is universal, an instinct, or, it may be, a mysterious revelation made by the Invisible to the heart of man, which finds its natural expression in the act of worship. But, blind in itself, the object worshipped will be proportioned to the degree of intellectual light possessed by the worshipper. The form depends on the intelligence, and the sentiment adapts itself to any form from the lowest African Fetichism to the highest and purest Jewish and Christian Monotheism. The sentiment itself is always the same, as unalterable and permanent as the nature of man, but its forms are variable and transitory. Man embodies in them his ideas or conceptions of the true, the just, the holy; but, as these ideas are progressive, he is obliged with each step in their progress to break his old forms become too strait for him, and to create new and broader forms, more in harmony with his advancing intelligence. Men began, in the lowest forms of Fetichism, with the worship of wood, stones, animals, four-footed beasts, and creeping things. From Fetichism they advanced in process of time to the worship of the sun, moon, and stars, or the hosts of heaven, and the elements of nature. At first man worships the outward, visible object itself, but gradually refining on the object, and rising to metaphysical conceptions, he takes it simply as a symbol of the invisible, and worships no longer the bull, but the spirit or manitou of the bull—no longer the sun, but the spirit of the sun. In this way he rises from Sabianism to Oriental, Egyptian, and Persian symbolism, and to the polished and graceful forms of Greek and Roman Polytheism. Refining and philosophizing still more on his ideas and the phenomena of nature, he ascends to the Jewish, and from the Jewish to the Christian Monotheism.

Man's natural tendency is to embody his ideas

and sentiments in fixed forms or institutions. He wishes to find to-day the friends of yesterday. He dreads change, and would render his acquisitions permanent and unchangeable. The jugglers, afterwards developed into a priesthood, take advantage of this, and labor to keep the forms of religion fixed and stationary, and to prevent all religious progress, all growth or expansion of religious ideas. This is especially the case in the East, where the sacerdotal religions obtain and give to society a theocratic organization and government. Originally the sacerdotal religions obtained even in Greece and Rome, but gradually the warrior caste emancipated themselves from the sacerdotal, established civil governments proper, and obtained for religion the freedom to follow the natural progress and development of the nation. There is a great progress in the moral and religious ideas of the Odyssey on those of the Iliad, and hence the two poems could never have been composed by one and the same man. The Roman Polytheism, again, is far in advance of the Grecian. Indeed Christianity is only one step in advance of Roman Polytheism,—a step to which the human mind naturally tended.

Each new form or institution of religion is not only an advance on its predecessor, but is the stepping-stone to newer and still greater progress. Each in turn is outgrown, ceases to be in harmony with the wants and intelligence of the age or country; and when it becomes so, men begin to criticize it, to point out its defects, its inconsistencies, and to break away from it. Do not be alarmed. These *critical* periods in history are no doubt terrible, such as one dreads to live in, but they are essential to the progress of man and society. People think religion is about to desert them, and they look upon the advanced minds longing for something purer, higher, truer, and broader, as their enemies, as the enemies of the gods, as infidels, blasphemers, and condemn them to drink hemlock, or to be crucified between two thieves. Such periods of criticism, of destruction of old forms, have occurred several times in the history of the human race. We meet one in Greece commenced by Socrates and continued by Plato; another which prepared the way for the introduction and establishment of the Christian Church; another which commenced in the sixteenth century of our era, when Catholicity had ceased to be in harmony with the wants and intelligence of the age, and which still continues. These periods of destruction and transition mark, not the decline of civilization, but its advance; and so far from being hostile to religion, they invariably prepare for it a more glorious future.

This theory of the progress of religion corresponded with my theory of the progress of mankind, and had for me many charms. I was prepared in advance to accept it, and did not at the time think of inquiring whether it really had any historical basis or not. No doubt had as yet arisen in my mind as to the truth of the doctrine of progress. A slight knowledge of history, as well as of philosophy, suffices to refute Benjamin Constant's theory. Truth is older than error, and Monotheism—the belief and worship of one only God—is older than Polytheism, older than Fetichism, and is, in fact, the earliest form of religion recorded in history. But the truth or falsity of the theory under this relation was not the point which struck me with the most force. That was not the problem which I was interested at the time in solving. The point in the theory which struck my attention, and influenced my studies and action, was the fact alleged, that man naturally seeks to embody his religious ideas and sentiments in institutions, and that these institutions serve as instruments of progress. What we now want, I said, is a new religious institution or church, one that shall embody the advanced intelligence of the age, and respond to all the new wants which time and events have developed. Every institution, in that it is an institution, has something fixed, inflexible, and inexpansive. Hence no institution can answer the wants of the race in all times and places. The various religions, Fetichism, Sabianism, Symbolism, Polytheism, Judaism, Catholicism, have all been good and useful in their day, when and where they harmonized with the wants and intelligence of the people; but they have all been outgrown, and the human race has cast them off, as the grown man casts off the garments of his childhood. Catholicity was good in its day, during the thousand years which intervened between the fall of the Roman Empire of the West and the rise of Luther and his associates; for during that period it was in harmony with the general intelligence, responded to the highest conceptions, and to the deepest wants of the soul then developed. It led the age, commanded respect, commanded obedience and love, because it aided the soul in its progress, inspired the heart with noble sentiments, and prepared its adherents to engage in grand and heroic enterprises for the human race. But fixed and inflexible, immovable and unalterable in itself, it ceased to be favorable to progress the moment it had brought the race up to its own level, and must from that moment become a let and a hindrance to progress,—a mischievous institution, which must be demolished and cleared away to make room for a new and better institution.

That Catholicity had been outgrown and ceased to be useful, was evinced by the Reformation. Protestantism was not a religion, was not a church, and in itself contained no germ of religious organization. It was not in any sense an institution. Its mission was simply one of destruction, as I wrote in *The Christian Examiner*, in 1834. But its rise proved that there were wants and lights which Catholicity did not meet—could not satisfy. What, then, is our mission? Not to revive Catholicity, already become superannuated in the sixteenth century, and struck with death by Luther, when he threw his inkstand in the face of the devil; not to continue Protestantism, which was simply critical, destructive, and without the slightest organic character or ten-

dency, or the least power to erect a temple of concord and peace, of union and progress.   What then?
It is to labor directly for a new religious institution, church, or organization, which shall embody the most advanced ideas and sentiments of the race, and be THE CHURCH OF THE FUTURE, by containing in itself what was wanting in the religions of the past, —the principle of its own progress.

CHAPTER IX.

I DID not lose sight of the great end I proposed,—
the progress of man and society, and the realization
of a heaven on earth. I was working in reference
to it even while I was pursuing my historical and
philosophical researches, and maturing my religious
theories. I had been forced to resort to religious
ideas and sentiments for the power to work effectually for it; and I now found that I must have a
religious organization, institution, or church, in order
to render these sentiments practically efficient. This
much I had gained from Benjamin Constant's great
work, and it was nearly all that I did gain from it.
The work of destruction, commenced by the Reformation, which had introduced an era of criticism
and revolution, had, I thought, been carried far
enough. All that was dissoluble had been dissolved.
All that was destructible had been destroyed, and it
was time to begin the work of reconstruction,—a
work of reconciliation and love.

Irreligious ideas and sentiments are disorganizing
and destructive in their nature, and cannot be safely
cherished for a single moment after the work of
destruction is completed When the work to be

done is that of construction, of building up, of organizing, of founding something, we must resort to religious ideas and sentiments, for they, having love for their principle, are plastic, organic, constructive, and the only ideas and sentiments that are so. They are necessary to the new organization or institution of the race demanded; and the organization or institution, what I called the church, is necessary to the progress of man and society, or the creation of an earthly paradise. The first thing to be done is to cease our hostility to the past, discontinue the work of destruction; abandon the old war against the Papacy, which has no longer any significance, and in a spirit of universal love and conciliation, turn our attention to the work of founding a religious institution, or effecting a new church organization, adapted to our present and future wants.

This we are now, I thought, in a condition to attempt.   Men are beginning to understand that Protestantism is no-churchism, is no positive religion; and while it serves the purpose of criticism and destruction, it cannot meet the wants of the soul, or erect the temple in which the human race may assemble to worship in concord and peace. Unitarianism has demolished Calvinism, made an end in all thinking minds of everything like dogmatic Protestantism, and Unitarianism itself satisfies nobody. It is negative, cold, lifeless, and all advanced minds among Unitarians are dissatisfied with it, and are craving something higher, better, more living. and lifegiving. They are weary of doubt, uncertainty, disunion, individualism, and crying out from the bottom of their hearts for faith, for love, for union. They feel that life has wellnigh departed from the world; that religion is but an empty name, and morality is mere decorum or worldly prudence; that men neither worship God, nor love one another. Society as it is, is a lie, a sham, a charnel-house, a valley of dry bones. O that the Spirit of God would once more pass by, and say unto these dry bones, "Live"! So I felt, so felt others; and whoever enjoyed the confidence of the leading Unitarian ministers in Boston and its vicinity from 1830 to 1840, well knows that they were sick at heart with what they had, and were demanding in their interior souls a religious institution of some sort, in which they could find shelter from the storms of this wintry world, and some crumbs of the bread of life to keep them from starving. Not only in Boston was this cry heard. It came to us on every wind from all quarters,—from France, from Germany, from England even; and Carlyle, in his *Sartor Resartus*, seemed to lay his finger on the plague-spot of the age. Men had reached the centre of indifference; under a broiling sun in the *Rue d'Enfer*, had pronounced the everlasting "No." Were they never to be able to pronounce the everlasting "Yes"?

Among them all I was probably the most hopeful, and the most disposed to act. If I lacked faith in God, I had faith in humanity. The criticisms on all subjects sacred and profane, the bold investigations of every department of life, continued unweariedly for three hundred years, by the most intrepid, the most energetic, and the most enlightened portion of mankind, had, I thought, sufficiently developed ideas and sentiments, and obtained for us all the light needed, all the materials wanted for commencing the work of reorganization, and casting broad and deep the foundations of the Church of the Future. All that was wanting was to collect the ideas which these three hundred years of criticism and investigation had developed, and mould them into one harmonious, complete, and living system, and then to take that system as the principle and law of the new moral and religious organization. Whence that system, formed from the union of various and isolated ideas, was to derive its life, its principle of unity and vitality, so as to be living and effective, I did not at the time specially consider. I supposed ideas themselves were potent, but, hard pressed, I probably should have said, they are potent by the potency of the human mind, or the Divinity in man.

There was a moment when I looked to Dr. Channing, the foremost man among the Unitarians, as the one who was to take the lead in this work of reorganization. His reputation in 1834 was high, and he loomed up at a distance in my eyes as the great man of the age; but a closer view, an intimate personal acquaintance with him, soon disabused me. Dr. Channing had done me great service in the beginning of my efforts to rise from the abyss of unbelief into which I had fallen ; he was my warm, considerate, and steady friend ever after to the day of his death. Ho consoled me, encouraged me, aided me in various ways; and I can never forget my personal obligations to him. I hold, and always shall hold his memory in grateful respect. But he was not the great man many supposed him to be. He was benevolent, philanthropic, and anxious to do all in his power for the good of mankind, especially for the relief of the poorer and more numerous classes. He had a just horror of Calvinistic theology, and warred to the last against the Calvinistic view of human nature. He rejected with indignation the doctrine of total depravity, asserted in eloquent terms the dignity of human nature, and entertained the loftiest conceptions of the greatness and capacity of the human soul. He asserted so frequently and so strongly the dignity of man, that one of his brother ministers said of him, with more point than truth, however: "Dr. Channing makes man a great god, and God a little man." He certainly, in revolting against the Calvinistic doctrine, which so unduly depresses the human to make way, as it supposes, for sovereign grace, ran to the opposite extreme, and as unduly depressed the Divine, and exaggerated the human. He is answerable for no small portion of the soul-worship, which was for a time the fashionabl idolatry of the metropolis of New England.

As a moral man, as a lover of his kind, as a sympathizer with the oppressed and the downtrodden, Dr. Channing was great, but he was never a clear and profound thinker. He was no philosopher, no theologian, and only moderately erudite. As a reasoner, he was feeble and confused; as a controversialist, he was no match for the Worcesters, Woods, and Stuarts in the ranks of his Calvinistic opponents. He was undoubtedly an eloquent sermonizer, and within his range the master of a style of great simplicity, sweetness, and beauty; but he lacked vigor and robustness, and left on his readers the impression that he was sickly and inclining to sentimentalism. He was an eloquent and effective declaimer, and was felicitous, when the matter did not lie beyond his depth, in summing up and clearly stating the various points in a question after it had been thoroughly discussed by more vigorous and original, but less polished and graceful, minds than his own. He was never, to my knowledge, a leader in the world of thought or of action, and his study apparently was to come after others, and to rebuke or applaud them as seemed to him proper; and as he usually chose his time for intervening with adroitness, he not unfrequently received the credit due to those who had gone before and enlightened him.

Dr. Channing exerted for a long time a very great influence, and he did, no doubt, good service in demolishing New-England theology, and in liberalizing the New-England mind; but he had no original genius or tendency. His nature was not expansive, and with all his generous sentiment he lived, as it were, shut up in himself. He inclined strongly to individualism, and distrusted all associated action, though sometimes tolerating, and even encouraging it. His sympathy with Unitarians, as a distinct sect or denomination, was not strong, and he gave them the prestige of his name chiefly because they suffered reproach. Unitarianism he regarded as useful, in that it was opposed to Calvinism; but he was far from regarding it as the last word of Christian truth. His own mind, I apprehend, remained unsettled to the day of his death. He felt that he was still seeking after the truth, and waiting for it to dawn on him and the world. "There is," he would often say in his conversations with me, "a higher form of Christian truth and love needed and to be revealed, than the world has yet seen; and I look with hope to the discussions and movements in the midst of which we live, to elicit and realize it for mankind." He looked for this new manifestation of Christian truth and love in a socialist direction. I do not think he had any tendency to return towards New-England orthodoxy, in which he was educated, as some Evangelicals have supposed. As far as I could discover, his tendency in the latter years of his life was to place less and less value on doctrines of any sort, and to make religion consist in sentiment alone. He rejected all creeds and confessions, rejected all church authority, and all church organization, though he died a member of the Church of the Disciples, founded by James Freeman Clarke, on the principle that true Christians are they who exclude no views, whether true or false, and are ever learning, and never able to come to the knowledge of the truth.

Dr. Channing was not and could not be the man to found the new order, and rival or more than rival a Moses, and a greater than Moses. Among my friends and acquaintances I found none. Perhaps the thought passed through my head that I was myself the destined man ; but I did not entertain it. I could not be more than John the Baptist, or the Voice of one crying in the wilderness, "Behold the Lord cometh :· prepare ye to meet him. " I might, perhaps, be the Precursor of the new Messias, but not the new Messias himself. My business was, not to found the new church, but to proclaim its necessity, and to prepare men's minds and hearts to welcome it.

You smile at my simplicity or at my lofty estimate of myself, but with less justice than you suppose. I was a believer in humanity, and the God I professed to worship was the God in man. I was with the Unitarians, and had not advanced nearer to Christianity than they were : most of them thought not so near. But the New-England Unitarians, though very excellent people as the world goes, hold nothing that made me appear absurd or ridiculous in thinking as I did. They are the descendants of the New-England Arminians of the last century, who rejected the Calvinistic doctrine of election and reprobation, the restriction of the atonement to the elect, the inamissibility of grace, and asserted universal redemption, free-will, and other points very nearly as settled by the Council of Trent. In the early part of the present century, it was found that nearly all the

Arminian churches and their ministers in New England had silently become Pelagian and Unitarian. They asserted human ability in relation to merit, and rejected both the Calvinistic and the Catholic doctrine of grace, denied the Atonement, the Incarnation, and the proper Divinity of the Word, and reduced Christianity very nearly to simple natural religion or philosophy, as every consistent reasoner must do, who adopts the Pelagian heresy. Some few among the Unitarians, as Dr. Noah Worcester and, perhaps, Dr. Channing, adopted Arian views, or at least regarded our Lord as a superangelic person; but the majority, at least of the preachers, regarded him as a man, with one simple nature, and that human nature, though a man extraordinarily, some said miraculously, endowed, and divinely commissioned to teach truth and righteousness, chiefly through the singular purity and holiness of his life. He taught nothing which, when once revealed, is above the ability of reason to comprehend, and was, in his moral perfection, in no sense above our aim or our reach. To be Christians in the full sense of the word, we must be what he was, sons of God, as he was the Son of God.

The Bible was regarded by Unitarians as containing, upon the whole, a faithful and trustworthy record of the revelations of truth which God at sundry times and in divers places had been pleased to make to mankind; but not as plenarily inspired, or as in all respects free from the errors and prejudices of the times in which it was written. Holy men spake of old as they were moved by the Holy Ghost, that is, by a pure and holy spirit or interior disposition, and may do so now. Men are as near to God to-day as they were two thousand years ago, and may, if they choose, have as intimate communion with him, and be as truly inspired by him.

In regard to another life, the Unitarians were not precisely agreed among themselves. A few held the orthodox view of a future judgment and the endless punishment of the wicked; now and then one thought there would be a final judgment, and that the wicked, those who died wicked, would be condemned, and then annihilated. Some believed in future disciplinary punishment, the restoration of the wicked, and the ultimate holiness and happiness of all men; others, and the majority, held that the future life would be simply a continuation, under other and perhaps more favorable conditions, of our present natural life, in which we should take rank according to the progress made here, and in which we might grow better and happier, or worse and more miserable forever. With these last, so far as I had any fixed views on the subject, I agreed.

The heaven the Unitarians promised in the world to come, was in the natural order,—a sort of natural beatitude, such as some Catholics have supposed might be enjoyed by those in the least unpleasant part of hell. It was not to consist in the beatific vision, or seeing God as he is in himself by the supernatural light of glory, but in a reunion of friends, in the exercise of the social and benevolent affections, and the study of the natural sciences, in discovering the secrets of nature, and in admiring the beauty and harmony of the Creator's works. In its details, it may differ from Mahomet's paradise, but hardly so in principle. Indeed there were those among us who openly claimed the Mahometans as good Unitarians, and were quite disposed to fraternize with them. It need therefore surprise nobody that one of the most brilliant and gifted of the early Unitarian ministers of Boston actually did go to Turkey, turn Mahometan, and become a Moslem preacher. He published in English a volume of Mahometan sermons, which I once read. I thought them equal to most Unitarian sermons I had seen or heard. Even John Wesley, the founder of Methodism, thought Islamism an improvement on the Christianity of the Greeks of Constantinople.

There was evidently nothing shocking to the Unitarian mind in my regarding myself as the Precursor to the new Messias. Why should there not be new Messiases? Indeed, was not Kossuth, vice-president of the American Bible Society, ex-governor of Hungary, when he came to this country a few years since, greeted, in so many words, as the "Second Messias," without a word of rebuke in public even from the so-called orthodox Protestant press? Did not Methodist schoolmasters in Cincinnati bring their young pupils to him that he might bless them? The truth is, I was quite modest in claiming for myself only the part of the Precursor, and many came to ask me if I was not myself a second Messias. The new moral world must have, of course, a great man, a representative man, to usher it in, to be its father and founder. If I had regarded myself as that man, and thus as superior, by all the difference between the first century and the nineteenth, to the Founder of Christianity, it would have argued rather my low estimate of Him than my high estimate of myself; and, in not doing so, I proved myself more modest than some who have come after me.

Not finding among my friends and acquaintances the "representative man," and waiting till he should reveal himself, I concluded to commence a direct preparation for his coming. One man, and one man only, shared my entire confidence, and knew my most secret thought. Him, from motives of delicacy, I do not name; but, in the formation of my mind, in systematizing my ideas, and in general development and culture, I owe more to him than to any other man among Protestants. We have since taken divergent courses, but I loved him as I have loved no other man, and shall so love and esteem him as long as I live. He encouraged me, and through him chiefly I was enabled to remove to Boston and commence operations. Dr. Channing and several of his personal friends, without knowing all my purposes, also assisted me. I was invited to Boston to preach to the laboring classes, and to do all I could to save them from the unbelief which had become quite prevalent among them. I accepted the invitation, proposing to myself to make of it an opportunity to bring out my religious and socialist theories, and to call public attention to the necessity of a new religious organization of mankind. I accordingly organized, on the first Sunday in July, 1836, " The Society for Christian Union and Progress."

The name I gave to the society was indicative of the principle of the future organization, and of the end I contemplated,—the union and progress of the race. I remained, with some interruption, the minister of this Society till the latter part of 1843, when I began to suspect that man is an indifferent church-builder, and that God himself had already founded a church for us, some centuries ago, quite adequate to our wants, and adapted to our nature and destiny. My Society at one time was prosperous, but in general I could not pride myself on my success; yet I saw clearly enough, that, with more confidence in myself, a firmer grasp of my own convictions, a stronger attachment to my own opinions because they were mine, and a more dogmatic temper than I possessed, I might easily succeed, not in founding a new Catholic Church indeed, but in founding a new sect, and perhaps a sect not without influence. But a new sect was not in my plan, and I took pains to prevent my movement from growing into one. What I wanted was, not sectarism, of which I felt we had had quite too much, but unity and catholicity. I wished to unite men, not to divide them—to put an end to divisions, not to multiply them.

The truth is, I was not, except on a few points,

settled in my own mind. I never concealed, or affected to conceal, that I regarded myself as still a learner, a seeker after truth, not as one who has found the truth, and has nothing to do but to preach it. I always told my congregation that I was looking for more light, and that I could not be sure that my convictions would be to-morrow what they are to-day. Whether I preached or wrote, I aimed simply at exciting thought and directing it to the problems to be solved, not to satisfy the mind or furnish it with dogmatic solutions of its difficulties. I was often rash in my statements, because I regarded myself not as putting forth doctrines that must be believed, but as throwing out provocatives to thought and investigation. My confidence was not in the individual mind, whether my own or another's, but in humanity, in the action and decisions of the general mind, the universal reason.

I was perfectly consistent in this; and my course, I thought then, and I think now, was the only honest course for a man who has not an infallible authority to which he can appeal, and in the name of which he is commissioned to speak. If the criterion of truth is the universal reason, or the reason of all men, not my individual reason; and if I am imperfect and yet progressive, never knowing the whole truth, yet able to know more to-morrow than I know to-day, how can I, as an honest man, regard my private opinions as dogmas, or put forth my personal convictions, as so much eternal and immutable truth? What as yet the universal reason has

not passed upon, what has not as yet received the
seal of approbation from universal and immutable
human nature, can be regarded only as private
opinion, which I have no right to ask others to
believe, or to assert as indisputable. I was in fact
too honest, too consistent, and too distrustful of
myself to succeed.

CHAPTER X.

MY "NEW VIEWS."

I WROTE and published, immediately after organizing my Society, a small work entitled, *New Views
of Christianity, Society, and the Church*, derived in
great part from Benjamin Constant, Victor Cousin,
Heinrich Heine, and the publications of the Saint-
Simonians. It was designed to set forth the reasons
which made a new church necessary, to assert the
principles on which it must be founded or the end it
must be established to effect, and to call attention to
the signs of the times favorable to its speedy
organization. The book made little sensation, and
had few readers. It met with no success flattering
to the pride or vanity of its author; yet the book is
remarkable for its protest against Protestantism, and
its laughable blunders as to the doctrines and
tendencies of the Catholic Church, to which I was
by no means hostile, but of which I was profoundly
ignorant. It is no less remarkable for its acceptance
and vindication, in principle, of nearly all the errors
into which the human race has fallen. It is the last
word of the non-Catholic world, and marks the limit
beyond which it cannot advance without recoiling.

In one respect, I misjudged my countrymen;

they had less understanding of their Protestantism than I gave them credit for. They were unable to recognize their own thoughts in the general and abstract form in which I stated them. The truth, I suppose, is, that Protestants, with individual exceptions, seldom reason on their Protestantism, or take the trouble to analyze it and understand what it really is. They do not reduce it to its ultimate principles, and appreciate them in their real and essential character. Perhaps they are not capable of doing it; perhaps they are too busy with the world to attempt it; perhaps, also, they have a lurking suspicion, that, should they attempt it, they would find it disappearing in the process, and themselves reduced to the necessity of choosing between Catholicity and no-religion. There is no doubt that, if they are determined to be Protestants, they are wise. Few who have thoroughly analyzed Protestantism, thoroughly mastered its distinctive principles, have been able to retain their respect for it.

I found my countrymen more attached to the Protestant name and traditions, and more hostile to the Catholic Church, than I had supposed them. I could not understand why they should cling so tenaciously to a mere shadow, or pursue so unrelentingly the dead. For my part, I was no Catholic, should never be a Catholic, but I felt no hostility to Catholicity. It had been respectable in its day, had done good service to mankind for a thousand years, and was now dead and buried. Why war against it? Rather strew fresh flowers on its grave, and breathe over its mouldering ashes a *requiescat in pace.* Foi Protestantism, regarded as a religion, I had had, since my brief trial of Presbyterianism, no respect, no affection. All that it had of religion was borrowed from the Church, and all it had of its own was simple negation. Undoubtedly it had, I conceded, been necessary in its time, when the work to be done was to demolish the old Church; undoubtedly it had done good service as a destroying angel, in breaking the chains in which the Papacy held the world, and in obtaining for the race the freedom to advance; but it had done its work, and was no longer justifiable or excusable. It had become mischievous, more mischievous than was Catholicity when Luther rose up against it. It could not command the intellect of the age, could not meet the wants of the heart, could not aid or direct the progress of the race. It was a dissolvent, but no harmonizer. It split by its everlasting protests, criticisms, and negations, the race into divisions, but had no power to reunite them, and make them of one mind and one heart. As a religious institution, it was a sham, and no reality. It only disgusted men with the very name of religion, and drove every living man, every man of free thought and loving heart, into doubt, infidelity, atheism; or chilled all his nobler feelings, rendered him indifferent to all elevated thought, or generous and noble deeds, and forced him to engross himself in the pursuit of wealth, or to seek dissipation in effeminating sensual pleasures.

As I recovered in some measure from my absolute unbelief, and saw and felt the necessity of religion as the agent of progress, I devoted myself to solving the problem of a religion which should be neither Protestantism nor Catholicity, but which should embody all that was true and holy in the latter, with the free spirit, the ideas, and sentiments which had been developed by the former. I had studied the new philosophy of Cousin, and had seized firm hold of its eclectic feature,—the feature which at that time struck me with the most force. Other elements of M. Cousin's philosophy afterwards had more charm for me; but when I first became acquainted with it in 1833, I knew little of metaphysics, and only attended to those things in the works I read, which I could appropriate to my purposes, or which I found solving, or appearing to solve, the problems with which I was more especially occupied.

For M. Cousin's ontology or his psychology, words of which I hardly understood the meaning, I cared little. Whether the method of philosophizing be intuitive or demonstrative; whether we derive all our ideas through the senses, or have a noetic faculty by which we may attain directly the non-sensible world, was for me a matter of comparative indifference. I did not and could not study philosophy for its own sake. But the eclectic character of the system arrested my attention, and M. Cousin's assertion, that all systems are true in what they affirm, false only in what they deny, or only in that they are exclusive, set my head at work. If this is

true in philosophy, it must be equally true in religious systems, and I immediately concluded with
Leibnitz, though I knew not then that Leibnitz had
so concluded, that all sects are right in what they
affirm, false in what they deny or exclude. Examine all sects, then, analyze them, get at the affirmative
or positive principle of each, and mould, in the
light of a higher unity, those principles into a
uniform and harmonious whole, and you will have
the pure truth without admixture of error. This is
true, so far as it concerns truth of the natural order,
or truth as a development of human nature; but it
will not apply to supernatural revelation, or even to
the natural order, only up to the present moment,
if we assume the progressive development of mankind, and the progressive nature of truth itself.
The former did not disturb me, for I had not yet
attained to a belief in supernatural revelation properly so called, and I made allowance for the latter.

With my principle of eclecticism I proceeded to
examine and ascertain the affirmative portion of
Catholicity, and the affirmative portion of Protestantism. I began my book by asserting the theory,
already developed, of the origin of religion in a
sentiment natural to man, and the progressive nature
of the forms with which man clothes it. Then I
considered Catholicism as the first form which the
religious sentiment assumed under Christianity.
This form embodied the noblest sentiments and the
most advanced intelligence of the age in which it
originated, and served the race for a thousand years.

But it was founded on an exclusive principle, and could not, therefore, answer for all times and all stages of human progress. I found, taking it as represented to me by Heine and the Saint-Simonians, that its principle was exclusive spiritualism, and the neglect or depression of the material order. It fitted men to die, but not to live; for heaven, but not for earth—promising a heaven hereafter, but creating none here. Then I proceeded to Protestantism, and found it, as distinguished from Catholicism, based on exclusive materialism, and the depression or the denial of the spiritual. It takes care of this life, but neglects that which is to come; amasses material goods, but lays up no treasures in heaven; rehabilitates the flesh, but depresses the spirit; elevates humanity, but obscures the Divinity. It is in principle the revival of Greek and Roman heathenism, and has culminated in the worship of a prostitute as the Goddess of Reason, and the conversion of the Church into the Pantheon, as in the French Revolution of 1789. Each system is wrong in what it excludes, and each is right in what it affirms. What is wanted is the union of the two in all that they have that is affirmative. And this union of Catholicism and Protestantism, of spiritualism and materialism, or spirit and matter, was what I meant by *union* in the name of my Society, and I asserted union as the condition of progress. As separate systems, both had exhausted their energies, and accomplished all they could for mankind, and the time had come for the union of the two, the spiritual and the material, the heavenly and the earthly, the eternal and the temporal, the Divine and the human, realizing the idea of the God-man, asserted by the Christian dogma; and their embodiment in an outward organization of mankind, which should secure to each full play for its activity in harmony with the other. Thus we should provide alike for soul and body at one and the same time, get rid of that dualism which has hitherto rent asunder both the individual and society, and been the source of life's tragedy, and restore love, harmony, peace, in the bosom of each,—the realization of the Atonement, or the Reconciliation.

How this union was to be effected outwardly, or what would be the precise form of this new organization, I did not clearly perceive, or pretend to be able to determine. The idea must go before its embodiment. My mission was not to effect the organization, but to develop and set forth the idea. Once get men fairly imbued with the idea, in love with it, convinced of its truth, and anxious for its external realization, and the great man, will appear, who, having realized it internally for himself, will realize it externally for the world,—a new Moses, a new Christ.

Wild, visionary, and absurd as all this may seem, it is nothing but a statement of the common belief of my non-Catholic countrymen. ·Protestantism in its origin pretended to be a return to the truth and simplicity of primitive Christianity, and a few Protestants, who are simply men of routine, may pretend the same even yet; but these are the old fogies of the Protestant world, and do not carry the age or the country with them. Protestantism is defended to-day as an advance on Catholicity in Christian truth and knowledge, and the Church is condemned as stationary, as inflexible, inexpansive, and neither advancing herself, nor permitting mankind to advance. She is denounced as behind the age, as not up with the times, and as bent on keeping men back in the narrow ideas, the ignorance and superstition, of the Dark Ages. She is condemned as being hostile to material civilization, as neglecting the body, as demanding the crucifixion of the flesh, as insisting on penance, mortification, and detachment from the world. Protestantism, on the other hand, is lauded as a progressive religion, a religion that allows full scope to human activity, that aids men forward in material progress, encourages industry, thrift, commerce, manufactures, enterprise, invents steamboats, railroads, lightning telegraphs, and makes all nature contribute to the earthly well-being of man. Are we not every day reminded of the alleged material superiority of Protestant nations to Catholic nations, as a proof of the truth of Protestantism, and of the falsity and mischievousness of Catholicity? There is no denying it.

Again, is it not the constant effort of all Protestants, who retain a sense of religion, to unite in their Church the human and the Divine, the earthly, and the heavenly, the material and the spiritual, the temporal and the eternal—to combine their love of the world with the love of God, and to find out an easier way to get to heaven than that by penance, mortification, self-denial, and detachment from the world? Everybody, up to the intelligence of the age, knows that it is so, and concedes it.

With regard to the Church, the great mass of my non-Catholic countrymen hold that it was divine only in the sense that the idea around which it is formed, and which it seeks to embody, was divinely revealed. They nearly all hold with Guizot, that "Christianity came into the world a naked idea," a doctrine, and, operating as such in men's minds and hearts, has led them to form or organize the Church. Even the mass of Episcopalians, approaching nearer to church views than any other sect at present among us, take the church from the doctrine, not the doctrine from the church. The whole tendency of the age is to regard religion as a development of man, of his higher nature, and the Church as the outward expression of the inward thought. This is the doctrine taught by the leading Protestant minds of France, Germany, Great Britain, and the United States. Even those who the most distinctly assert divine revelation, regard it as quickening thought and aiding its development, rather than as teaching any distinct, formal, objective doctrines. I was, then, really only up to the level of Protestantism, and in principle did not differ essentially from my Protestant contemporaries. I drew, perhaps, conclusions where they drew none and held themselves in suspense.

My views were hardly new or singular; but the

manner in which they were received was instructive, and satisfied me that my Protestant countrymen,
though disclaiming all authority in matters of belief,
and professing to discard all authoritative tradition,
were little accustomed, except in worldly affairs, to
free, independent, distinct thought.　For the most
part, their belief, I found, was practically a prejudice.
They had never thought out their doctrines, and
they took them merely on trust, and that, too, without
ever troubling themselves to inquire whether they
accorded or not with what they held to be the principles of reason.　They held all my views, though
mixed up with much extraneous and contradictory
matter.　Yet they recoiled, or affected to recoil,
with horror from my statements, and bespattered me
with cant phrases and epithets, to which, I presume,
not one in ten attached any definite meaning; and,
of those who did attach such meaning, not one in a
hundred believed it, or was not prepared in the next
breath to contradict it.

I was convinced that I had gone too fast for the
public, and that there remained a greater preliminary
work to be done than I had supposed.　To effect
something in regard to this preliminary work, I
established, in January, 1838, a Quarterly Review,
which I conducted almost single-handed for five
years, and in 1840 published " Charles Elwood; or,
The Infidel Converted," a philosophico-religious work,
strung together on a slight thread of fiction.　My
Quarterly Review was devoted to religion, philosophy, politics, and general literature.　It had no

creed, no distinct doctrines to support on any subject whatever, and was intended for free and independent discussion of all questions which I might regard as worth discussing, not, however, with a view of settling them, or putting an end to any dispute. I had purposes to accomplish, but not, and I did not profess to have, a body of truth I wished to bring out and make prevail. My aim was not dogmatism, but inquiry; and my more immediate purpose was to excite thought, to quicken the mental activity of my countrymen, and force them to think freely and independently on the gravest and most delicate subjects. I aimed to startle, and made it a point to be as paradoxical and as extravagant as I could, without doing violence to my own reason and conscience. Whoever reads the five volumes of that Review, nearly all written by myself, with the view of finding clear, distinct, and consistent doctrines on any subject, with the exception of certain political questions, will be disappointed; but whoever reads it to find provocatives to thought, stimulants to inquiry, and valuable hints on a great variety of important topics, will probably be satisfied. I did what I aimed to do, effected my purpose, and, though its circulation was limited, its influence was such as to satisfy me. The Review should be judged by the purpose for which it was instituted, not merely by the speculations it contains. Many of them, no doubt, are crude, rash, and thrown out with a certain recklessness which nothing, if I had aimed to dogmatize, could justify, but as designed simply to set other minds to thinking, may, perhaps, escape any great severity of censure.

None of my countrymen are less disposed to accept entire the speculations, theories, and utterances of that Quarterly Review, than I am, and yet I believe it deserves an honorable mention in the history of American Literature; and the opinions it enunciates on a great variety of topics are substantially such as I still hold on the same topics. On other points I should have been right if my facts had been true. It will be generally found, to speak after the manner of the logicians, that my *major* was sound, but my *minor* often needed to be denied, or distinguished. There is much in these volumes, especially the later ones, to indicate that my mind did not remain stationary, that I was beginning to look in the direction of the Catholic Church, and that I had, after all, less to change on becoming a Catholic than was commonly supposed at the time. The public read me more or less, but hardly knew what to make of me. They regarded me as a bold and vigorous writer, but as eccentric, extravagant, paradoxical, constantly changing, and not to be counted on; not perceiving that I did not wish to be counted on, in their sense, as a leader whom they could safely follow, and who would save them the labor of thinking for themselves. My aim was to induce, to force, others to think for themselves, not to persuade them to permit me to do their thinking for them. This aim was just and proper in one who knew he had no authority to teach.

CHAPTER XI.

SAINT-SIMONISM.

If I drew my doctrine of Union in part from the Eclecticism of Cousin, I drew my views of the Church and of the reorganization of the race from the Saint-Simonians,—a philosophico-religious, or a politico-philosophical sect that sprung up in France under the Restoration, and figured largely for a year or two under the monarchy of July. Their founder was Claude Henri, Count de Saint-Simon, a descendant of the Duc de Saint-Simon, well known as the author of the *Memoirs.* He was born in 1760, entered the army at the age of seventeen, and the year after came to this country, where he served with distinction in our Revolutionary War under Bouillé. After the peace of 1783, he devoted two years to the study of our people and institutions, and then returned to France. Hardly had he returned before he found himself in the midst of the French Revolution, which he regarded as the practical application of the principles or theories adopted by the Reformers of the sixteenth century, and popularized by the philosophers of the eighteenth. He looked upon that revolution, we are told, as having only a destructive mission, necessary, important, but inadequate to the wants of humanity; and instead of being carried away by it, as were most of the young men of his age and his principles, he set himself at work to amass materials for the erection of a new social edifice on the ruins of the old, which should stand and improve in solidity, strength, grandeur, and beauty forever.

The way he seems to have taken to amass these materials was to engage with a partner in some grand speculations for the accumulation of wealth, and speculations too, it is said, not of the most honorable, or even the most honest, character. His plans succeeded for a time, and he became very rich, as did many others in those troublous times; but he finally met with reverses, and lost all but the wrecks of his fortune. He then for a number of years plunged into all manner of vice, and indulged to excess in every species of dissipation, not, we are told, from love of vice, any inordinate desire, or any impure affection; but for the holy purpose of preparing himself by his experience for the great work of redeeming man, and securing for him a paradise on earth. Having gained all that experience could give him in the department of vice, he then proceeded to consult the learned professors of l'Écol Polytechnique for seven or ten years, to make himself master of science, literature, and the fine arts in all their departments, and to place himself at the level of the last attainments of the race. Thus qualified to be the founder of a new social organization, he wrote several books, in which he deposited the germs of his ideas, or rather the germs of the future, and most of which have hitherto remained unpublished.

But now that he was so well qualified for his work, he found himself a beggar, and had as yet made only a single disciple. He was reduced to despair, and attempted to take his own life; but failed, the ball only grazing his sacred forehead. His faithful disciple was near him, saved him, and aroused him into life and hope. When he recovered, he found that he had fallen into a gross error. He had been a materialist, an atheist, and had discarded all religious ideas as long since outgrown by the human race. He had proposed to organize the human race with materials furnished by the senses alone, and by the aid of positive science. He owns his fault, and conceives and brings forth a new Christianity, consigned to a small pamphlet entitled *Nouveau Christianisme*, which was immediately published. This done, his mission was ended, and he died May 19, 1825, and I suppose was buried.

Saint-Simon, the preacher of a new Christianity, very soon attracted disciples, chiefly from the pupils of the Polytechnic School, ardent and lively young men, full of enthusiasm, brought up without faith in the Gospel, and yet unable to live without religion of some sort. Among the active members of the sect were at one time Pierre Leroux, Jules and Michel Chevalier, Lerminier, my personal friend, Dr. Poyen, who initiated me and so many others in New England into the mysteries of Animal Magnetism.

Dr. Poyen was, I believe, a native of the island of Guadeloupe, a man of more ability than he usually had credit for, of solid learning, genuine science, and honest intentions. I knew him well, and esteemed him highly. When I knew him, his attachment to the new religion was much weakened; and he often talked to me of the old Church, and assured me that he felt at times that he must return to her bosom. I owe him many hints which turned my thoughts towards Catholic principles, and which, with God's grace, were of much service to me. These and many others were in the sect, whose chiefs, after the death of its founder, were Bazard, a Liberal, and a practical man, who killed himself, and Enfantin, who, after the dissolution of the sect, sought employment in the service of the Viceroy of Egypt, and occupies now some important post in connection with the French railways.

The sect began in 1826, by addressing the working classes, but their success was small. In 1829 they came out of their narrow circle, assumed a bolder tone, addressed themselves to the general public, and became in less than eighteen months a Parisian *mode*. In 1831 they purchased the *Globe* newspaper, made it their organ, and distributed gratuitously five thousand copies daily. In 1832 they had established a central propagandism in Paris, and had their missionaries in most of the departments of France. They attacked the hereditary peerage, and it fell; they seemed to be numerous and strong, and I believed for a moment

in their complete success. They called their doctrine
a religion, their ministers, priests, and their organization, a church; and as such they claimed to be
recognized by the State, and to receive from it a
subvention as other religious denominations. But
the courts decided that Saint-Simonism was not a
religion, and its ministers were not religious teachers.
This decision struck them with death. Their prestige
vanished. They scattered, dissolved in thin air, and
went off, as Carlyle would say, into endless vacuity,
as do, sooner or later, all shams and unrealities.

Saint-Simon himself, who, as presented to us by
his disciples, is a half mythic personage, seems, so
far as I can judge by those of his writings that I
have seen, to have been a man of large ability and
laudable intentions; but I have not been able to find
any new or original thoughts of which he was the
indisputable father.   His whole system, if system
he had, is summed up in the two maxims: "Eden
is before us, not behind us," or the golden age of
the poets is in the future, not in the past; and,
" Society ought to be so organized as to tend in the
most rapid manner possible to the continuous moral,
intellectual, and physical amelioration of the poorer
and more numerous classes."   He simply adopts the
doctrine of progress set forth with so much flash
eloquence by Condorcet, and the philanthropic doctrine with regard to the laboring classes, or the people,
defended by Barbeuf, and a large section of the
French Revolutionists. His religion was not so
much as the Theophilanthropy attempted to be

introduced by some members of the French Directory. It admitted God in name, and in name
did not deny Jesus Christ, but it rejected all
mysteries, and reduced religion to mere socialism.
It conceded that Catholicity had been the true
Church down to the Pontificate of Leo X, because
down to that time its ministers had taken the lead
in directing the intelligence and labors of mankind,
had aided the progress of civilization, and promoted
the well-being of the poorer and more numerous
classes. But since Leo X, who made of the Papacy
a secular principality, it had neglected its mission,
had ceased to labor for the poorer and more numerous classes, had leagued itself with the ruling
orders, and lent all its influence to uphold tyrants
and tyranny. A new church was needed,—a church
which should realize the ideal of Jesus Christ, and
tend directly and constantly to the moral, physical,
and social amelioration of the poorer and more
numerous classes; in other words, the greatest happiness in this life of the greatest number: the principle of Jeremy Bentham and his Utilitarian school.

His disciples enlarged upon the hints of the
master, and attributed to him ideas which he never
entertained. They endeavored to reduce his hints
to a complete system of religion, philosophy, and
social organization. Their chiefs, I have said, were
Bazard and Enfantin. Amand Bazard was born in
Paris in 1791, and at the age of twenty-two married
the daughter of Joubert the Conventionalist. He
was a rigid republican, and the principal founder

of the French Carbonari. He held an eminent rank in the French secret societies, was Venerable of the Lodge of the Amis de la Vérité, and after the foundation of the Carbonari was President of the Haute Vente, and of the Vente Suprême, and most of the orders circulated in the association were from him. He was the life and soul of nearly all the movements, plots, and conspiracies in behalf of republicanism under the Restoration. He was in those times, though less before the public, very much what Mazzini is in ours. In October, 1825 he became acquainted with the little band of disciples left by Saint-Simon, and joined himself to them, and was the ablest and most competent man, so far as it regards external organization and direction, the sect ever had. He was a politician, a revolutionist, and stamped his own character on the school.

Barthélemy Prosper Enfantin, the son of a banker, born at Paris 1796, was a man of a different stamp, better fitted for thinking, or rather dreaming, than acting. Bazard evidently adopted Saint-Simonism as an instrument to be used, or as an engine which he hoped to use in accomplishing, his own political and social purposes; Enfantin appears to have really believed in the mission of his master, and to have entered sincerely, with all his soul, into his new religion. He was endowed with rare philosophical genius, was of a contemplative turn of mind, and of great natural religious fervor. He was firm, conscientious, and would, for no prospect of gain or the success of his sect, make the slightest compromise of principle, or sacrifice a single iota of what he held to be right. Had he been a Catholic, he would have suffered martyrdom, or been a saint, whom the faithful would have delighted to hold in honor through all ages. As it was, he was too scrupulous to make the compromises necessary for success in a scheme that could not afford to be honest; and the larger portion of his associates regarded him as a bigot, a fanatic, and laid the blame of their divisions and failures to his obstinacy; to what I should call his sincerity, firmness, and consistency.

These two men elaborated the Saint-Simonian doctrine and the Saint-Simonian religion. Bazard took the lead in what related to the external, political, and economical organization; and Enfantin, in what regarded doctrine and worship. The philosophy or theology of the sect or school was derived principally from Hegel, and was a refined Pantheism. Its Christology was the unity, not union, of the Divine and human; and the Incarnation symbolized the unity of God and man, or the Divinity manifesting himself in humanity, and making humanity substantially divine: the very doctrine, in reality, which I myself had embraced, even before I had heard of the Saint-Simonians, if not before they had published it. The religious organization was founded on the doctrine of the progressive nature of man, and the maxim that all institutions should tend, in the most speedy and direct manner possible, to the constant amelioration of the moral, intellectual, and physical condition of the poorer and more numerous classes. Socially, men were to be divided into three classes, artists, *savans*, and industrials, or working men, corresponding to the psychological division of the human faculties. The soul has three powers or faculties : to love, to know, and to act. Those in whom the love-faculty is predominant, belong to the class of artists ; those in whom the knowledge-faculty is predominant, belong to the class of *savans*, the scientific and the learned ; and, in fine, those in whom the act-faculty predominates, belong to the industrial class. This classification places every man in the social category for which he is fitted, and to which he is attracted by his nature. These several classes are to be hierarchically organized, under chiefs or priests, who are respectively priests of the artists, of the scientific, and of the industrials, and are, priests and all, to be subjected to a Supreme Father, *Père Suprême*, and a Supreme Mother, *Mère Suprême.*

The economical organization is to be based on the maxims, "To each one according to his capacity," and, "To each capacity according to its work." Private property is to be retained, but its transmission by inheritance or testamentary disposition must be abolished. The property is to be held by a tenure resembling that of gavelkind. It belongs to the community, and the priests, chiefs, or brehons, as the Celtic tribes call them, to distribute it for life to individuals, and "to each

individual according to his capacity." It was supposed that in this way the advantages of both
common and individual property might be secured
Something of this prevailed originally in most nations, and a reminiscence of it still exists in the
village system among the Sklavonic tribes of Russia
and Poland; and nearly all jurists maintain that the
testamentary right, by which a man disposes of his
goods after his natural death, as well as that by
which a child inherits from the parent, is a municipal, not a natural right.

The most striking feature in the Saint-Simonian
scheme was the rank and position it assigned to
woman. It asserted the absolute equality of the
sexes, and maintained that either sex is incomplete
without the other. Man is an incomplete individual
without woman. Hence a religion, a doctrine, a
social institution, founded by one sex alone, is incomplete, and can never be adequate to the wants
of the race or a definitive order. This idea was also
entertained by Frances Wright, and appears to be
entertained by all our Women's Rights folk of either
sex. The old civilization was masculine, not male and
female as God made man. Hence its condemnation.
The Saint-Simonians, therefore, proposed to place by
the side of their sovereign Father, at the summit of
their hierarchy, a sovereign Mother. The man to be
sovereign Father they found, but a woman to be
sovereign Mother, *Mère Suprême*, they found not.
This caused great embarrassment, and a split between
Bazard and Enfantin. Bazard was about marrying

his daughter, and he proposed to place her marriage under the protection of the existing French laws. Enfantin opposed his doing so, and called it a sinful compliance with the prejudices of the world. The Saint-Simonian Society, he maintained, was a state, a kingdom within itself, and should be governed by its own laws and its own chiefs without any recognition of those without. Bazard persisted, and had the marriage of his daughter solemnized in a legal manner, and for aught I know, according to the rites of the Church. A great scandal followed. Bazard charged Enfantin with denying Christian marriage, and with holding loose notions on the subject. Enfantin replied that he neither denied nor affirmed Christian marriage; that, in enacting the existing law on the subject, man alone had been consulted, and he could not recognize it as law till woman had given her consent to it. As yet the society was only provisionally organized, inasmuch as they had not yet found the *Mère Suprême.* The law on marriage must emanate conjointly from the Supreme Father and the Supreme Mother, and it would be irregular and a usurpation for the Supreme Father to undertake alone to legislate on the subject. Bazard would not submit, and went out and shot himself. Most of the politicians abandoned the association, and Père Enfantin, almost in despair, despatched twelve apostles to Constantinople to find in the Turkish harems the Supreme Mother. After a year they returned and reported that they were unable to find her; and the society, condemned by the

French courts as immoral, broke up—and broke up because no woman could be found to be its mother: and so they ended, having risen, flourished, and decayed in less than a single decade.

The points in the Saint-Simonian movement that arrested my attention, and commanded my belief, were what it will seem strange to my readers could ever have been doubted,—its assertion of a religious future for the human race; and that religion, in the future as well as in the past, must have an organization, and a hierarchical organization. Its classification of men according to the predominant psychological faculty in each, into artists, *savans*, and industrials, struck me as very well; and the maxims, " To each according to his capacity," and, " To each capacity according to its works," as evidently just, and desirable, if practicable. The doctrine of the Divinity in humanity, of progress, of no essential antagonism between the spiritual and the material, and of the duty of shaping all institutions for the speediest and continuous moral, intellectual, and physical amelioration of the poorer and more numerous classes, I already held. I was rather pleased than otherwise with the doctrine with regard to property, and thought it a decided improvement on that of a community of goods. The doctrine with regard to the relation of the sexes, I rather acquiesced in than approved. I was disposed to maintain, as the Indian said, that " woman is the weaker canoe," and to assert my marital prerogatives; but the equality of the sexes was asserted by nearly all my friends, and I remained generally silent on the subject, till some of the admirers of Harriet Martineau and of Margaret Fuller began to scorn equality, and to claim for woman superiority. Then I became roused, and ventured to assert my masculine dignity.

It is remarkable that most reformers find fault with the Christian law of marriage, and propose to alter the relations which God has established both in nature and the Gospel between the sexes; and this is generally the rock on which they split. Women do not usually admire men who cast off their manhood, or are unconscious of the rights and prerogatives of the stronger sex; and they admire just as little those "strong-minded women," who strive to excel only in the masculine virtues. I have never been persuaded that it argues well for a people when its women are men, and its men women. Yet, I trust I have always honored, and always shall honor, woman. I raise no question as to woman's equality or inequality with man, for comparisons cannot be made between things not of the same kind. Woman's sphere and office in life are as high, as holy, as important as man's, but different; and the glory of both man and woman is, for each to act well the part assigned to each by Almighty God.

The Saint-Simonian writings made me familiar with the idea of a hierarchy, and removed from my mind the prejudices against the Papacy generally entertained by my countrymen. Their proposed organization I saw might be good and desirable, if their priests, their supreme Father and Mother, could really be the wisest, the best—not merely the nominal, but the real chiefs of society. Yet what security have I that they will be? Their power was to have no limit save their own wisdom and love but who would answer for it that these would always be an effectual limit? How were these priests or chiefs to be designated and installed in their office? By popular election? But popular election often passes over the proper man, and takes the improper. Then as to the assignment to each man of a capita proportioned to his capacity to begin life with, what certainty is there that the rules of strict right will be followed? that wrong will not often be done both voluntarily and involuntarily? Are your chiefs to be infallible and impeccable? Still the movement interested me, and many of its principles took firm hold of me, and held me for years in a species of mental thraldom, inasmuch as I found it difficult, if not impossible, either to refute them or to harmonize them with other principles which I also held, or, rather, which held me, and in which I detected no unsoundness. Yet I imbibed no errors from the Saint-Simonians, and I can say of them as of the Unitarians, they did me no harm, but were, in my fallen state, the occasion of much good to me.

CHAPTER XII.

HORRIBLE DOCTRINES.

THE Saint-Simonians asserted a new Christianity. I held that their new Christianity was not new, and that it was only a just interpretation of the old Christianity as it lay in the mind of its Author. This was my chief point of difference with them. They asserted a religious future for mankind, and so did I. They asserted the necessity of a new religious institution or organization of society, and so did I. They maintained that the object or end of this new institution should be the amelioration, moral, intellectual, and physical, of the poorer and more numerous classes, or the creation of a heaven upon earth for all men, and so did I. But, as to the practical means of realizing this end, I had my doubts and misgivings.

I had come to the conclusion that the amelioration of the laboring classes could not be effected by themselves alone, or by appealing solely to them. It could be effected only by the coöperation of all classes of society, or, as I said, not without a slight touch of mysticism in my thought, the coöperation of the race. The organization of the race in a manner to secure this end, was what I meant by the new church.

The Christian thought, as it existed in the mind of Jesus of Nazareth, I maintained, was coincident with Democracy. His kingdom was to be set up in this world; his mission was to establish the reign of justice and love on the earth. He claimed to have come from God, because his mission was to the poor and oppressed. "The Spirit of the Lord," he said, "is upon me, because he hath anointed me to preach glad tidings to the poor, to heal them that are bruised, to bind up the broken-hearted, to set the captives free." To the disciples of John the Baptist, sent to ask him whether he was the Messias promised, or whether they were to look for another, he said: "Go tell your master, the poor have the Gospel preached unto them." He declared the poor blessed, heirs of his kingdom, and pronounced a woe upon the rich, declaring it "easier for a camel to go through the eye of a needle, than for a rich man to enter into the kingdom of heaven." He rebuked all cant, sham, or make-believe goodness, and declared to the Scribes and Pharisees, the saints of his day, that publicans and harlots would enter into the kingdom of heaven before them. He discarded all the titles and distinctions created by human pride and vanity, recognized no earth-born nobilities, no pomp of rank or earthly majesty, but looked on simple naked humanity, and accepted and honored man for his real or intrinsic worth. He loved man as man, and died for his redemption. The great law of his religion was love of man. "By this shall all men know that ye are my disciples, if ye love one another." "A new commandment give I unto you, that ye love one another." "We know," said his beloved disciple, "that we have passed from death unto life, because we love the brethren." Nor was this love to be confined to one's own family, friends, or nation. We were to love our enemies, and bless them that curse us, do good to them that hate us. We must love our neighbor as ourselves, and count every man our neighbor to whom we can be of service, as was the Samaritan to the Jew who fell among thieves. Jesus proclaimed the worth of man as man, taught the great law of love, and proposed the universal brotherhood of the race,—Liberty, Equality, Fraternity: the noble device of the Democratic banner.

Here was that Christian Democracy, as I called it, which constituted the substance of my preaching for ten or eleven years. I was not alone in this. It was substantially the doctrine of Dr. Channing, and that section of the Unitarians that took him for their leader; and it was held more or less distinctly by the whole movement party of the time, in both Europe and America. It had a powerful champion in the unhappy Abbé de Lamennais, both before and after his excommunication by Gregory XVI, and was maintained by all the leading Liberals of the European continent. Indeed, it had penetrated very widely even into the Catholic camp, and in 1848 we found in France even priests ready to assert the identity of Democracy and Christianity; and some, I believe, went so far as to call our blessed

Lord the first Democrat, as in the old French Revolution individuals were found to call him the great *Sans Culotte*, and to speak of him as "le Citoyen Christ." Even the pious and philosophical Rosmini seemed, in his work on the Five Wounds of the Church, to look towards it; and many of the Italian clergy who favored the Republican Revolution which compelled the flight of the Holy Father from Rome to Gaëta, held it. It can be detected, in some of its phases, in Padre Ventura's famous Funeral Oration on Daniel O'Connell. It is, as the Cardinal Archbishop of Rheims has well remarked, "the great heresy of the nineteenth century." It is not singular, then, that I, believing in progress, and therefore regarding the latest thought as the truest and best, should have adopted it.

The doctrine, moreover, is not without its side of truth, especially as I defended it. Democracy, in the sense I defined and defended it, regarded the end for which government should be constituted and administered, rather than the origin and form of the government itself. I never myself held the doctrine of the native underived sovereignty of the people. When I believed in no God, I believed in no government; for I could never understand why the people collectively should not be under law as well as the people distributively. I always said with St. Paul, *Non est potestas nisi a Deo.* When I renounced my atheism, I derived all power from God, the source of all law and of all justice. I might, and probably did, even as I do now, derive it from

God through the people, as the medial origin of government, and thus accept Mr. Bancroft's definition, that "Democracy is eternal justice ruling through the people;" but the popular doctrine which puts the people in the place of God, and asserts not only people-king, but people-God, I never held, and it is one of the few errors of my times into which I have never fallen. I had to combat the people too often. I had to make too frequent war on popular prejudice and popular errors, to believe that whatever is popular is true, right, and just. I had found majorities too often in the wrong, to believe them either infallible or impeccable. Did not the people, the majority, condemn Socrates to drink hemlock? Did not the people cry out against One greater than Socrates, "Crucify him, crucify him"? And did not the majority actually crucify him between two thieves?

But Democracy as designating the end of government, I did hold; that is, I held that government should be constituted and administered for the common good of the governed as men, irrespective of the accidents of rank, birth, position, or condition. This I held, and hold still. This is the simple dictate of reason or the law of nature, and is the common doctrine of all the doctors of the Church in all ages and nations. All governments not constituted and administered for the common good of the governed, are illegitimate, whatever their form or historical origin, and are unable to bind the consciences of their subjects. Hence, the Church has always inclined to the side of the poorer and more numerous classes, and has always treated with disfavor, and in her own sphere has never recognized, the privileges and privileged orders introduced and sustained by the feudal system. She treats men as men, and admits, in her dealing with them, no noble or ignoble classes. She has one law of justice, one and the same office and discipline for the prince and the peasant, the noble and the plebeian, the lord and the vassal, the rich and the poor, the master and the slave. In this sense, the Church, Christianity, is democratic, and the law of nature, also, is democratic; and it was in this sense that I defined Democracy to be "the supremacy of man over his accidents:" that is, it imposes on government the obligation to consult the good of man as man, irrespective of the accidents of birth, wealth, rank, position, or condition.

In this sense only did I ever profess to be a Democrat, and in this sense I am a Democrat now, though I dislike the term, and disclaimed it as long ago as 1841. The proper term is *republican*, which designates any government, whatever its form, that is constituted and administered in sole reference to the public good, or the good of the governed in distinction from the private good of the governors. Whether the democratic form, such as is demanded by modern Liberals and Revolutionists, be or be not the form best adapted to secure the public good, is an open question, which admits of much being said on both sides. Probably, there are no two countries in Christendom so little favorable to the poorer and more numerous classes, or in which wealth has so much influence, and it is so great a misfortune to be poor, as Great Britain and the United States. They do not, as the ancient heathen nations did, actually kill their poor or sell them into slavery, but they despise, abhor them, shut them up in work-houses, and treat them as criminals. Democratic, or democratically-inclined, governments are for the most part cruel and hard-hearted. Like corpora-tions, they have no souls, and are incapable of tender-ness. They have their advantages, but also their disadvantages, and probably are less favorable to public prosperity than is commonly imagined.

I found my countrymen attached to Democracy in the sense that the people are the original source of all power, sovereign, as *The Democratic Review* expressed it, "in their own native might and right." In this sense, Democracy has its expression in universal suffrage and eligibility. But in this sense, I said, it is a bitter mockery, if the people are not practically equal as individuals. Political equality may be a blessed thing; but, to be real, anything more than a delusion, it must rest for its basis on social equality: equality in wealth, position, edu-cation, ability, influence. Man against man and money is not an equal match. Man ignorant, rude, uncultivated, cannot enter into the political contest on equal terms with the educated, the cultivated man, with all the advantages society can give him. How pretend that you and I are equal, when you can influence a thousand votes, while I can hardly control my own, unless I have the spirit of a martyr? The immense majority of American voters vote with no real will or independence of their own. A few individuals contrive to manage the people, and some two or three hundred more determine even our national elections, and the politics of the country.

If, then, you will have Democracy, if you insist on the Democratic form, have the courage to go farther, and the good-sense to adopt the measures necessary to prevent your universal suffrage and eligibility from being a mere sham. You must do more than you have done; you must establish and maintain the substantial equality of conditions, so that not merely the *rights*, but the *mights*, of men shall be equal. With this thought, I wrote and published in my Review for July, 1840, an essay on the Laboring Classes, which had a louder echo than I had counted on. It was published during the heat of the presidential electioneering campaign, and I was regarded at that time as a prominent member of the Democratic party. The Whig, or opposing party, seized it, reprinted it, and circulated it by thousands, if not by hundreds of thousands, for the purpose of damaging the party with which I was connected. I was denounced in the press, from the pulpit and the rostrum. My friends shook their heads, and were very sorry that I had been so imprudent; and not a voice was raised in my defence, or in mitigation of the censure with which I was visited.

The Democratic journals threw me overboard, and defended themselves as well as they could, by disowning me, and declaring it unfair and unjust to hold the party responsible for my eccentricities and extravagances.

The doctrines of my essay were received by my countrymen with one universal scream of horror, partly affected, no doubt, for party purposes, but partly real and sincere. There was no question that I had gone beyond the point the public could be induced to go with me. Yet I had only drawn from the Democratic and Protestant principles, which I had never heard questioned from my youth up, their legitimate consequences; I had only drawn from the premises supplied by the dominant public opinion, their strictly logical conclusions. I felt the blame, if blame there was in the case, was not mine. If my Protestant and Democratic countrymen said, " Two and two," wherefore could it be wrong for me to add, " make four"? With Protestantism I denied the Church and the priesthood; and with the Democracy I denied the distinction of classes, of castes, of noble and ignoble, and asserted the political equality of all men. I added only a change in the transmission and distribution of property to the new generation, necessary to render political equality a practical fact, a reality, not an illusion. What sin against either had I committed?

The essay was an honest, undisguised, fearless, and not ineloquent expression of thoughts which had been fermenting in my mind, and pressing for years for utterance. In it I poured out my soul, such as it was, and kept nothing back. I made my confession to the world, a clean breast of it; and I think my convalescence dates from that moment. But I can hardly read the essay over without being myself shocked, and wondering at my temerity in publishing it. Yet never did I speak more truly my honest thought, or more consistently with myself. Place me where I stood then; place me outside of the Catholic Church, and make me regard that Church as exclusive, as a spiritual tyranny, as all my Protestant countrymen maintain she is, and give me faith only in progress by the natural forces of man, and I would to-day repeat and indorse every paragraph and every word I then wrote.

"Mankind," I wrote, "came out of the savage state by means of the priests. Priests are the first civilizers of the race. For the wild freedom of the savage, they substitute the iron despotism of the theocrat. This is the first step in civilization, in man's career of progress. It is not strange, then, that some should prefer the savage to the civilized state. Who would not rather roam the forest, with a free step and unshackled limb, though exposed to hunger, cold, and nakedness, than crouch an abject slave beneath the whip of the master? As yet civilization has done little more than break and subdue man's natural love of freedom—than tame his wild and eagle spirit. In what a world does man even now find himself, when he first awakes and feels some of the workings of his manly nature?

He is in a cold, damp, dark dungeon, and loaded all over with chains, with the iron eating into his soul. He cannot make one single free movement. The priest holds his conscience, fashion controls his tastes, and society with her forces invades the very sanctuary of his heart, and takes command of his love, that which is purest and best in his nature, which alone gives reality to his existence, and from which proceeds the only ray that pierces the gloom of his prison-house. Even that he cannot enjoy in peace and quietness—hardly at all. He is wounded on every side, in every part of his being, in every relation in life, in every idea of his mind, in every sentiment of his heart. Oh, it is a sad world, a sad world to the young heart just awakening to its diviner instincts! A sad world to him who is not gifted with the only blessing which seems compatible with life as it is,—absolute insensibility. But no matter. A wise man never murmurs. He never kicks against the pricks. What is is, and there is an end of it; what can be may be, and we will do what we can to make life what it ought to be. Though man's first step in civilization is slavery, his last step shall be freedom. The free soul can never be wholly subdued; the ethereal fire in man's nature may be smothered, but it cannot be extinguished. Down, down, deep in the centre of the heart, it burns inextinguishable and forever, glowing intenser with the accumulating heat of centuries; and one day the whole mass of humanity shall become ignited, be full of fire within and all over as a live coal; and then—slavery, and whatever is foreign to the soul itself, shall be consumed.

" But, having traced the inequality we complain of, to its source, we ask again, What is the remedy ? The remedy is to be sought first in the destruction of the priest. We are not mere destructives. We delight not in pulling down; but the bad must be removed before the good can be introduced. Conviction and repentance precede regeneration. Moreover, we are Christians, and it is only by following out the Christian law and the example of the early Christians, that we can hope to effect anything. Christianity is the sublimest protest against the priesthood ever uttered, and a protest uttered by both God and man, for he who uttered it was God-man. In the person of Jesus, both God and man protest against the priesthood. What was the mission of Jesus but a solemn summons of every priesthood on earth to judgment, and of the human race to freedom ? He discomfited the learned doctors, and with whips made of small cords drove the priests, degenerated into money-changers, from the temple of God. He instituted himself no priesthood, no form of religious worship. He recognized no priest but a holy life, and commanded the construction of no temple but that of the pure heart. He preached no formal religion, enjoined no creed, set apart no day for religious worship. He preached fraternal love, peace on earth, and good-will to men. He came to the soul enslaved, ' cabined, cribbed, confined,' to the poor child of mortality, bound hand

and foot, unable to move, and said in the tones of a God, 'Be free, be enlarged, be there room for thee to grow, and expand, and overflow with love.'

"In the name of Jesus, we admit, there has been a priesthood instituted, and, considering how the world went, a priesthood could not but be instituted; but the religion of Jesus repudiates it. It recognizes no mediator between God and man but him who died on the cross to redeem man; no propitiation for sin but a pure love which rises in a living flame to all that is beautiful and good, and spreads out in light and warmth for all the chilled and benighted sons of mortality. In calling every man to be a priest, it virtually condemns every possible priesthood; and in recognizing the religion of the New Covenant, the religion written on the heart, of a law put within the soul, it abolishes all formal worship.

"The priest is universally a tyrant, universally the enslaver of his brethren, and therefore it is that Christianity condemns him. It could not prevent the reëstablishment of a hierarchy, but it prepared its ultimate destruction, by denying the inequality of blood, by representing all men as equal before God, and by insisting on the celibacy of the clergy. The best feature of the Church was its denial to the clergy of the right to marry. By this it prevented the new hierarchy from becoming hereditary, as were the old sacerdotal corporations of India and Judea.

"We object not to religious instruction. We object not to the gathering together of the people on one day in seven to sing and pray, and listen to a discourse from a religious teacher; but we object to everything like an outward visible church, to everything that in the remotest degree partakes of the priest. A priest is one who stands as a sort of mediator between God and men; but we have one Mediator, Jesus Christ, who gave himself a ransom for all, and that is enough. It may be supposed that the Protestants have no priests; but, for ourselves, we know no fundamental difference between a Catholic priest and a Protestant clergyman, as we know no difference of any magnitude, in relation to the principles on which they are based, between a Protestant Church and the Catholic Church. Both are based on the principle of authority, both deny in fact, however it may be in name, the authority of reason, and war against freedom of mind; both substitute dead works for true righteousness, a vain show for the reality of piety, and are sustained as the means of reconciling us to God, without our being required to be godlike. Both, therefore, ought to go by the board."

I spoke here of Protestantism as I knew it, but of Catholicity as it was represented to me by Protestants. The Catholic Church had been misrepresented to me, and, when I came to examine her, I found that she did require us to be godlike, as the condition of our actual reconciliation with God; that she did require of us true righteousness, intrinsic justice and sanctity, and that this was precisely the most formidable objection which the Reformers urged against her. My statement as against Protestantism was true and just, in so far as Protestantism pretends to be a church; but, as against the Catholic Church, was, of course, untrue.

The first step was to demolish the outward visible Church, and make away with the priesthood—annihilate the priest. The next step was to "resuscitate the Christianity of Christ. The Christianity of the Church has done its work. We have had enough of that Christianity. It is powerless for good, but by no means powerless for evil. It now unmans us and hinders the growth of God's kingdom. The moral energy which is awakened it misdirects, and makes its deluded disciples believe that they have done their duty to God when they have joined the Church, offered a prayer, sung a psalm, and contributed of their means to send out a missionary to preach unintelligible dogmas to the poor heathen, who, God knows, have unintelligible dogmas enough already, and more than enough. All this must be abandoned, and Christianity, as it came from Christ, be taken up and preached—and preached in simplicity and power.

"According to the Christianity of Christ no man can enter the kingdom of God, who does not labor with all zeal and diligence to establish the kingdom of God on earth; who does not labor to bring down the high, and bring up the low; to break the fetters of the bound, and to set the captive free; to destroy all oppression, and to establish the reign of justice, which is the reign of equality, between man and man ; to introduce new heavens and a new earth, wherein dwelleth righteousness, wherein all shall be as brothers, loving one another, and no one possessing what another lacketh. No man can be a Christian who does not labor to reform society, to mould it according to the will of God and the nature of man ; so that free scope shall be given to every man to unfold himself in all beauty and power, and to grow up into the stature of a perfect man in Christ Jesus. No man can be a Christian who does not refrain from all practices by which the rich grow richer, and the poor grow poorer, and who does not do all in his power to elevate the laboring classes, so that one man shall not be doomed to toil while another enjoys the fruits ; so that every man shall be free and independent, sitting under his own vine and fig-tree, with none to molest or to make afraid. We grant the power of Christianity in working out the reform we demand ; we grant that one of the most effectual means of elevating the workingmen is to Christianize the community. But you must *Christianize* it. It is the Gospel of Jesus that you must preach, not the gospel of the priests."

After this the resort must be to the government as the agent of society, or the instrument of carrying out its ideas. Through the government we must break up the banks and great business corporations, destroy the modern credit system, and introduce those changes in regard to the descent and distribution of property proposed by the Saint-Simonians. These were the principal offensive points in my essay, though some attacks in it on the factory system, and on the middling classes of society, represented as far more hostile to the workingmen than the aristocracy, were not very acceptable. I am not surprised that my doctrines were denounced as horrible, but I am surprised to find such men as Theodore Parker, Wendel Phillips, and Henry Ward Beecher, continuing to preach the most horrible of them, and almost with public approbation.

CHAPTER XIII.

IT required no great effort to defend these doctrines on Protestant and Democratic principles. No one but a Catholic can consistently assert the Church in the sense in which I opposed it, and the denial of the priesthood is an essential element of Protestantism. It is only figuratively that Protestantism has an altar or a sacrifice, and without both there is no priest. Protestants have ministers and preachers, but no priests, and they seldom or never call their preachers or pastors by that name.

But this abolition of the Church and the priesthood was necessary to my view of the new religious organization of mankind. The error of the past had been in the double organization of society, the one temporal, the other spiritual. "The mission of Jesus," I wrote in explanation and defence of my essay, "was twofold." One purpose of his mission was to make an atonement for sin, and prepare the soul for heaven in the world to come. The other purpose was to found a holy kingdom on the earth, under the dominion of which all men should finally be brought. This holy kingdom, which Christ came to found on the earth, has been mistaken for the

outward visible Church; and the Church has therefore been held to be a spiritual body, a body
corporate, independent in itself, and distinct from
the body politic, or civil society. This has given
rise to a double organization of mankind: one for
material interests, called the State, and under the
control of the civil government proper; the other
for spiritual purposes, called the Church, and
governed by laws and officers of its own, distinct
from those of the State.

"Now to this we strenuously object. We would
establish the kingdom of God on the earth, but we
would not have a double organization of mankind.
We would have but a single organization; and this
we would call, not the Church, but the State. This
organization should be based on the principles of
the Gospel, and realize them as perfectly as finite
men can realize them. The kingdom of God is an
inward, spiritual kingdom. In plain language, it is
the dominion of truth, justice, and love. Now we
would build up this kingdom, not by founding an
outward visible church, but by cultivating the principles of truth, justice, and love in the soul, and by
bringing society and all its acts into harmony with
them. Our views, if carried out, would realize, not
the *union*, but the *unity* of Church and State. They
would indeed destroy the Church as a *separate* body,
as a distinct organization; but they would do it by
transferring to the State the moral ideas on which
the Church was professedly founded, and which it
has failed to realize. They would realize that idea

of a 'Christian Commonwealth,' after which our
Puritan fathers so earnestly and so perseveringly
struggled."

The new church, or religious institution, I had
asserted in my New Views to be necessary, it will be
recollected, was to be based on the union, or rather
unity, of the spiritual and the material; and therefore, to be consistent, I must reject the double
organization which had obtained under Catholicity,
and was attempted to be continued under Protestantism. The error of the old Church was, that it was
organized in the interest of the spiritual to the
exclusion of the material; the error of the State
had hitherto been that it was organized in the interests of the material to the exclusion of the spiritual.
The new order must unite the two, the spiritual and
the material, in a single organization, as the soul
and body are united and form one living man.

In 1836 I was disposed to call the new organization the Church instead of the State; in 1840, I
was disposed to call it the State rather than the
Church; but my principles, doctrines, and opinions
were the same at both epochs. It made no difference
as to the character of the organization itself, by
whichever name it was called; it remained precisely
the same; but by calling it State instead of Church,
I could obtain for it more support. Many would
labor to organize the State on what I regarded as
Christian principles, and to realize in its constitution
and administration the purposes of the Gospel as I
understood it, that would have stood aloof or even

opposed me, if I had called upon them to aid me in founding a new church. Moreover, I saw or thought I saw in the American political constitution the germ of the very organization I was in pursuit of. This was the view taken by my most distinguished and influential friends. It was thought that, by uniting with the Democratic party, at once the conservative and the movement party of the country, and indoctrinating it with our philosophical, theological, and humanitarian views, we could make it the instrument of realizing our ideas of men and society. I adopted this the more readily, because my philosophical studies, which I had begun to prosecute in earnest, had led me to the rather important conclusion that man cannot found institutions absolutely new, that he can develop, but not create, and, therefore, the new must have its root in the old. The future can be only the development and perfection of the past. I must then either begin with the old Church and develop and modify that to the new wants, or I must do the same with the State. The former is impracticable, because the old Church is founded on the ideas of immobility and unchangeableness, and therefore excludes the idea of its own development or progressiveness. This was not the case with the State, especially in this country. The American State contemplates progress, and provides for its own amendment. What we had then to do, was to imbue the Democratic party with our ideas of Christian Democracy, in order to wield the whole political power of the Union in favor of the end contemplated, and to make the State a truly Christian State, or to develop it into that organization of mankind which was to rule the future. It was with this view that my "Quarterly Review," after the publication of its first number, in January, 1838, supported the Democratic party, and labored to imbue it with the doctrines of what was then called the Boston School.

This doctrine of the single organization of mankind, or the unity of Church and State, had many friends among the profoundest thinkers and most approved writers of the country, and is more or less distinctly held by our Abolitionists, and Philanthropists, who seek to make the State the agent for realizing their spiritual ideas and moral doctrines. It was implied in the Reformation itself, and attempted to be realized by Calvin in Geneva, and by the Puritan colonists of New England. It had been defended by Mr. Alexander H. Everett in *The North American Review*, and by an able writer in *The Christian Examiner*, the organ of the Unitarians, long before I broached it. It was embraced by the Saint-Simonians, and held by all the Socialists, who did not reject the State for Phalansteries or Communities. Indeed, it is reasonable and just, if you recognize only the natural order. At the time I held it, though I accepted all the Christian mysteries in a sense of my own, I had no conception of the supernatural order. God and nature, or God in nature, embraced all the being or existence I admitted. The supernatural was either God as transcending creation, of which no revelation had been made, or it was the metaphysical, the supersensible, as Coleridge seemed to maintain. I had not the least conception of a created order of supernatural existence, or life above the natural; and with only a single order of life, the double organization of mankind could not and cannot be defended. That is defensible only on the condition that there are two orders, the one natural and the other supernatural, and that man lives or may live in this world both a natural and a supernatural life. The Catholic Church is the supernatural organization of the supernatural order,—an order that cannot be represented by the State, which is and can be only the natural organization of the natural. From my standpoint at the time, I was perfectly right in rejecting the Church as an organization distinct from the State.

My doctrines touching the Church and the priesthood were not those by which I gave the most offence. The really horrible doctrines in the eyes of the public were my supposed doctrine on marriage, my condemnation of the system of wages, and my proposition to change the laws which govern the descent and redistribution of property. I have cited the passage relating to marriage. What was running in my head when I wrote it, I no longer remember. I did not at that time deny the indissolubility of the marriage contract. My language was construed to mean a denial of marriage, and the assertion of what is called the "Free-Love" system; but I certainly held no such system, if I ever had done so, after my connection with the Fanny-Wright school had ceased. In defending myself at the time, I took the Catholic ground, without much consistency, that marriage is a sacrament and indissoluble; and alleged that what I complained of was the viciously-organized state of society, which makes marriages mercenary, and renders it, to a great extent, impossible for them to be founded on love or mutual affection. I suspect that there was a slight touch of sentimentalism, and no very clear or definite meaning in what I wrote. There might have been some nonsense, but there was no looseness.

The proposition with regard to property was thrown out avowedly, not for adoption, but for discussion. It was simply the doctrine of the Saint-Simonian school, which I have already stated. It did not interfere with private property, or dispossess a single proprietor during his lifetime, or interfere with his free use of his property as long as he lived. It proceeded on the assumption that a man's right of property ceases with his natural life, and therefore that he has no natural right to dispose of his property by will or testament, to take effect after his death; and that the right of inheritance in the child to the property of the parent is a municipal, not a natural right, or right founded in the law of nature. These assumptions are generally conceded or maintained by jurists; and, thus far, I proposed nothing new. It was then perfectly competent for the State to abolish the present legislation on the subject, and to enact a new law of descent, and a new Statute of

Distribution. The only question that could arise between me and my opponents was a question, not of right, but of expediency. Is the proposed change expedient? I contended that it was, if we meant to maintain political equality really as well as nominally; and I think even now that, on this hypothesis, I was right. My error was in taking that equality seriously, and in supposing that it would be possible to induce my countrymen to adopt the measures necessary to make it a reality. The objection to my proposition was, not that it was wrong in principle, or would be hurtful in practice, but that it was simply impracticable. Equality is a fine thing to profess, to declaim about, but it is the last thing men will consent to adopt, except in name. It is not displeasing when applied to those above us, but is very disgusting, unreasonable, unnatural, when applied to those below us. I am as good as you, does very well; but, you are as good as I, is quite another affair, and few will accept it, who have not the supernatural virtue of Christian charity.

The gravamen of my offence was my condemnation of the modern industrial system, especially the system of labor at wages, which I held to be worse, except in regard to the feelings, than the slave system at the South. In this I adopted the views of the socialists of France and other countries. The revolution we wanted now was, not a revolution against the king or the crown, but against the Bourgeoisie or middling class. They who in the European revolutions of 1848 clamored for *la République démocratique et sociale,* held only the views I had advocated in my essay on the laboring classes; and they were the only consistent party that I was able to detect in those revolutions. A Democratic government that leaves untouched all the social inequalities, or inequalities of condition, which obtain in all countries, always struck me as an absurdity; and I have seen no reason to change my opinions on that point. The political history of my own country tends to confirm them. In 1840 I had not wholly ceased to believe it possible to introduce such changes into our social and economical arrangements as would give to the political equality asserted by American Democracy a practical significance. I have got bravely over that since.

I took, in regard to society, even as late as 1840, the Democratic premises as true and unquestionable. They were given me by the public sentiment of my country. I had taken them in with my mother's milk, and had never thought of inquiring whether they were tenable or not. I took them as my political and social starting-point, or *principium,* and sought simply to harmonize government and society with them. If I erred, it was in common with my Democratic countrymen, and I differed from them only in seeking what they did not seek, to be consistent in error. Democratic government was defended on the ground that it recognized and maintained the equality of all men, and was opposed to the system of privilege, class, or castes. It asserted equality as a natural right, and assumed that the

introduction and maintenance of equality between
man and man is desirable, and essential to the moral,
intellectual, and physical well-being of mankind on
earth. Taking this, without examination, to be true,
I concluded very reasonably that we ought to
conform society to it; and that whatever in society
is repugnant to it, and tends to prevent its practical
realization, is wrong, and should be warred against.
My countrymen did not understand me, because
they were not in the habit of generalizing their own
views, and testing them by the light of first principles. They could reason well enough on particulars,
or in particular instances, but not as to the whole of
their political and social ideas. They could accept
incongruous ideas, and felt no inconvenience in supporting anomalies and inconsistencies. They could
defend with equal earnestness perfect equality in
theory, and the grossest inequality in practice, and
call it common-sense. I could not do that. Either
conform your practice, I said, to your theory, or
your theory to your practice. Be Democrats
socially, or do not claim to be so politically. Alas!
I did not know then that men act from habit,
prejudice, routine, passion, caprice, rather than
from reason; and that, of all people in the world,
Englishmen and Americans are the least disturbed
by incongruities, inconsistencies, inconsequences, and
anomalies—although I was beginning to suspect it.

Starting from the Democratic theory of man and
society, I contended that the great, the mother-evil
of modern society was the separation of capital and

labor; or the fact that one class of the community owns the funds, and another and a distinct class is compelled to perform the labor of production.   The consequence of this system is, that owners of capital enrich themselves at the expense of the owners of labor.   The system of money wages, the modern system, is more profitable to the owners of capital than the slave system is to the slave-masters, and hardly less oppressive to the laborer.   The wages, as a general rule, are never sufficient to enable the laborer to place himself on an equal footing with the capitalist.   Capital will always command the lion's share of the proceeds.   This is seen in the fact that, while they who command capital grow rich, the laborer by his simple wages at best only obtains a bare subsistence.   The whole class of simple laborers are poor, and in general unable to procure by their wages more than the bare necessaries of life.   This is a necessary result of the system.   The capitalist employs labor that he may grow rich or richer; the laborer sells his labor that he may not die of hunger, he, his wife, and little ones; and as the urgency of guarding against hunger is always stronger than that of growing rich or richer, the capitalist holds the laborer at his mercy, and has over him, whether called a slave or a freeman, the power of life and death.

An examination into the actual condition of the laboring classes in all countries, especially in Great Britain and the United States, where the modern industrial and commercial system is carried farthest, proves this reasoning to be correct. Poor men may indeed become rich, but not by the simple wages of unskilled labor. They never do become rich, except by availing themselves in some way of the labors of others. Dependent on wages alone, the laborer remains always poor, and shut out from nearly all the advantages of society. In what are called prosperous times he may, by working early and late, and with all his might, retain enough of the proceeds of his labor to save him from actual want; but in what are called "hard times," it is not so, and cases of actual suffering for want of the necessaries of life, nay, of actual starvation, even in our own country, are no rare occurrences. It would be difficult to estimate the amount of actual suffering endured by the honest and virtuous poor in every one of our larger towns and cities, and which neither private nor public charity can reach.

The evil does not stop here. The system elevates the middling class to wealth, often men who began life with poverty. A poor man, or a man of small means in the beginning, become rich by trade, speculation, or the successful *exploitation* of labor, is often a greater calamity to society than a wealthy man reduced to poverty. An old established nobility, with gentle manners, refined tastes, chivalrous feelings, surrounded by the prestige of rank, and endeared by the memory of heroic deeds or lofty civic virtues, is endurable, nay respectable, and not without compensating advantages to society in general, for its rank and privileges. But the upstart, the *novus homo*, with all the vulgar tastes and habits, ignorance and coarseness, of the class from which he has sprung, and nothing of the class into which he fancies he has risen but its wealth, is intolerable, and widely mischievous. He has nothing to sustain him but his money, and what money can purchase. He enters upon a career of lavish expenditure, and aids to introduce an expensive and luxurious style of living, destructive of genuine simplicity of manners, and of private and social morals. Moral worth and intellectual superiority count for nothing. Men, to be of any account in their town or city, must be rich, at least appear to be rich. The slow gains of patient toil and honest industry no longer suffice. There is in all classes an impatience to be rich. The most daring and reckless speculations are resorted to, and when honest means fail, dishonest, nay, criminal, means are adopted. The man of a moderate income cannot live within his means. His wife and daughters must have the house new furnished, or a new house taken up town, and must dress so as to vie with the wives and daughters of the millionnaires of Fifth Avenue. Nobody is contented to appear what he is, or to enjoy life in the state in which he finds himself. All are striving to be, or to appear, what they are not, to work their way up to a higher social stratum, and hence society becomes hollow, a sham, a lie.

Between the master and the slave, between the lord and the serf, there often grow up pleasant personal relations and attachments; there is personal intercourse, kindness, affability, protection on the one side, respect and gratitude on the other, which partially compensates for the superiority of the one and the inferiority of the other; but the modern system of wages allows very little of all this: the capitalist and the workman belong to different species, and have little personal intercourse. The agent or man of business pays the workman his wages, and there ends the responsibility of the employer. The laborer has no further claim.on him, and he may want and starve, or sicken and die—it is his own affair, with which the employer has nothing to do. Hence the relation between the two classes becomes mercenary, hard, and a matter of arithmetic. The one class become proud, haughty, cold, supercilious, contemptuous, or at best superbly indifferent, looking upon their laborers as appendages of their steam-engines, their spinning-jennies, or their power-looms, with far less of esteem and affection than they bestow on their favorite dogs or horses; the other class become envious, discontented, resentful, hostile, laboring under a sense of injustice, and waiting only the opportunity to right themselves. The equality of love, of affection, cannot come in to make amends for the inequality of property and condition.

To remedy these evils, I proposed to abolish the distinction between capitalists and laborers, employer and employed, by having every man an owner of the funds as well as the labor of production, and thus making it possible for every man to labor on a capital of his own, and to receive according to his works. Undoubtedly, my plan would have broken up the whole modern commercial system, prostrated all the great industries, or what I called the factory system, and thrown the mass of the people back on the land to get their living by agricultural and mechanical pursuits. I knew this well enough, but this was one of the results I aimed at. It was wherefore I opposed the whole banking and credit system, and struggled hard to separate the fiscal concerns of the government from the moneyed interests of the country, and to abolish paper currency. I wished to check commerce, to destroy speculation, and for the factory system, which we were enacting tariffs to protect and build up, to restore the old system of real home industry. The business men of the country saw as clearly as I did whither my propositions tended, and took the alarm; and as the business interests, rather than the agricultural and mechanical interests, ruled the minds of my countrymen, I had my labor for my pains. I went directly against the dominant sentiment of the British and American world, and made war on what it holds to be its chief interest and its crowning glory. Here was the gravamen of my offence. I had dared take Democracy at its word, and push its principles to their last logical consequences; I had had the incredible folly of treating the equality asserted as if it meant something, as if it could be made a reality, instead of a miserable sham. It was the attacks I made on the modern industrial and commercial system, that gave the offence. Mr. Bancroft, who had been one of my stanchest friends, could not go with me in my views of property, though he did not object to my views with regard to the Church and the priesthood. John C. Calhoun, of South Carolina, told me that in what I had said of the priests I was right. "You have," he said, "told the truth of them. But your doctrine as to the descent and distribution of property is wrong, and you will do well to reëxamine it." I was not wrong, if the premises from which I reasoned were tenable ; and I am unable even to-day to detect any unsoundness in my views of the relation of capital and labor, or of the modern system of money wages. I believe firmly even still that the economical system I proposed, if it could be introduced, would be favorable to the virtue and happiness of society. But I look upon its introduction as wholly impracticable, and therefore regard all thought and effort bestowed on it as worse than thrown away. We must seek its equivalent from another source, in another order of ideas, set forth and sustained by religion.

My political friends, as may well be believed, were indignant, if not precisely at my views, at my inopportune publication of them. I had injured my party, and defeated by my rashness the success of its candidates. They came to the conclusion that whatever my honesty, my zeal or ability, I was deficient in the essential qualities of a party leader. In this they were right, but they reasoned from wrong premises. I had my own purpose in publishing my essay on the laboring classes; and what they supposed I did from rashness, mere wantonness, I did with deliberation, with "malice aforethought." I have seldom, if ever, published anything in the heat of blood, or without being well aware of what I was doing, and I must bear the full responsibility of doing it. That is, I have always acted from reason, not impulse; my reason may or may not have been a good one, but it always seemed to me a good one at the time, and generally was a good one from the position I occupied.

I had, at the persuasion of friends, given my support, such as it was, to the Democratic party, with the hope of making that party the instrument of carrying out my views. A short experience convinced me that that hope was chimerical. I was convinced of it by the changes I detected taking place in myself. I found myself acquiring a prominent position in the Democratic party, and in a fair way of becoming one of its trusted leaders; but in proportion as I acquired the confidence of the party, I found myself less disposed to insist on my doctrines of Social Reform, and less and less at liberty to be myself, and follow my own convictions. I might gain political preferment, I might aspire to the highest posts in the State and Nation, and even gain them: at least I had the vanity to believe I could, if I chose. The road to them was open and plain before me, and I understood as well as any other man in the country the means to be used to gain them; but, in gaining them, I must give up my per-

sonal freedom and independence, and follow as well
as lead my party. I felt, too, for a moment, the
workings of political ambition, and dared no longer
trust myself. Let me go on as I am going a
little longer, and I shall forget all my early purposes,
abandon the work to which I have consecrated my
life, or become so involved in the meshes of party,
or form so many political relations, that I can no
longer be free to return to my work without compromising my friends, my party, and perhaps myself.
The best and shortest way, because the honestest
and most straightforward, is, now before I become
deeper involved, to come out and publish in the most
startling form possible my whole ulterior thought,
without circumlocution or reticence. If the party
accept my views, which of course they will not, well
and good; if not, as will be the case, the party ties
will be broken, and I shall be free to publish my
honest convictions without fear of compromising any-
body but myself. I shall be free to act as I think
proper, unshackled by party obligations, or even
personal friendships. Such were my reasons, avowed
to those who shared my confidence, before the
article was written. For my party, the act was
impolitic; for myself, it was necessary and prudent.
I look back upon it to-day as the least discreditable
act I had hitherto performed; and there was in it
something bordering on moral heroism, which has
not been without its reward.

When I published my essay, I supposed it would
close my literary as well as my political career. But

the manner in which I was assailed aroused for a
moment my indignation, and made me resolve contra:y to my original intention, to defend myself, and
to show that I could more than regain before th
public the position I had lost. I defended my e. say
at length and with vigor in the following number of
my Review, and silenced the noisy clamors raised
against me. I retained and enlarged my audience,
and assumed a higher tone and position than I had
ever before held, though not without making the
greatest intellectual efforts, and using all the arts of
popularity I was capable of. I felt in those times
that, to be popular or unpopular, is simply a matter
of one's own choice. In the three years that
followed I gained more than I had lost, and I never
stood higher, commanded more of the public attention, or had a more promising career open before me,
than at the moment when I avowed my conversion
to Catholicity. I did not value reputation for its
own sake—I have never done so; and if I labored
to recover the ground I had lost, it was simply to
prove that I could do so when I chose. It cost me
not a pang to throw all away on becoming a Catholic, and to be regarded as henceforth of no account
by my non-Catholic countrymen, as I did not doub
I should be. There is something else than reputation worth living for.

The publication of my Essay on the Laboring
Classes marked the crisis in my mental disease. In
it I had made my confession to the public; I had
made, as I have already said, a clean breast of it,

and had no further concealment. I had thrown off
a heavy load which had been accumulating for
years, and felt relieved. From that moment a
change came over the temper of my madness. I
had gone as far in the direction I was going as I
could go. I had reached the last stage in that
journey, and there I must stop and remain, or re-
trace my steps. I had one principle, and only one,
to which, since throwing up Universalism, I had
been faithful,—a principle for which I had perhaps
made some sacrifices: that of following my own
honest convictions whithersoever they should lead
me. I had drawn from the premises furnished me
by my non-Catholic and Democratic countrymen,
their strictly logical conclusions, and these same
countrymen had recoiled from them with horror.
Either they are wrong in doing so, or their premises
are false. Suppose I examine these premises, and
see if this Protestant and Democratic theory of man
and society, to which the world seems tending, is not
itself founded in error.

The electioneering campaign of 1840, carried on
by doggerels, log cabins, and hard cider, by means
utterly corrupt and corrupting, disgusted me with
Democracy as distinguished from Constitutional
Republicanism, destroyed what little confidence I
had in popular elections, and made me distrust
both the intelligence and the instincts of "the
masses." I sat down to the scientific study of
government, in its grounds, its origin, its forms, and
its administration. I read for the first time Aristotle

on Politics; I read the best treatises, ancient and modern, on government within my reach; I studied the constitutions of Greece and Rome, and their history, the political administration of ancient Persia, the feudal system, and the constitutions of modern states, in the light of such experience and such philosophy as I had, and came to the conclusion that the condition of liberty is order, and that in this world we must seek, not equality, but justice. To the maintenance of order in the State, and justice between man and man, a firm, strong, and efficient government is necessary. Liberty is not in the absence of authority, but in being held to obey only just and legitimate authority. Evidently, I had changed systems, and had entered another order of ideas. Government was no longer the mere agent of society, as my Democratic masters had taught me, but an authority having the right and the power to govern society, and direct and aid it, as a wise Providence, in fulfilling its destiny. I became henceforth a conservative in politics, instead of an impracticable radical, and through political conservatism I advanced rapidly towards religious conservatism. So I date my beginning to amend, from the publication of my so-called "horrible doctrines."

CHAPTER XIV.

MAN NO CHURCH-BUILDER.

I **HAD** settled it that there is no true liberty withou
order, and no order without a constituted authority
Then, since no progress without liberty, my new
church, necessary to the maintenance of order,
instead of coming after progress and being its result,
must precede it, and be the condition of effecting it.
I cannot effect the progress of man and society without the new organization. That I settled long ago.
But how without that progress obtain the new organization, or the new church itself?

Here was a problem I had neglected to solve,—
a problem, too, of no little difficulty. It will be easy
enough to effect the progress when I have the means
in my hands, but how am I to get the means? I
cannot effect my end, the creation of a heaven on
earth, without means: how any more without means
create my new church, by which I am to effect that
end? Whence proceeds the organic power to erect
the new institution, which is to elevate the human
race above their present condition, and to set them
forward in an endless career of progress? I have
heretofore maintained that ideas are potent, and
proceeded on the supposition that they have the

intrinsic force to actualize themselves. Ideas, I was accustomed to say with my friend, Bronson Alcot, the American Orpheus, when once proclaimed, will take unto themselves hands, build the new temple, and instaurate the new worship; but ideas in themselves are not powers, have no active force, and can be rendered real and active only as clothed with concrete existence by a power distinct from themselves. Suppose, then, that I really have the true ideas, suppose that I see clearly and distinctly what is to be done, it by no means follows that I have the power to do it—to concrete the ideas, to actualize them, to embody them in a real and living organization of the race.

Certain it is that man, speak we of the race or of the individual, has no proper creative power. He can work only on and with materials furnished to his hands. The great things he does, he does only by availing himself of the great active forces of the universe in which he is placed. The forces that propel the machinery he constructs are not his own, nor of his own creation; they are forces that already exist, and exist and operate without any dependence on either his intellect or his will. The water that drives his mill, the steam that propels his ship in defiance of wind and tide, the electricity that sends his messages instantaneously round the globe, and brings back an answer, are all powers created to his hand, and he only adapts them to his use. Undoubtedly, the power of association is great, but it is at best only the sum of the separate powers associated. Association generates no new power; it only collects, concentrates, and utilizes the powers of the individuals embraced in the association. The power of the race is only the power of all men, the combined power of the individuals who compose it; for, aside from the individuals, from all men, there is no actual man, no actual humanity. The race, as distinguished from individuals, is only an idea, only ideal, not actual, man; for man is actual, concrete existence only in men. In my new association or organization, I may have the sum of the life that the race already lives or has attained to, but no augmentation of life. The organization can, then, give me, give the human race itself, nothing above what we already have. How, then, with nothing more than what we already have, am I to get my new organization, and in it the means and conditions of future progress, or of becoming more than we are?

Man is now below what I would have him, and behind the goal I propose for him. I propose his progress; I propose to elevate him in virtue and happiness. But if he is below what I would have him, how, with him alone, am I to elevate him? Man is what he is, and, with only man, how am I to make him, or is he to become, more than he now is? Man only equals man. From man I can get only man, and, with man alone, I have and can have nothing above man. No man can rise above himself, or lift himself by his own waistband. Archimedes is reported to have said, "Give me whereon to stand, and I will move the world;" but there is no law of mechanics by which you can raise a body without something distinct from it on which to rest the fulcrum of your lever. The ship cleaves its way through the ocean, or the bird through the air, only by finding a counter-pressure or resisting force in the fluid cleaved. There can be no motion without rest, no movable without the immovable. Nothing cannot make itself something, and the imperfect, without borrowing from what is not itself, cannot make itself perfect. *Ex nihilo nihil fit.* My new church, then, if it is to elevate the race and be the means of their progress, must embody a power above that which they now have. Whence is that power to come? How am I to obtain it, and obtain it as I must, without my new church, and obtain it as the condition of organizing it?

Undoubtedly, there is such a phenomenon as growth. We see it in vegetables, in animals, in man; but all growth is by accretion, by assimilation from abroad. The acorn develops and grows into the oak, only by virtue of the substance it assimilates from the soil, air, and light. It must have food, appropriate food; and it is only through assimilating the food by a living process determined by the internal law of the oak, that it grows and expands into the tree. So of the whole animal world. No animal can grow or even live by itself alone. Thus is it in the material order, as all men know and concede. Else why the necessity of food, of drink? The spiritual and material correspond, for the material does in its order but copy or imitate the spiritual. Neither in body nor soul, then, can man grow or make progress,—for progress is nothing but growth,—with himself alone, or without assimilating to himself appropriate food from abroad. Progress there may be, and undoubtedly is, and this progress is effected by processes determined by the internal law or nature of man, but not without the aid of that which is not man. Here I derived no little aid from the writings of Pierre Leroux.

Pierre Leroux, a French philosopher and politician, member of the National Assembly in 1848, whose name was frequently heard under the Republic which ended in the present French Empire, in connection with the socialists and the Banquets of Love, was originally affiliated to the Saint-Simonians, and retains, or did at my latest information, many of the principles of their school. He is a man of learning, in whose head ferments a marvellous variety of ideas, and who, with the exception of Malebranche, must be regarded as the ablest and most original philosopher France has produced. As a writer, he lacks the repose, the classic grace, the sustained elegance and finish of M. Victor Cousin, but he is free, bold, and energetic. His writings are voluminous. For some time he edited the *Revue Encyclopedique*, in connection with J. Reynaud. He commenced in 1886 the *Encyclopédie Nouvelle*, not yet finished; subsequently he edited, in connection with George Sand and the late Abbé de Lamennais, the *Revue Indépendante*, in which George Sand first published her *Consuelo*. He has published a uew French translation of Plato, though whether made by him or by some of his disciples under his direction, I am not informed; and a remarkable work in its way, entitled *L'Humanité*. My personal knowledge of his writings is confined to this last-mentioned work, to his *Réfutation de l'Eclectisme*, and his articles in the New Encyclopedia. He was a fellow-pupil with M. Victor Cousin, in L'École Normale, and since the Revolution of July, has appeared as his rival and bitter opponent.

The *Réfutation de l'Eclectisme* was first published in 1839, but I first read it in 1841. It had a marvellous effect in revolutionizing my own philosophical views, or rather of emancipating me from my subjection to the Eclectic school founded by MM. Cousin and Jouffroy. Like most English and Americans of my generation, I had been educated in the school of Locke. From Locke I had passed to the Scottish school of Reid and Stewart, and had adhered to it without well knowing what it was, till it was overthrown by Dr. Thomas Brown, who, in the Introductory Lectures to his philosophy, revived the skepticism of Hume, and drove me into speculative Atheism, by resolving cause and effect into invariable antecedence and consequence, thus excluding all idea of creative power or productive force. Still young, I rushed into pure sensism and materialism, and was prepared intellectually to join with Fran es Wright and her followers, when they appeared. Gradually I had elaborated a sort of philosophical sentimentalism, depending on the heart rather than the head, bearing some analogy to the tendencies of Bernardin de St. Pierre, Madame de Staël, Benjamin Constant, Châteaubriand, Adam Smith, and the German Jacobi. In this half-dreaming state, with vague feelings, and vaguer notions, I encountered the philosophical writings of M. Cousin, first, I think, in 1833, and yielded almost entirely to the witchery of his style, the splen l r of his diction, the brilliancy of his generalizations, and the real power of his genius, although I made from first to last certain reserves.

M. Victor Cousin was born in 1792, and his original destination was literature; but captivated by the *Leçons* of M. Laromiguière and M. Royer-Collard, he resolved to devote himself to philosophy. He was first *répteitéur*, and then professor of philosophy in the Normal School, subsequently professor of the History of Philosophy in the Faculty of Letters at Paris. His first Course, which has been published, was given in 1816, and is most remarkable as the production of a young philosopher not twenty-five years of age. His Course for the half year of 1828, and his full Course for 1829, and his *Fragments Philosophiques*, collected and published in 1826, with an elaborate preface, were the first of his writings that came into my hands; and they remain, as modified in subsequent editions, his principal philosophical works up to the present time. He has edited the works of Proclus and Descartes, and the previously unpublished works of Abelard, preceded by a history of the Scholastic Philosophy. He has also published a translation into beautiful French, hardly inferior to the original Greek, of the Complete Works of Plato, with an Introduction and Notes to most of the Dialogues, in thirteen volumes octavo, with the promise of a new Life of the author, and a Critical Judgment of his philosophy, which have not yet appeared. Latterly he has published a new edition of one of his earlier Courses under the title of *Le Vrai, Le Beau, et Le Bien*, The True, The Beautiful, and The Good, and some admirable Studies of the literature of the seventeenth century grouped around Pascal, the Duchess de Longueville, Madame de Sablé, etc. As he grows older, he seems to turn more towards religious ideas, and to manifest less disrespect for Christianity and the Church. In politics he is a constitutionalist, or what was formerly termed a *Doctrinaire ;* and, under the Republic of 1848, he acted for the most part with the conservative majority. I was not the first of his disciples in this country, but I was among his most ardent admirers, and perhaps contributed more than any other one man to draw the attention of American thinkers to his philosophy.

Gioberti, in a note of two hundred pages or more to the third volume of his *Introdusione allo Studio della Filosofia*, has pointed out and refuted in a masterly manner the errors of M. Cousin's doctrine on ontology, creation, and moral liberty, but he speaks, in my judgment, too slightingly of his philosophical genius, as he does also of Leroux's. Whoever has read attentively the philosophical writings of the illustrious Italian, cannot fail to perceive that he has been far more indebted to these two Frenchmen, whom he affects to despise, than it pleases him to acknowledge. Neither can I agree with the Italian that Jouffroy, the most distinguished of M. Cousin's early disciples, had a truer and loftier philosophical genius than his master. Yet Jouffroy, who died too young for philosophy, or for his own fame, was no doubt a superior man, a clear, systematic, and logical thinker, with an amiable disposition and a transparent soul, who never ceased to regret the loss of his early Catholic faith, which I would gladly believe he recovered before his death; but he never rose above the Scottish school, and died uttering his protest against philosophy. His great merit, and the highest proof he gave of his philosophical genius, was in perceiving the worthlessness of the philosophy he had been teaching, and its vast inferiority to the Catechism he had rejected. He had not, however, the genius that penetrates through the mass of errors, and seizes the great, living, and eternal truth, which so many philosophers misapprehend, misinterpret, and misapply. But, be all this as it may, I acknowledge willingly my indebtedness in philosophy to both M. Victor Cousin and to M. Théodore Jouffroy, who have served me hardly less by their errors than by their truths.

M. Cousin had labored to combine the method of the psychologists with that of the new German school of Schelling and Hegel. He starts with the facts of consciousness, and professes, by careful observation and rigid induction, to rise to the ideas of the True, the Beautiful, and the Good, and then, from these necessary, absolute ideas, as he calls them, to descend to the region of psychology, and by their light to verify anew the facts of consciousness, previously analyzed. But these absolute ideas, what are they? M. Cousin makes them the constituent elements of reason. But of what reason? The Divine or the human? If of the Divine, how does our intelligence grasp them? If of the human, how determine their objective validity, or, to use the language of the schoolmen, their existence *a parte rei?*. M. Cousin's answer is confused and unsatisfactory. Reason, he maintains, is indeed constituted by these ideas, they are its constituent elements; but the reason they constitute is the spontaneous and impersonal reason, not our personal or reflective reason. Therefore these absolute ideas are objective in relation to our personality, that is to say, to our principle of voluntary activity, *le moi*, the me. But what is this impersonal, spontaneous reason, operating without our voluntary activity? Is it essentially distinct from the personal or reflective reason? M. Cousin tells us that it is not; that there are not two reasons; that spontaneity and reflection are simply two modes in which one and the same reason operates. Then this one reason—is it objective or subjective? Is it the Divine reason, or is it a faculty of the human soul?

M. Cousin maintains that it is the Divine reason, and at the same time a faculty of the human soul.

But here is a grave difficulty. How make the Divine reason, indistinguishable from the Divine Being or Essence, a human faculty, and therefore essentially human, without identifying God and man, and falling into pure pantheism or pure atheism? To escape this difficulty, M. Cousin attempts to distinguish between God and reason, between the Divine Being and the Logos, and to present the Divine reason, not as God, but as the Word of God. In this, however, he misapprehends the Christian dogma of the Trinity, on which he professes to found his distinction, and falls into a grave ontological error. In the Christian dogma of the Trinity, the distinction of being is denied, and the Logos is asserted to be one in essence with the Father. Besides, the Logos, if not one in essence with God, and therefore really and truly God, is creature; for between God and creature there is no middle existence. What is not creature is God, and what is not God is creature. If your spontaneous reason is God, then you make God and man identical; if you distinguish it from God, you make it creature, simply human reason, a faculty of the human soul, and therefore remain still in the region of psychology. Your absolute ideas are only subjectively absolute, and the inquiry returns, How establish their objectivity, or existence *a parte rei?*

This question M. Cousin has never to my knowledge answered, and therefore has never really advanced beyond the subjectivism of Kant, which, elsewhere, he so effectually refutes. It was always an objection in my mind to his philosophy. His absolute ideas of the True, the Beautiful, and the Good, which he labors to identify with God, were, after all, on his hypothesis, only abstractions, and could give me only an abstract God, and no living God, no real God at all. Here Leroux, who is regarded by not a few as an atheist, and who does fall, in his *Humanité*, into the Hegelian pantheism, came to my aid, by directing my attention to the simple analysis of thought, or to what M. Cousin calls "the fact of consciousness." M. Cousin himself had said, thought, or the fact of consciousness, is a phenomenon with three elements, subject, object, and their relation. The subject is always *le moi*, or the thinker, the object is always *le non-moi*, or something standing over against the subject, and independent of it; and the relation is the form of the thought. M. Leroux adopts this, and shows that thought is a synthesis and the resultant of two factors. The subject cannot think without the concurrence of the object, and the object cannot be thought without the concurrence of the subject, or thinker. The subject and object are both given simultaneously in one and the same thought or act, and therefore the reality of the one is as certain as that of the other. The object affirms itself in the fact of consciousness as object, as distinct from, and independent of, the subject; and the subject recognizes itself as subject, as thinker, and therefore as distinct from and opposed to the object. This stripped philosophy of its mystery, divested it of its endless abstractions and vain subtilties, and harmonized it with the common-sense of mankind.

Man cannot think without an object, and, being finite, he can never be his own object. Only God can be the object of his own intelligence, or be intelligent without other than himself; man, whatever else he is, is a dependent being, and is in no instance, in no respect, alone sufficient for himself. He is not intelligent in himself, because he is not intelligible in himself. There is and can be no intelligence where there is no intelligible, or nothing that can be known. We cannot see where there is nothing to be seen. What is not is not intelligible. That which does not exist cannot be an object of thought; for it is not, and therefore cannot present anything to the mind, can present no resistance or counterpressure to the mental force. The object, then, is always real, and no thought ever is or ever can be totally false or purely subjective. A further question may be raised, indeed, as to the light by which the object is thought, or as to the intelligible medium of thought,—a question which Malebranche attempted to solve by what he called "vision in God," and which M. Cousin comes near solving in asserting that absolute ideas are intuitive. But M. Cousin fails precisely where Plato before him failed, by not distinguishing the idea as archetype in the Divine reason from idea as the essence or reality of the thing, regarded as the object of our science. He fails to distinguish reason as Divine from reason as a human faculty, and to point out the real relation which subsists between them. He makes only a modal distinction, which is not sufficient to save him from pantheism, and fails to perceive that the Divine reason is the human reason only through the medium of the Divine creative act,—*mediante actu creativo divino.* The Divine reason, indistinguishable from the Divine Essence or Being, at once creates the human reason, and presents itself as its light and its immediate object. We see all things in God, as we see visible objects in the light which illuminates them, though not simply as ideas in the Divine mind, as Malebranche appears to have held; for we see existences themselves in their concreteness and reality, not merely their ideas, or possibility of being created.

Having settled it, that man does not suffice for himself in the intellectual order, that he cannot even think himself without thinking what is not himself, or without the concurrence of the object with the subject, I learned from Leroux that the same principle extends to all our acts, and that no act of life is possible without the concurrence of the object. Man lives and can live only by communion with what is not himself. In himself alone, cut off from all not himself, he is neither a progressive nor a living being. His body must have food from without, and so must his heart and his soul. Hence his elevation, his progress, as well as his very existence, depend on the object. He cannot lift himself, but must be lifted, by placing him in communion with a higher and elevating object,

This will be the more evident, if we bear in mind that the fact, any fact, of human life is the joint product of the subject and object, and therefore partakes of the character of each. This is a fact of no inconsiderable importance, and enables us to explain many things certain from observation, from human experience, but which philosophy has hitherto failed to explain. "Evil communications corrupt good manners," is a proverb as old as human experience, but has philosophy hitherto explained it? Why is it that association with the great and good improves our manners and our morals? I meet a great and good man, I hold intercourse or communion with him, and am never after what I was before. I feel that a virtue has gone forth from him and entered into my life, so that I am not, and never can be again, the man I was before I met him. What is the explanation of this fact? How happens it that I am benefited by my intercourse with the good, and injured by my intercourse with the bad? How is it that one man is able to influence another, whether for good or for evil? What is the meaning of *influence* itself? Influence, inflowing, flowing-in,—what is this but the very fact I assert, that our life is the joint product of subject and object? Man lives, and can live only by communion with that which is not himself. This must be said of every living dependent existence. Only God can live in, from, and by himself alone, uninfluenced and unaffected by anything distinguishable from his own being. But man is not God, is not being in himself, is not complete being, and must find out of himself both his being and its completeness. He lives not in and from himself alone, but does and must live in and by the life of another.

Cut off man from all communion with external nature, and he dies, for he has no sustenance for his body, and must starve; cut him off from all communion with moral nature, and he dies, starves, morally; cut him off from all moral communion with a life above his own, and he stagnates, and can make no progress. All this everybody knows and concedes. Then, to elevate man, to give him a higher and nobler life, you must give him a higher and nobler object, a higher and nobler life with which to commune. To elevate his subjective life, you must elevate his objective life. From the object must flow into him a higher virtue, an elevating element. Thus far I followed Leroux, but I did not and could not follow him in all his applications of the great principle he had helped me to grasp and understand. He sought to apply the principle in an un-Christian sense; I saw, or thought I saw, in it the means of placing myself more in harmony with the common beliefs of Christendom, without violence to my reason.

"Man," said Leroux, "lives by communion with his object—with nature, with his fellow-men, and with God. He communes with nature through property, with his fellow-men through family and the State, and with God through humanity." In the first two statements he is right, and asserts a solid basis for property, family, and the State, three institutions which are indispensable to human life; and which, however they may be warred against, are really as indestructible as human nature itself. But in the third statement he adds nothing, for, to commune with God through humanity is nothing else than to commune with our kind, or with other men in the family and the State. Man can live, and the majority of men do live, with only the first two communions named, but he can so live only the life of the human animal,—an unprogressive life, which can never rise to the Divine. Leroux knew this, and as he believed firmly in progress, in the progressiveness of the race, nay, of nature, indeed of all natures, he asserted as its condition, communion with God; but as he conceived God as actual only in existences, he asserted for us only the communion with God through humanity, which was in effect simply no communion with God at all, and supplied and could supply no objective element to our life above that which we already have, and cannot as men but have.

Leroux never fairly understood his own philosophy. His analysis of thought had given him the foundation of true realism in opposition to the Kantian subjectivism or idealism; but the moment he had finished his analysis of thought, and proved to us that the life of every man is the joint product of subject and object, and therefore partaking alike of the character of each, he fell into the precise error which I have pointed out in the case of Cousin, that of confounding the ideal with the real. He even went farther, and asserted, in violation of his whole ontology, the power of the ideal, which he himself identifies with the possible, to realize or actualize itself,—the very error I had detected in myself, and which he more than any other had enabled me to detect. Subsequently, I believe, in his refutation of Hegel, he professes to refute this error; but in his *Refutation of Eclecticism*, and his huge work on *Humanity*, he asserted God as the Void of the Buddhists, the infinite possibility of the universe, which the universe is continually actualizing, and hence its progress. Yet he had asserted direct intuition of God, that we think God, and God must really be, or we could not think him.

All the contradiction or absurdity of his theology I did not at the moment perceive, because my mind was taken up with his doctrine, that human life is the resultant of two forces, of the intercommunion of subject and object, from which I drew a further conclusion than that drawn by Leroux himself. I drew from it the conclusion that man is not and cannot be in himself progressive, and that his progress depends on the objective element of his life, or, in other words, on his living in communion with God, and not only in a natural communion, as held by Leroux, but also in a supernatural communion. If God vouchsafes us no communion with him but that which we have with him in our own natures and the natural objects in relation with which we are placed, we cannot advance beyond or rise above what we are, for of that communion we have never for a moment been deprived, and never could have been deprived. God, as the divine object of our life, must present himself in a higher order, or we are not elevated above or advanced beyond what we already are. I was obliged, then, either to give up all my hopes of progress, or abandon my doctrine of no God but the God in man, or the identity of the human and the Divine. I must recognize God as superior to humanity, independent of nature, and intervening as Providence in human affairs, and giving us, so to speak, more of himself, than he gives in nature. Here, though still far enough from the truth, I had entered into the order of religious ideas, and was headed, for the first time in my life, in the direction of real Christian beliefs, and began to sus pect that I might believe as the Christian world had always believed, without abandoning my reason, or doing it the least violence. This filled me with an inexpressible joy. I need not always stand alone, and pine in vain for sympathy with my kind. I, too, may one day enter the brotherhood of believers.

CHAPTER XV.

Pierre Leroux was not, like myself, wholly ignorant of Catholic theology, and he was able to give me some glimpses of what is called by my Puseyite friends, "the Sacramental System." He knew the Catholic doctrine of grace, and made use of it in explaining his doctrine of progress. His aim was to find a philosophical equivalent for the infused habits of grace, asserted by the Church, but rejected by all classes of Protestants, and which I had not at that time even so much as heard of; but in his effort to do this, and to show that what Catholics mean by infused habits, is attainable by the natural communion of man with man, or of the individual with the race, he enabled me to see that grace might be infused, in accordance with the law of all life, and without the slightest violence to nature or reason.

According to the law of all dependent life, man lives not by himself alone, but by communion with an object not himself; and his actual life partakes alike of the object and the subject, of which it is the joint product. In the fact of life, the object is not passive, but active, as active, to say the least, as the subject; for, if purely passive, it would offer nc counteraction to the subject, and be practically no object at all. The object acts on the subject no less than the subject on the object. They mutually act and react on each other, and in their mutual action and reaction the fact of life is generated. The object by its action flows into the subject, and becomes a real element of the life of the subject. If, then, we suppose the object supernaturally elevated, the life of the subject will be elevated also, and his progress secured. Now, as I held that the Divine, though distinguishable in reality from the human, could flow into us only through the human, I saw that, by a Providential elevation of individuals by the Creator to an extraordinary or supernatural communion with himself, they would live a divine life, and we by communion with them would also be elevated, and live a higher and more advanced life. Thus the elevation and progress of the race would be provided for in accordance with the law of life, by the aid of these individuals Providentially elevated, and called by Leroux, " Providential Men."

In this, though I had by no means reached the Catholic thought, I was enabled to conceive the natural and the supernatural as corresponding one to tho other; and that it is possible for God to afford us supernatural aid without violence to our natures, and without suspending, superseding, or impairing the laws of our natural life. This, to one who had been accustomed to hold that nature and grace, reason and revelation, can be asserted only as mutually repugnant one to the other, that the one cannot be asserted, as Calvinism, indeed all Evangelicalism, had taught me, without denying the other, was no slight advance. Moreover, it placed me in harmony with the universal belief of the race, for the human race has universally attributed all its elevation and progress to God through inspired Prophets, Apostles, Messiases,—in a word, Providential men, or men raised up and extraordinarily endowed by the Creator, to aid his creature, man, in his ceaseless march through the ages. In an essay on Conversatism and Reform, published January, 1842, but written in the previous November, I say :—

"Errors are peculiar to no one class of men. They who are called Reformers, and they who are called Conservatives, both err; not because they advocate or oppose progress, but in their adoption and application of means to obtain the end common to them all. They are all brethren, their faces are really all the same way; but they all, in no small degree, mistake the most effectual means of setting humanity forward. Our Transcendental theologians, save so far as they are animated by an intenser zeal than their opponents, are no more the party of the future, are no more reformers, than the others. They err by mistaking, in no small degree, both the end and the means. Their merit consists in their assertion of the inspiration of all men, and thereby declaring that all men stand in intimate relation with their Maker. This is a great and glorious truth, but by no means the whole truth. Their opponents, in rejecting this truth, are wrong, and are mischievous in their influence. But these opponents contend for another truth equally great, and equally, if not more, essential,—the special inspiration of individual messengers, as the Providential agents of the progress of the human race.

" The tendency of the Transcendental theologians is to overlook the agency of these special messengers, these Providential men, and to assert the sufficiency of the inspiration common to a'l men. Hence Bibles and Messiases are to them but natural occurrences, and entitled to no special reverence or authority. Through the aid of Bibles and Messiases they have grown so large, that they fancy Bibles and Messiases are no longer necessary—nay, that they were never necessary. We have no sympathy with this tendency. Undoubtedly, all men stand in intimate relation with their Maker; undoubtedly, all men are inspired, for all men love; undoubtedly, many of the great essential elements of religious faith have been so far assimilated to the life of humanity as to be now natural religion, and therefore no longer needing, with the more advanced nations of the earth, a positive supernatural revelation either to assert them or to confirm their authority; but, after all, it is mainly through the agency of specially inspired and extraordinarily endowed individuals, that the race itself is improved, and through Bibles, Prophets, Messiases, Revelators, that it has attained its present growth. God is nearer to us than Transcendental theology teaches. He is near us, not merely in the fixed and uniform laws of nature, but also in his Providence, taking free and voluntary care of us, and tempering all events to our strength and convictions. God is not a resistless fate, an iron destiny, inaccessible to human prayers, which no tears, no entreaties, no contrition, can move; but a merciful Father, who hears when his children cry, and is ready, able, and willing to supply all their wants. True, we see him not, know him not, save in his manifestations, save in the effects he produces, and so far as by his power and love he enters into his creatures. But this we know, that we have never sought help of him in vain, and have never gone to him with a broken and contrite spirit without finding relief. We see a special as well as a general Providence in the history of individuals and of the race. All is not the result of natural tendencies. Moses, no doubt, embodies in himself all the tendencies of his people, but how much more! These tendencies did not produce him and his legislation, for ages on ages were needed for his people to come up to his level, to reach the point where his legislation must cease to be an ideal for humanity. The absurdest of all theories is that which would make Moses the natural production of his age and people, and that people utterly incapable of comprehending him, so sunk in ignorance as, the moment his presence was withdrawn, to fall down and worship a golden calf.

" We have, indeed, no sympathy with Jewish exclusiveness, none with the doctrine which teaches that God disinherited all nations but the Jewish,

and, we may add, just as little with the modern
doctrine, that,

'Out from the heart of Nature roll'd
The burdens of the Bible Old;
The Litanies of Nations came,
Like the Volcano's tongue of flame,
Up from the burning core below,—
The Canticles of Love and Woe.'

"This is to mistake the effect for the cause.
These litanies came not from the 'burning core
below,' but they came from God, and kindled that
'burning core.' They originated not in the human
heart, sprang not from the efforts of the soul to utter
or to satisfy its own inherent wants; but they came
from abroad, to create in the soul a deep want for
God, and to make the heart and the flesh cry out
for the living God. Tell us not that nature has
produced the Bible. Man has not degenerated, he
lives in as close communion with nature as ever—
has the same senses, the same soul, the same 'burning
core,' and yet out from his heart no Bible rolls its
'burdens.'

"Christianity is no natural production. It had,
no doubt, its reason in the age in which it was born;
it was, no doubt, that to which all preceding progress pointed, which all the previous tendencies of
the race demanded as their fulfilment; but if it
was the mere natural and inevitable result of previous development of the human race, why appeared
it not first where that development was most manifest? Why was not its first appearance in Athens,

Rome, or Alexandria, the Temples, the Mysteries, or the Schools, instead of a by-corner of the world, in an obscure hamlet, in the person of an obscure peasant, followed by humble fishermen and despised publicans? Had the tendencies of the age reached farthest, and become most manifest, the development of the race most advanced with the fishermen and boatmen of the Lake of Genesareth? Undoubtedly, Christianity was the last word of Oriental and Grecian philosophies, a word for the utterance of which all previous Providences had been preparing the way, but a word which none but God could utter; and not till he had uttered it in thunder-tones from his dwelling in the heavens, and his well-beloved Son had echoed it from the cross and the tomb, could the nations hear it, and leap at the sound.

"Nor let it be supposed that, in clinging to the Bible and to Jesus, men are mere conservatives, that they have no aspirations. Some of the truths of the Bible have been assimilated; a portion, if we may so speak, of the Divine life of Jesus, has become the life of Christendom. Some portion of the Christian Ideal has been realized. But not all. There are depths in that old Hebrew book which no human plummet has sounded; heights in the life of Jesus which no human imagination has scaled. In contending for the Christianity of the Bible and of Jesus, we are not looking back, but forward; for we are contending for truths far, far in advance of our age. Here is the truth of those who war ugainst what is called Transcendental theology. They ser, as well they may, in the rich store-houses of the Gospel, of the Bible, of Christ, enough for the warmest heart, the profoundest intellect, the loftiest aspiration. Their error, if error they have, is in misinterpreting Christianity, in not being true to the law they acknowledge, in not laboring with sufficient faith and energy to realize the Ideal of Christ. They are hearers, and not doers of the word. They are as the man who seeth his face in a glass, and then goeth away and forgetteth what manner of man he was. Let them really bring out the Christian Ideal, and labor with energy and zeal to form Christ, the hope of glory, in the individual and in the race, and they will be true and efficient reformers. Their works will live after them.

"Nor, again, let it be supposed that they who cling to the authority of revelation, are necessarily inimical to the rights of the mind, or to progress in the knowledge of truth. The Christian Ideal, so far as realized, needs no foreign authority. The human mind is equal to it. But what is the authority for that Ideal so far as it is as yet unrealized? The individual reason? Alas! we have seen enough of mere individual reason. It is impotent when it has not for its guide and support the reason of God, speaking not only to the heart, but through revelations and the traditions of the race. The great doctrine we are laboring to establish, the reforms we would effect, we confess our inability to demonstrate by mere individual reason. We ask for them, both on

our own account and on account of others, a higher
authority than mere individual reason.   That reason
may be sufficient for here and there one; but how
can it suffice for the ignorant, the bigoted, the
superstitious, the incredulous, the wicked,—the men
in whom conscience slumbers, love sleeps, and only
the world with its impurities is awake?   Alas! man's
word is impotent to arouse them, man's authority too
weak to command even their attention.   They may
speculate with us, or debate with us, but not act with
us, not live with us for God or for man.   You must
go to them with a higher authority than your own,
speak to them in a Name above all names, and which
they dare not resist, or your preaching and efforts
will be fruitless.   Deprive the preacher of the
authority of God, let him go forth in his own name,
not as the messenger of God, and men will laugh at
his truths, and mock at his most earnest expostula-
tions.   No.   They are sorry reformers who would
reduce God to nature, and the authority of his word
to that of the individual reason, varying with every
individual, and with every age."

I was far enough from being free from grievous
errors, and as yet had not once thought of seeking the
old Church; but it is clear that I had made some
progress, and had embraced, without ceasing to exercise my reason freely, or failing in my pledge to
myself, of being faithful to my own rational nature,
the great principles and facts which placed me on
the route to the Catholic Church.   I found I could
reasonably accept the ideas of Providence, special as

well as general, supernatural inspiration, supernatural revelation, and Christianity as an authoritative religion, and must do so, or be false alike to history and my hopes of progress. I felt, as I had felt from my boyhood, that I had need of an authoritative religion; and that a religion which does not and cannot speak with Divine authority, is simply no religion at all.

I did not, indeed, conclude, from the possibility of the Providential men I asserted, that they have actually been raised up and sent; I did not, from the fact that God can give us the needed supernatural aid through them, without violence to nature and reason, and in accordance with the great law of all life, conclude that therefore he actually does so give it. I never yet was so poor a logician as to do that. I was always ready and anxious to believe, providing I could see my way clear to do so without violence to reason, or the abnegation of my own manhood. I never wanted reasons for believing: what I wanted was, to have the real or imaginary obstacles to believing removed. More than this, I never needed, never sought; and, therefore, precisely as were removed my reasons against believing, I believed.

Most people, born and reared in Christian countries, who reject Christianity, are very much in the condition I was. They reject Christianity, not because they see no good reasons for believing, but because they see, or think they see, many and stronger reasons against believing. They refuse to believe, because they do not understand how supernatural assistance can be rendered without violence to nature;

or an authoritative revelation, or a revelation that is to be regarded as authority for reason, can be accepted and submitted to without an abandonment of reason. Such had been the case with me, and, consequently, as this obstacle to believing was removed, I believed without seeking any *further reason for believing.

This was not wholly irrational or unphilosophical. To believe is normal, to disbelieve is abnormal. When the mind is in its normal state, nothing more is ever needed for belief than the removal of the obstacles interposed to believing; for, if we consider it, the mind was created for truth. Truth is its object, and it seeks and accepts it instinctively, as the new-born child seeks the mother's breast, from which it draws its nourishment. Place the mind and truth face to face, with nothing interposed between them, and the truth evidences itself to the mind, and the mind accepts it, without seeking or needing any further reason. The assent termed knowledge follows immediately from the joint forces of the intelligible object and the intelligent subject. So in belief. Practically, it is never a reason for believing, but the removal of reasons against believing, that is demanded. Hence, we always believe what a man tells us, when we have no reason for not believing him: and the business of life could not go on were it otherwise. For belief. reason never requires anything but the mutual presence, with nothing interposed between them, of the credible object and the creditive subject.

I held then, as I hold now, that the office of proof, or even demonstration, is negative rather than affirmative. Neither ever goes farther than to remove the *prohibentia*, or obstacles to assent. Demonstration, the most rigid and the most conclusive, only shows the object without envelope or disguise, and motives assent only by removing every reason for not assenting. The assent itself is always immediate and intuitive. Truth needs no voucher, · and, when immediately presented to the mind, evidences or affirms itself. The will may be perverse, and withdraw the intellect from the contemplation of truth; prejudice or passion may darken the understanding, so that it does not for the moment see or recognize the object; but, whenever the truth is immediately present, and reason looks it full in the face, it knows that it is truth without further evidence, without anything extrinsic to prove that it is truth. To deny this would be to deny to the soul the faculty of intelligence, the faculty of knowing at all. To know a thing is to know that it is true, for nothing but truth is or can be an object of knowledge. To say that you know a thing, and yet do not know whether it be true or not, is only saying that you do not know the thing at all. No man does or can know falsehood, for falsehood is nothing, is a nullity, a mere negation, and therefore no intelligible object. False. hood is intelligible only in the truth it denies, and is known only in knowing that truth. In so far as any proposition is false, it is unintelligible, and never known. In all errors we know only the element of truth which they contain; and the part of error is simply the part of our ignorance, the part in which nothing is known. To know something, and to know it to be true, is one and the same thing; and this is what is meant when we say truth is the object of the intellect. Hence, no logical process is ever needed to prove to the mind that the object it immediately apprehends is truth, or is true. That it is true or truth is included in the fact that the mind apprehends it as its object, or knows it. To suppose the contrary, to suppose that a logical process is needed to demonstrate that the object in immediate relation to the mind is, true, would be absurd; for it would demand an infinite series of logical processes to every single act of knowledge or mental assent. There is no reasoning except from premises or principles, and no valid reasoning from either false or unknown principles. How are these premises or principles to be obtained? Not by reasoning, not by a logical process, for, without them, no reasoning, no logical process is possible, and no such thing as proof or demonstration conceivable. They must, then, precede reasoning, be intuitive, that is, evident of themselves. Then, nothing is necessary, in the last analysis, to knowledge but the immediate pres ence to each other of the intelligible object and the intelligent subject. So is it in the case of knowledge or science in the natural order, where the object is immediately intelligible to reason.

The principle must hold true, as far as applicable, in the supernatural order, and in regard to faith as

well as in regard to science. Faith or belief is
assent to propositions not immediately known, on the
authority affirming them; that is, it is assent on
testimony. The understanding does not assent to
them because it sees immediately their truth, as in
case of science or knowledge, but because it sees the
sufficiency of the authority or testimony affirming
them. The immediate object of belief is the veracity
of the witness, or the fact that the authority in the
case can neither deceive nor be deceived; and here
the assent is immediate as soon as the obstacles are
removed, because to believe is normal. If the supernatural and the natural correspond one to the other,
as it is here assumed that they do, the same holds
true of belief in the supernatural order. We cannot
believe the supernatural things revealed without
what are called motives of credibility; but these
motives do not, so to speak, motive the assent of the
mind to the veracity or sufficiency of the authority
affirming them. They only show that the authority
is credible; that is, remove all the reason we may
have, or imagine we have, for regarding it as incredible or untrustworthy. The assent to its veracity
or sufficiency when these reasons are removed, is
immediate, by the joint forces of the credible object
and creditive subject as in the natural order. My
conduct, then, in believing in the supernatural order
the moment my reasons against believing in it
were removed, and I saw its accordance with nature
and reason, was not rash or precipitate, but truly
reasonable and philosophical, in accordance with the

principle of all belief, and, indeed, of all science.
I asked, and I needed, nothing more.

My doing so was justified, also, by the view
which I then took, and still take, of the inspiration
of the human race. I held that the race lives
by immediate communion with God, therefore inspired by him, and hence in its normal state aspires
to him. Man lives by immediate communion with
God as his object, and theref re the objective element of his life is divine, and through this objective
element his life is the life of God. Man thus in his
natural life even partakes of God, and this partaking of God I called inspiration. I did not mean
by this that the race is supernaturally inspired;
I only meant what the Scriptures say, that "there is
a spirit in men, and the inspiration of the Almighty
giveth understanding;" or, in other words, that man
is intelligent, is a rational existence, only by virtue
of the immediate presence of God, simultaneously
the creator, the object, and the light of his reason.
This is the doctrine I now hold, and which I am
supposed to have borrowed from Gioberti, but which
I held before Gioberti had published it, and long
before I had seen his writings or heard his name.
Cousin and Leroux had held something like it, but
made it, in their explanation of it, a pantheistic
doctrine. They did not distinguish with sufficient
care between the human reason and the reason of
God; and while they made the immediate presence
of God in the soul the condition of our intelligence,
they did not regard that presence as creating our

reason, or faculty of intelligence, and becoming immediately, in the act of creating it, its object and its light; but left it to be inferred that it is God himself who knows and loves in us: which is virtually pantheism. I distinguished where they did not, and held that it is not God who knows and loves in us, but God in us who creates in us our power to know and to love. The Divine reason is not our reason, but, so to speak, the reason of our reason. It creates our reason, and is its immediate light and object. This doctrine is well known to the theologians under the names of the presence of God in all his works, and the Divine concurrence in all the acts of his creatures. All theologians teach that it is in God we live, and move, and are, and that his reason is the light of our reason. Hence St. John, speaking of the Word or Logos, one with God, says, he was "the true light which enlighteneth every man coming into this world."

Saying with Eliu in the book of Job, " There is a spirit in men, and the inspiration of the Almighty giveth understanding," " *Spiritus in hominibus et inspiratio Omnipotentis dat intelligentiam*," I concluded the human race is inspired. God gives understanding, not only in the sense that he creates the faculty, but also in the sense that he is its object. In being the object of the intellect, he is also that of the will, and affirms himself both as the True and the Good, as alike the object of knowledge and of love. Hence it is we understand and love, know and aspire. This affirming himself as the True and the Good in natural reason is natural inspiration, and the cause of the universal aspiration of the race to God as the Infinitely True and the Supremely Good. In this inspiration and this aspiration of the race, I detect the dignity and authority of the race. In it I find the worth and legitimacy of reason, and vindicate my right to take the reason of the race as a legitimate ground of belief. The reason of the race may be safely followed, because it is the inspiration of the Almighty, who can neither deceive nor be deceived. The race has always recognized, in some form, supernatural communion with God, and held that it is only by virtue of this supernatural communion, that is, a communion in a higher sense than that by which we are rendered capable of knowing and loving in the natural order, that the race is elevated and set forward in its career of progress. Then, to believe in the reality of this communion, in the fact of this supernatural aid or assistance, is not an irrational belief, or a belief on an inadequate authority. The race has always believed that men are elevated and set forward by supernatural assistance, obtained through the agency of specially inspired individuals, or what I call Providential men. Wherever you find man, you find him with some sort of religion; and all religions, the lowest and most corrupt, as well as the highest and purest, recognize a supernatural element in human life, and claim, each for itself, the assent of mankind, on the ground of being the channel or medium through which it is attained, or flows into the natural, and supernaturalizes human action. This is the essential, the vital principle of all the religions which are or ever have been. Take this away, and you leave nothing to which the common-sense of mankind does or can give the name of religion. As this supernatural element may flow in without violence or injury to the natural, what reason have you to assert that this common belief of mankind is false or unreasonable? For you, who concede an authoritative religion, propounded and interpreted by an authoritative church, what higher authority is or can there be for believing anything, than the reason of the race? It is your highest reason after the immediate and express word of God; and not to believe it without a higher reason for discrediting it, is not to follow reason, but to reject reason.

My conduct, then, was not unreasonable, but reasonable; and the joy I felt at finding myself believing in the supernatural providence of God, was no silly joy, but such as I might well indulge, for it proceeded from the recognition by the soul, thought as yet but partially and dimly, of the object to which I had always aspired. I had made the greatest step I had yet made, in this recognition of the fact that the human race is advanced by the aid of Providential men. In it I seemed to assert my own freedom, and, what is more, the freedom of God. No matter how I had reasoned or talked, I had regarded God as a *Fatum*, or an Invincible Necessity, creating from the necessity of his own being, and hedged in and bound by the invariable

and inflexible laws of nature. This is more generally the case with our modern philosophers, and
so-called free thinkers, than is commonly supposed.
The real obstacle in many minds to the acceptance
of Christian faith, is the want of belief in the freedom
of God.   Read the works of all your non-Catholic
philosophers, and you will find that they nowhere
admit Providence, or the free intervention of God
in the affairs of the universe he has himself created.
What they call the providential is always the fixed,
the invariable, the inexorable, the fatal.   They
reject miracles, the supernatural, or voluntary inter-
positions on the part of the Creator, because they
are assumed to be marks of change, of variability,
and forbidden by the laws of nature.   I had, in
asserting Providential men, risen above this difficulty, and become able to understand that, while
God binds nature, nature cannot bind him; that
being in himself sufficient for himself, no necessity
compels him to operate externally, or to create a
world; and therefore creation itself must be, on his
part, a free, voluntary act, and much more so his
intervent on in the government of what he has
created.   This threw a heavy burden from my
shoulders, and in freeing God from his assumed
bondage to nature, unshackled my own limbs, and
made me feel that in God's freedom I had a sure
pledge of my own.   God could, if he chose, be
gracious to me ; he could hear my prayers, respond
to my entreaties, interpose to protect me, to assist
me, to teach me, and to bless me.   He was free to

love me as his child, and to do me all the good his infinite love should prompt. I was no longer chained, like Prometheus, to the Caucasian rock, with my vulture passions devouring my heart; I was no longer fatherless, an orphan left to the tender mercies of inexorable general laws, and my heart bounded with joy, and I leaped to embrace the neck of my Father, and to rest my head on his bosom. I shall never forget the ecstasy of that moment, when I first realized to myself that God is free.

CHAPTER XVI.

I HAD now settled it in my own mind, that the progress of man and society is effected only by supernatural assistance, and that this assistance is rendered by Almighty God, in perfect accordance with nature and reason, through Providential men. M. Cousin had emitted the theory, that the great man is great because he, better than any of his contemporaries, collects and represents, or impersonates, the ideas and sentiments of his own age; but I adopted the opposite doctrine, that the truly great man is great because he makes his age, determines the ideas and sentiments of the race, and by his own elevation lifts them to a higher plane. Truly great men are superior to their age, and give it what it has not, and cannot draw from its own funds.

I placed, as yet, our Lord in the category of great men, Providential men, along with Abraham, Moses, Zoroaster, Confucius, Socrates, Plato, etc., but I considered him greater than any of them, and, indeed, as completing the line of Providential men, and supplying all that was wanting in those who went before him. I ventured even to call him God-man in a special sense, and thought, for a moment, that, by my doctrine of Communion, by virtue of which the object becomes identical with the subject in the fact of life, I could explain the chief mystery of the Incarnation, and, indeed, all the principal Christian dogmas, and find a common ground on which Trinitarians and Unitarians, Orthodox and Heterodox, Conservatives and Reformers, the believers in revelation and the advocates of natural reason, could all meet in peace and love, and unite as one man to effect the amelioration and progress of society. It was a brave dream, but only a dream, from which I soon awoke.

I made at the time a distinction between being and life, and held, after Leroux, that being actualizes itself in life or living. I fell here into the fundamental error of all, or nearly all, modern, and no little of ancient, philosophy. The starting-point of Leroux's doctrine, and which I accepted from him, that thought is a phenomenon that includes simultaneously subject, object, and their relation, consistently carried out, implies realism as opposed to idealism. It implies that we know the object, because we think it, and we think it simply because it is, and is immediately present to our intellect. I saw and understood this well enough; but, in applying it to being, to ontology, I forgot it, as Leroux himself did. The primitive objective element of thought is indeed being, I said, real being too, but not actual being. Real being and actual being identified give us then: 1, Pure being, *das reine Seyn* of Hegel, which is simply possible being; 2, Idea, or possible being, advanced to the state of type, or mental conception; and 3, Life, *das Wesen*, or being actualized, being advanced from the state of possibility to living being, or complete actuality. These three moments, states, or terms, I had the simplicity to regard as the real significance of the Christian Trinity. Truth is always simpler than error, and requires far less effort to explain or understand it. This possible, or, as Leroux said, virtual being, which precedes both Idea and Life, Leroux identified with the Void of the Buddhists, and represented as standing opposed to the *Plenum* or *Pleroma* of the Gnostics. It was, then, in reality only possible, not actual; but it appears not to have occurred to him any more than it did to me, that the possible without the actual is a mere abstraction, and, like all abstractions, a nullity. Suppose all actual being wanting, and you can conceive of nothing as possible. Suppose no living, actual God, and the possibility of God ceases to be supposable. Hence, Aristotle and all theologians call God *actus purissimus*, most pure act, and deny that in him, in reference to his being or perfections, there is any *possibility*, or anything *in potentia*, not yet actual, but susceptible of becoming actual. He is eternal, and eternally most full and perfect being. He is so, or he is not at all.

The possible may be considered either in relation to God, or in relation to the creature. In relation to God, it is simply his power to create creatures not actually created; and in relation to creature, it is the creature's power as second cause to do what it has not yet done. Creatures which God may create, but does not, may be said to exist virtually in him, as ideas in his own mind, but, as so existing, they are not distinguishable from his Divine being, or essence itself. So the things we may do, but have not yet done, are the virtuality of our nature, and indistinguishable from it. Abstracted from God, the creatures he may create or the ideas he may clothe with existence, are simple nullities, and inconceivable; and so, when abstracted from our power, are the things we may as second causes do, but as yet have not done. It is the actuality of God that renders creation possible, and it is only in the intuition of that actuality, that possible creatures or perfections are conceivable. It is also in the fact of our actuality that we are, or can be conceived, capable of acting, doing, or producing.

As plain and as conclusive as all this is, very few philosophers ever apprehend it; or, if they apprehend it, they apprehend it only as a barren fact, and see no use to be made of it. The great Leibnitz, in commenting on St. Anselm's argument for the existence of God from the idea present to our minds of the most perfect being, says, it would be conclusive if it were previously established that the rea' existence of most perfect being, or God, is possible ' Storchenau, a disciple of Wolf, as Wolf was a disciple of Leibnitz, and whose work has been, and I believe still is, used as a text-book of philosophy even in some Catholic Colleges, seems to hold that possible being is anterior to real being, and to precede the actual, living God, by a superior possible God, just as if the actual, living God is not the reason, ground, and condition of all possibility. If God were not, nothing would be possible, not even his own existence. There is nothing real or possible anterior to God or independent of him. It is he himself in the infinite fulness of his own being that makes creation possible, as it is his own creative act that renders it actual; and that abstract being which we call the nature of things, is concrete in him, and is his own eternal, universal, immutable, and indestructible essence.

The source of the error of placing the possible before the actual, and presenting it as infinite virtuality actualizing itself in the universe, and rising, as Hegel, and after him Cousin, says, to self-consciousness in the consciousness of man, or in our consciousness of our own existence, is in the assumption that it is the subject, not the object, that determines the form of the thought. Cousin and Leroux both say, and say truly, that thought is a phenomenon embracing simultaneously and indissolubly three elements: subject, object, and their relation. They say truly, too, that the relation is the form of the thought. But they both maintain that the subject determines the form, and thus with Kant make the categories forms of the human understanding, and assume that we think things so and so, not because they are so, but because such is the nature or character of our intellect. They hold object is actualized in our thought, and is only a virtuality when we do not think it. As we never see ourselves in ourselves, and recognize our own existence only as mirrored in the act of thinking, we exist for ourselves only so far as we enter into and manifest ourselves in the act. As, prior to the act of thinking, neither subject nor object actually exists for us, either, independent of our thought, is only a virtuality, not an actuality. Thought therefore is their actualization, and this actualization of subject and object in thought, *pensée*, is what Leroux meant by life, as distinguished from being. Now, as the form of this life is determined by the subject, we are forced, in applying it to God, to deny that he is actual or living God prior to his being thought, and to regard him as actual or living God only in so far as concreted in our life. Hence the modern Pantheism, which represents God as realizing or actualizing himself in idea, idea as realizing itself in the race, the race as realizing itself in individuals, and individuals as realizing themselves in the act of thinking, that is, feeling, knowing, and loving: a superb system of transcendental nullism. The mother error is in supposing that the subject determines the form of the thought, and therefore is the condition of the actualization of the object, as well as of itself. This supposes that both when unthought are virtualities, not actualities. But there is no thought save by the concurrence of both subject and object. In the generation of thought, both subject and object must act. What is not actual cannot act, and therefore both subject and object must be actualities

prior to thought, and, therefore, when unthought.
The subject in thought is not alone active, or active
at all save in concurrence with the activity of the object. The object depends on the subject to be
thought if you will, but not to be, or to be actual,
for it can be thought only on condition that it exists
prior to the thought, and its action precedes the
action of the subject.

The common error of philosophers is in supposing
that it is the subject that affirms the object, while it
is the object that affirms or evidences itself to the
subject. This is the condemnation of our psychologists, or those who seek the principle of philosophy,
or *primum philosophicum*, in the fact of consciousness,
or an affection of the soul, or subject; and the reason
why all sound philosophy is and must be ontological,
taking its principle in the fact that the object is, and
affirms itself in the fact of consciousness along with
the subject, and as the condition of its activity. In
all human life, the action of the object precedes and
renders possible the action of the subject. A thing
does not exist because we think it, but we think it
because it is intelligibly—actively—present to our
intelligence, or intellectual faculty. It is, then, not
the intelligence that determines the intelligibility of
the object, but the intelligibility of the object tha
determines the intelligence; and therefore the object,
not the subject, that determines the form of the
thought. Things evidence themselves to us, and we
see them because they are, and as they are *a parte
rei*; for, if it were not so, we could see what is not, or

what does not exist, which would be absurd. What is not, or exists not, is not intelligible.

All this was implied in the doctrine that thought is invariably and indissolubly a synthesis of object, subject, and their relation, though I did not at the time clearly perceive it. Had I done so, I should have perceived that the distinction made between being and life, and the doctrine that both subject and object are actualized in thought, are inadmissible. The object flows in its action into the life of the subject, but not the subject into the object. Both are actual prior to the generation of the thought. But, overlooking this fact, I proceeded on the erroneous assumption, that being, whether of the object or the subject, when unthought, is latent, virtual, not actual, and is actualized in thought, and therefore that, in the thought, both subject and object are identical. This actualization of subject and object in the act of thinking, is what I called life as distinguished from being. This life I called the life of the subject, because its form is determined by the subject, and hence I maintained that both subject and object live and are one in our life.

Applying this doctrine to our Lord, and seeking to explain by it the mystery of the Incarnation, or to get at the fact covered or intended by that mystery, I took the Incarnation as a fact of life, not of nature. The Christian world calls our Lord God-man. This is true, if you speak of him in his actuality, in his life, not in his nature. Suppose the man Christ Jesus,—for man he was according to the most

orthodox teaching,—was taken up, miraculously, if
you will, into a supernatural communion with God, so
that God, as in the case of every Providential man,
became his object in a supernatural sense; then,
since life partakes alike of subject and object, and is
the union or identification of the two, his life must
be strictly a Divine-human life, and he in the life he
lives truly God-man, as the Christian world has
always believed. Is not here the Incarnation, the
actualization of the Divine in the human? And as
it is evidently a miraculous communion of the human
with the Divine, is not this the Miraculous Conception and Birth of our Lord?

But you have only the Divine-human life, not the
hypostatic union of the two natures in one person.
Yet I have two natures united, identified in one life;
and as these natures live only by virtue of their intercommunion, I have the union of both the living
God and living man in one life. It is the life that
redeems and saves. Whatever emphasis may be
laid on the death of Christ, it is evident from the
Scriptures that his death is referred to only as the
completion and crown of his life. He came into the
world that we might have life, to beget in us life, a
new, a higher, a diviner life. That he redeems the
world by infusing life into our life through communion with himself, is the belief of Christendom. As
the Father hath life in himself, and as the Son lives
by the Father, so his disciples live by him. It is the
life that saves; and what else is the real significance
of salvation through an Incarnate Saviour, or the

union in our Lord of this twofold redeeming and saving life?

As the Father hath life in himself, so hath he given to the Son to have life in himself. The Son, by his supernatural or miraculous communion with the Father, lives a Divine-human life; so the Apostles and Disciples, by communion with the Son, lived the same life, and through him became one in life with the Father and with one another, and were elevated above their natural life, and set forward in the career of progress. Here, I said, is the Christian doctrine of Holy Communion, or Eucharistia. The whole mystery of the Christian religion has been supposed to turn around the mystery of Holy Communion; and in this communion the Scriptures teach, and the Church has always held, that the communicant really receives the flesh and blood of our Lord. "Except ye eat my flesh, and drink my blood, ye have no life in you." The flesh profiteth nothing, and the Church never teaches that we must eat the flesh or drink the blood of Christ in a gross, carnal sense, as we eat meat bought in the shambles. What is meant is, that we really receive, and have incorporated into our life, the Divine-human life of our Lord. This is done by communion with him, and through him with God the Father. Thus he becomes to us, through communion, the mediator or medium between God and men, as St. Paul calls him. Thus, from the central point of communion I can explain the Incarnation, the Mediatorial life of Christ, and the principal Christian dogmas, as I attempted to show in a Letter on the *Mediatorial Life of Christ*, addressed to Dr. Channing, which I wrote and published in the summer of 1843.

But we who live at this day do not communicate directly with Christ our Lord. We do it, and can do it, only through the medium of others. The Apostles and Disciples lived in personal intercourse with him, and therefore communed with him directly and immediately as their object. By this direct and immediate communion, his Divine-human life became infused into their life. Others, by communion with them, partake of the same life. The succeeding generation participates in it by communing with its predecessor. Thus by communion the life may be infused through all men living contemporaneously, and transmitted to the latest posterity. The Apostles become thus the medium of its reception, diffusion, and transmission. Here is the meaning of Apostolic Succession.

This Divine-human life is one and identical in all who receive it, for it is a real life, really lived, not merely desired by the heart, or assented to as a doctrine by the reason. It enters really into the life of individuals as the life of their life. All life is organic; and, consequently, all who live this life are moulded or formed into one body, living one and the same life, the life of Christ, and therefore rightly termed his body, the CHURCH, as the Scriptures expressly teach. Hence I have the Church, not as an association, an organization, or mere aggregation of individuals, but as an organism, one and Catholic,--one because its life is one, and Catholic because it includes all who live the life, of whatever age or nation, and because all men in every age and nation may by communion live it. The life of Christ is not only life, but the principle of life, and operating in the body, assimilates individuals, as the human body assimilates the particles of the food eaten. It is then no sham, no illusion, but the real body of Christ, a real living organism, and in some sense a continuation of the Incarnation.

But as the Church includes all who are assimilated by its central life, and as it is only the real reception of that life that elevates and advances one, it is clear that out of the Church no one can be saved. There is no other name given under heaven [the name of Jesus] among men whereby we can be saved; and as he saves us only by communicating his Divine-human life, according to the universal law of life, the doctrine of exclusive salvation is and must be strictly true.

But, as the life of the Church is a higher than natural life, higher than the life of the race, since it is a Divine-human life in a supernatural sense, it is and must be authoritative, not only for my individual reason, but also for the human race itself. It is the highest manifestation of both the Divine and the human, and therefore is, in both Divine and human things, the highest authority under God, nay, is the authority of God himself. Hence the AUTHORITY of the Church, and the reasonableness and obligation of individuals and of all men to submit to her—to believe what she teaches, and to do what she commands. I found here the authority I had been so long seeking for; a real, legitimate, not a sham or a usurped authority, to which reason could submit without abnegating itself, or ceasing to be reason.

Moreover, the Divine-human life which creates or constitutes the Church, and is its authority, the authority of the indwelling Holy Ghost,—for I identified the interior life of the Church with the Paraclete,—is transmitted in the Church from the Apostles, and has been operative at every moment of time from the Incarnation to the present. The life of the Church now is identically the life of the Church in the first age, by virtue of an uninterrupted communion with the Apostles. Each successive generation communes with its predecessor, and derives its life from it. This is the principle of the tradition, or transmission of life, called under one aspect the Apostolic Succession, and under another, Apostolic Tradition. As Apostolic or Ecclesiastical tradition is the tradition of the Divine-human life, it is always authoritative with all the authority of that life itself. Hence the authority of Tradition, as opposed to the Protestant principle of private judgment. The error of Protestantism was, in that it broke with Tradition, broke with the past, and cut itself off from the body of Christ, and therefore from the channel through which the Christian life is communicated. Protestantism was a schism, a separation from the source and current of the Divine-human life which redeems and saves the world, and

Protestants are therefore thrown back upon nature, and able to live only the natural life of the race,—saving the portion of Christian life they brought away with them at the time of the separation, and which, as not renewed from its source, must in time be exhausted.

In the same way I explained all the Christian dogmas I was acquainted with, and found that, do what I would, I must admit that the great current of Christian life had flowed and still flowed down through the Catholic Church. It is evident to every Catholic reader that this theory, elaborated with skill, indeed, and not without some speciousness, is far enough from being an adequate expression of Catholicity. But, as far as it went, it was not false or unworthy of consideration. It indeed demonstrated or proved no peculiar or distinctive Catholic doctrine, and was far enough from being a complete theory, or adequate to its own demands; but it was, in the main, true philosophy, and enabled me to grasp certain laws of life which Christianity accepts, and in accordance with which it acts. It removed, and removed philosophically, all my objections to the more obscure or the more offensive dogmas of the Catholic Church, and showed me how she could operate, in accordance with nature, the elevation of nature, and blend the Divine redeeming and saving life in with the human, and make them in the Christian one life. It did not give me the Catholic dogmas, nor even the Catholic Church in her deeper significance, but it did prepare me, by the grace of God, to receive them. My philosophy had answered all my objections to the Catholic system, if I may so speak, and had supplied me with all the principles which that system presupposes, and which prove that it harmonizes with the dictates of reason and the demands of nature. There is in the Christian Church and in Christian communion infinitely more than in my doctrine of life and communion; but there is nothing opposed to that doctrine, or which makes it necessary for a Catholic to exclude it. The law of life I asserted is a real, a genuine, and a universal law; the communion I asserted is a real and genuine communion, and is included even in the doctrine of Christian communion; but in Christian communion there is an immediate communion with Christ, an increase of life from the Incarnate God, the very source and fountain of all Christian life, not merely a communion with him as he enters into the life of others. Yet there is a communion with him in the way I supposed, a transmission of his life; and the Church, in the sense I have explained, is a reality, and Church Authority, Tradition, Apostolic Succession, etc., as I alleged, are real and true. These are all included in Catholic theology, though they do not, as I supposed, constitute it.

In making this application of the doctrine of Life, as I did, my mind was intent mainly on one point, that of the real infusion of a Divine element into human life, by which that life should be supernaturally elevated, and rendered progressive. I saw that the law of life explained the possibility and practicability of this; but I did not perceive, in the application of it, how far I departed from the doc trine, that both subject and object when unthought are merely latent or virtual, not actual; because in reality, though I accepted that doctrine from Leroux, as found in connection with the truth he helped me to grasp, it never had any hold on my mind, and never received any attention from me. Back of it in my mind was the true doctrine, that the object, though it may create or actualize the subject, is itself actual antecedently to human thought, as is evident from the fact that I held to Providence, and asserted the free intervention of God in human affairs, that the Father has life in himself, and therefore lives independently of the subject, and that he performs the miracle of raising the man Christ Jesus into a supernatural communion with himself. It is evident that, however I might have spoken when treating the ontological question, I was not a Pantheist, that I held that God is free and independent, and confined the law of life I set forth to created existence. Leroux erred by making the law universal, and by regarding all being not developing itself in human thought, as not actual. These errors I never embraced except in mere words; they never really entered into my thought, and I held from the first, that the law was applicable only to created or dependent existence, and that the subject and object are actual powers and therefore act, not that they are rendered actual by acting. Undoubtedly, the intellect can be actual only in acting; but it is inherently active by virtue of the immediate and permanent intuition and creative presence of the Intelligible, which is God; but it is actual power to know, before knowing this or that particular object as after, and therefore is not actualized in any degree by knowing.

Making these reserves, the doctrine of life or communion is true, and, taken in connection with the history or traditions of the race, does all that I alleged. I was not thus far deceived. It gave me the Church in the sense I asserted. My only error was in supposing that the Church and her doctrines were only what I explained them to be. The Christian mysteries lay infinitely deeper than I supposed. But the real advantage to me of the doctrine was, not in its erroneous explanation of the ontological origin of the Divine-human life, but in its enabling me to perceive a law of life, in accordance with which it could be infused into us, and supernaturalize our life, by giving to our actions a supernatural principle, as well as a supernatural end. This service it rendered me, and this service it may render to all who comprehend it; and hence it is, in my judgment, a true and useful preparation for the reception of the Gospel.

CHAPTER XVII.

A STEP FORWARD.

IT may well be believed that I did not arrive at
these conclusions immediately and at a single bound.
The transition from one order of thought to another
is seldom effected at once. Man is a bundle of
habits and prejudices, as well as a being endowed
with reason. His progress from one system to another is usually gradual, and remains for a long
time incomplete. A ray of light has flashed on his
mind, but he does not at once take note of all the
objects it illumines. I saw, at first, very little in
Leroux to my purpose, and it was only some time
after I had read him that I saw the bearing of his
doctrine of life or communion, as I modified it, on
theological questions. My mind was forced to take
the direction which it did, and to make the applica
tion of it I have briefly sketched, by a couple of
Lectures by Theodore Parker, to which I listened
in the autumn of 1841. The Lectures were the first
part of the volume, which Mr. Parker subsequently
published, entitled, *A Discourse of Matters pertaining . to Religion*, and contained nothing except a
learned and eloquent statement of the doctrine
which I had long defended, and which I have called

the Religion of Humanity. But, strange as it may seem, the moment I heard that doctrine from his lips, I felt an invincible repugnance to it, and saw, or thought I saw, at a glance, that it was unphilo sophical and anti-religious.

Mr. Parker at that time was one of my highly prized personal friends, a young man, full of life and promise. There was no young man of my acquaintance for whom I had a higher regard, or from whom I hoped so much. He had very respectable intellectual ability, was learned, witty, and eloquent. His ideas were perhaps a little crude, and his taste needed a little chastening, but his fancy was lively, his imagination brilliant, and his rhetorical powers were of the first order. He had devoured an immense number of all sorts of books, and could discourse not badly on almost any subject. He was more brilliant than solid, less erudite than he appeared or was thought to be, and, in translating a work from the German of De Wette, made some sad blunders; but he was still young, and his attainments were unquestionably above the average standard of American scholarship. His powers of sarcasm and declamation were, however, superior to his powers as a reasoner, and his attachment to his own opinions was stronger than his love of truth. His greatest defect was lack of inherent loyalty. He would, perhaps, walk boldly to the dungeon, the scaffold, or the stake, in defence of the cause he had espoused, or an opinion he had once emitted, but he closed resolutely his mind, his heart, and his eyes to the reception of any light which might require him to revise and modify views to which he had once committed himself. He might be a fanatic, and die in defence of his opinions, but never a martyr to the truth, even in case it and his opinions should happen to coincide. He had the pride of the Stoic, but not the humility of the Christian. His boldness, firmness, courage, and independence were striking, and would have deserved very high reverence, if they had been exhibited in the cause of truth, not simply in the cause of Mr. Theodore Parker. Nevertheless, he has not belied his early promise, and is undeniably one of the most distinguished Protestant ministers in the United States.

As soon as I listened to his Lectures, I perceived that, though we apparently held the same doctrines, there was and had been a radical difference between us. We had both, it is true, placed the origin and ground of religion in a religious sentiment natural to man; but while I made that sentiment the point of departure for proving that religion is in accordance with nature and reason, and therefore of removing what had been my chief difficulty in the way of accepting supernatural revelation, he made it his starting-point for reducing all religion to mere naturalism, or, as Carlyle calls it, "natural-supernaturalism," another name for downright Pantheism, or rather, Atheism. He held and applied it nakedly, in an unbelieving spirit; I held it in connection, with many elements of my early traditional faith, and applied it in a believing spirit. When an countering the doctrine, he was in the access of his wrath against religion, or, as he said, "popular theology," produced by the reaction of his reason against Calvinism, in which he had been born and reared, and of his heart against the inefficiency and hollowness of the sleek and decorous morality which formed the burden of fashionable Unitarian preaching; and he seized upon it as an instrument for demolishing the Christian temple, overthrowing the altar of Christ, and of sweeping away the Bible, and all creeds, dogmas, forms, rites, and institutions of religion. He was mad at religion, and, as the *Sartor Resartus* would say, he wished to turn men in utter nakedness out into this bleak and wintry world, to rely on themselves alone, and to support themselves as best they might from their own native resources. But I had long since got through that stage in my disease, had long since subdued my wrath, and now longed to approach nearer and nearer to the Christian world, not to remove farther and farther from it. I had learned to loathe doubt, to have a horror of unbelief, and was ready to be an orthodox believer the moment that I could see my way to believe without violence to my human nature, or the abnegation of my reason.

I have already said it was not arguments for belief I wanted, but the removal of the obstacles I encountered, or imagined I encountered, in the way of believing. Just in proportion as these were removed, Christian belief seemed to rise spontaneously in my heart and soul. The doctrine of the origin of religion in a religious sentiment natural to man, which in my mind had really meant no more than that religion is adapted to man's nature and meets an inherent want of his soul, had removed the most formidable of these obstacles, and placed me with my face towards Christianity. It had never been in my mind, in fact, either the origin or the ground of religion, but simply an answer to my principal objection to religion; and therefore I could and did include in religion more than I did or could deduce from it by a logical process. Mr. Parker, on the contrary, really made it the origin and ground of religion, the source and basis of all that he included in that term; and therefore with him it led legitimately and necessarily to sheer naturalism. He made it the basis of his theology, and therefore his theology became simply anthropology; I made it the basis of solving an objection to Revelation, and therefore remained free to accept Christian theology. Each applied it according to his wants and tendencies of the moment.

But these distinctions I had not explicitly made before listening to Mr. Parker; yet, as soon as I looked at the doctrine in its nakedness, as he presented it, I saw that it could not support the superstructure which I had in my own mind erected; that, though it embodied a fact, an important fact, it could offer no foundation for real objective religious belief. So far as I had really built on it, my system was worth nothing, and was and could be only a vain effort to devise a religion without

God, ending at best in mere soul worship, or the worship of my own internal sentiments and affections projected. From the internal sentiment alone it is impossible to conclude the existence of any external object, for the sentiment, taken as sentiment, is only an affection or modification of the subject, and indistinguishable, substantially, from the subject itself. Philosophy has never yet discovered a passage from the subjective to the objective. Both must be given simultaneously, in one and the same intuition, or neither can be asserted. To make religion solely dependent on a sentiment natural to man, is to make it purely subjective, purely human, a development of human nature, and therefore to suppose a religion which presents no real object of worship, which implies no God, no obligation, or sense of duty. This would be absurd; for religion, if religion there be, necessarily implies belief in God, and the recognition of our obligation to worship him. In it is embraced, as essential to its very existence, the idea of intercommunion between God and man, of object and subject, and it is denied the moment that you reduce it to the subject alone, or to the object alone; or, what is the same thing, identify as one in substance, God and man, object and subject. Never was language more grossly perverted than by Cousin, when he called the Pantheist Spinoza, religious, and made his errors flow from an excess of piety. The Pantheism of Spinoza is as far removed from religion as the Subjectivism of Kant, the Egoism of Fichte, or the Atheism of D'Holbach.

Unless you can assert the two terms, God and man, as substantially distinct, or as two distinct substances, bearing to each other the relation of Creator and creature, Sovereign and subject, you cannot assert religion in any sense at all.

Mr. Parker, I saw, was right in his application of the doctrine, that religion originates in a sentiment natural to man, and that I must either go with him, and reject all religion deserving the name, or seek the ground of religion elsewhere. This induced me to reëxamine what it was that I had really, thus far, made the basis of such religious belief as I had. In doing this, the vast importance and reach of the doctrine of Leroux, in regard to thought or life as the joint product of the intercommunion of subject and object, when applied to religion, began to dawn on my mind, and I made the applications of that doctrine which I have already set forth. I found, too, that I had never really built so exclusively on the doctrine of Benjamin Constant as in my mental confusion I had supposed, and that I had really approached in principle nearer to the Christian world than I had myself imagined. While admitting still the religious sentiment as in some sense natural to man, and therefore proving that man may be religious without violence to his nature, indeed, in harmony with it, I now explicitly rejected that sentiment as the origin and ground of religion, and denied that religion is simply the result of its development. I placed the origin and ground of religion in the relation of Creator and creature, of God and man, made known to man by God himself, and held it to be the infusion, through communion, of a supernatural life into natural human life. In this sense I reviewed Mr. Parker's Lectures, when published in a volume. In reviewing the volume and refuting its pantheism, naturalism, or infidelity, I found myself advancing step by step towards real Christian belief. I was impressed, as I never had been before, with the utter insufficiency, the nothingness, of the system to which I had been more or less attached for nearly twenty years, and which, I must say, had never satisfied my reason. I caught glimpses of Christian truths which were to me both new and cheering, and I saw, though dimly as yet, that the deeper philosophy was with the orthodox, not with the heterodox. I began to discover that the doctrine of the Church in the Catholic sense was far profounder and truer than the doctrine of No-Church asserted by Dr. Channing and my Unitarian friends. I obtained the main conceptions of the Church, and of her principal dogmas, which I have set forth in the foregoing chapter, and went so far as to assert the problem of our age is, "Catholicity without the Papacy."

This problem I thought I could solve by my doctrine of life. My first step was to proclaim that doctrine, and the Catholicity it had led me to adopt. The great thing was to revive Church principles, to induce people to regard the Church as an organism, and to effect, if possible, the reunion of Christendom, now broken into fragments, not on a new

Church basis, but really on what had been the basis of the Church from the beginning. Filled with this thought, I consented to become one of the editors of *The Christian World*, a new weekly journal, published by a brother of the late Dr. William Ellery Channing, and which I trusted to be able to make the organ of my views. I commenced in that journal a series of essays on *The Mission of Jesus*, which attracted no little attention. The design of these essays was to develop and apply to the explanation of Christianity my doctrine of life or communion. I did not in the outset see very clearly where I should land, but I hoped to do something to draw attention to the Church as a living organism, and the medium through which the S n of God practically redeems, saves, or blesses mankind. The first and second essays pleased my Unitarian friends, the third drew forth a warm approbation from a Puritan journal, the fourth threw the Tractarians into ecstasies, and the *New York Churchman*, then edited by the well-known Dr. Seabury, announced in its prefatory remarks to some extracts it made from it, that a new era had dawned on the Puritan city of Boston; the fifth, sixth, and seventh attracted the attention of the Catholic journals, which reproduced them, or portions of them, with approbatory remarks. The eighth, which was to answer the question, Which is the true Church or Body of Christ? the publisher of *The Christian World* refused to insert, and therefore was not published. A Catholic editor kindly offered me the use of his columns. but I respectfully declined his offer. The essay was the concluding one, and as I hesitated, and evaded a direct answer to the question raised, I was not sorry that I had a good excuse for not publishing it.

Till I commenced writing this series of essays, I had no thought of ever becoming a Roman Catholic; and it was not till I saw my articles copied into a Catholic journal, that even the possibility of such a termination of my researches presented itself to my mind. I found myself with my starting-point led by an invincible logic to assert the Catholic Church as the true Church or living body of Christ. To be logical, I saw I must accept that Church, and accept her as authoritative for natural reason, and then take her own explanation of herself and of her doctrines as true. All my principles required me, and my first impulse, in the enthusiasm of the moment, was, to do it; yet I hesitated, and it was over a year before I made up my mind to submit myself to her instructions and directions.

My doctrine of life or communion did not include in itself, as I supposed, the whole of Catholicity; but, in assuming it to be true, and a fair expression of the rational elements of Catholic theology, there was no great error. It did not bring me into the Catholic Church, but it did bring me to the recognition of those great principles, which, taken in connection with the unquestioned historical facts in the case, required me either to renounce my reason, or go farther and accept the Church and her doctrines, in her own sense, not merely in the sense in which I had asserted them in my philosophy. But this I was not at once prepared to do; and for the first time in my life I refused to follow out my principles, so long as I held them, and to accept their last consequences.

I have been accused of precipitancy and rashness in submitting myself to the Catholic Church, but the fact is that I betrayed inexcusable weakness in not submitting to her much sooner than I did. I was quite willing to accept the Church in the abstract, and defend, in a general way, Catholicity as I understood it; but I had so long been accustomed to consider the claims of the present Catholic Church as out of the question, that I found it difficult to make up my mind to accept them. I was unwilling to believe that the Reformation had had no reason against her, and that the whole Protestant movement had been wholly wrong from the beginning. I was not prepared either in words or deeds to condemn outright the whole Protestant world, so large a portion of mankind, and that, as I had been accustomed to believe, the more moral, enlightened, and energetic portion. I had formed but a poor opinion of Roman Catholics, and was far from being willing to cast in my lot with them. I had, indeed, few Catholic acquaintances, and had only Protestant representations from which to form my opinion, but I had not as yet learned to question the substantial truthfulness of those representations. One or two modern Catholic controversial works had fallen in my way, and I had attempted to read them, but they did not impress me favorably. They were written, as I thought, in a dry, feeble, and unattractive style, and abounded with terms and locutions which were to me totally unintelligible. Their authors seemed to me ignorant of the ideas and wants of the non-Catholic world, engrossed with obsolete questions, and wanting in broad and comprehensive views. Their method of arguing struck me as mere special pleading, turning on mere technicalities and verbal distinctions, evading the real merits of the questions debated, aud puzzling rather than convincing the reason of their opponents. They struck me as cunning, as subtile, as adroit disputants, not as great, broad, or open-hearted men, who win at once your confidence in their intelligence and sincerity, and in the truth and honesty of their cause; and, in point of fact, Catholic controversialists are generally regarded by Protestants very much in the light I regarded them, that. is, of lawyers speaking from their brief. This, however, it is only fair to say, is not the fault of the Catholic party.

Then I had been accustomed to regard the Catholic nations of Europe, since the time of Leo X, as unprogressive, and the mass of their populations us ignorant, degraded, enslaved, cowardly, and imbecile. I found Catholics, I thought, at the head of none of the great intellectual, political, social, literary, or scientific movements of the age. The great, energetic nations of the day were the non-Catholic nations, Great Britain, Russia, and the United States. Even in so-called Catholic nations the ruling or governing mind had ceased to be Catholic. The majority of the French population were Catholic, but intellectual, literary, scientific, political France was non-Catholic. The great French philosophers, writers, thinkers, those who directed the mind of the kingdom and represented it to foreigners, were far enough from being attached to the Church. French journalism was, almost without exception, anti-Catholic. The men who made the old Revolution, rejected the Church, and instituted the Reign of Terror, were but a small minority of the nation, and yet what availed the opposition of the Catholic masses against them? So in every Catholic State, power, learning, science, energy, is in the hands of non-Catholics, and the Catholic portion, though the immense majority, are governed by the non-Catholic minority. Where, I asked, is the Catholic who takes, in any nation, the lead in any branch of literature or science? I did not attribute, I could not attribute, this supposed inferiority of Catholics to nature or to Catholicity, but to the mistaken policy of the Catholic clergy, who must have lost the deeper sense of their religion, become men of routine, and incapable of comprehending or meeting the wants of the age. Trained up in scrupulous ignorance of the world, in a superannuated scholasticism, they were unfitted to act on the age, and to take the direction of the great movements of the race. Finding the intelligence ot the age against them, they had set their faces against intelligence; finding efforts to extend freedom, and to carry on the progress of man and society directed by their enemies, they had condemned those efforts, thrown themselves on the side of absolutism, and labored to keep the masses in ignorance and slavery, that they might keep them in the faith. Taking this view, and only partially understanding its explanation, how could I but shrink from uniting with the present Catholic Church?

Nor was this all. To pass from one Protestant sect to another is a small affair, and is little more than going from one apartment to another in the same house. We remain still in the same world, in the same general order of thought, and in the midst of the same friends and associates. We do not go from the known to the unknown; we are still within soundings, and may either return, if we choose, to the sect we have left, or press on to another, without serious loss of reputation, or any gross disturbance of our domestic and social relations. But to pass from Protestantism to Catholicity is a very different thing. We break with the whole world in which we have hitherto lived; we enter into what is to us a new and untried region, and we fear the discoveries we may make there, when it is too late to draw back. To the Protestant mind this old Catholic Church is veiled in mystery, and leaves ample room to the imagination to people it with all manner of monsters, chimeras, and hydras dire. We enter it, and leave no bridge over which we may return. It is a committal for life, for eternity. To enter it seemed to me, at first, like taking a leap in the dark; and it is not strange that I recoiled, and set my wits to work to find out, if possible, some compromise, some middle ground on which I could be faithful to my Catholic tendencies without uniting myself with the present Roman Catholic Church.

I had, indeed, found the Church as authoritative for natural reason, but I had not established her absolute infallibility: at least I did not see that I had. The Divine-human life which constituted the Church and was its informing principle, was indeed infallible, but as we receive this life only by communion with those who live it, and as, according to the philosophy I then held, it is the subject that determines the form of the life or fact of conscious-ness, I could well concede that more or less of error might find its way into the concrete conceptions even of Catholics; and as I had as yet failed to recognize the office of the Papacy, and supposed the infallibility of the Pope a doctrine which no enlightened Catholic accepted, for all the Catholics and Catholic books I was acquainted with took good care to state that it was no article of faith, I might, without any very great inconsistency, hold that the Catholic Church had committed some mistakes, and impaired her Divine-human life. I had long been convinced that the Church in communion with the See of Rome had been the true body of Christ down to the age of Leo X, and I regarded the Apostolic See as the central source of the Christian life; but the body seemed to me to have been broken into fragments. and to exist no longer in its integrity. The Roman Catholic Church was undoubtedly the larger fragment, tho one through which the main current of the Divine-human life continued to flow; but no man would dare say that nothing of that life is or can be lived outside of her communion, and I had found no Catholic that held there could be absolutely no salvation outside of it. The several sects, when broken off, retained a certain amount of Christian life,—that amount which Christendom had already assimilated; as is evident the moment you compare a Christian of any sect with a Pagan, a Mahometan, or any man born and living outside of Christian civilization. Moreover, all communion of the sects with one another, and even with the Roman Church, has not been absolutely interrupted. There is more or less even of personal intercourse between them, and, besides, there is intercommunion through similar laws and institutions, and through a common literature and science. They all belong, in some sort, to one and the same family, and all, in a measure, live the one life of Christ. Though the divisions, separations, and schisms greatly enfeeble it, they do not absolutely extinguish it at once; they only weaken it, and prepare by evil communications its final extinction. The real difficulty is not that the Christian world does not live the life at all, but that it does not live it in its unity and fulness. Undoubtedly they who are attached to the Roman Catholic fragment have the advantage; but, instead of uniting ourselves with them, we should labor, from the point where Providence has placed us, to effect in the surest and speediest manner possible the reunion of all the fragments, and thus restore the body of Christ to its original unity and integrity.

Here I came for a moment in contact with the so-called Oxford or Tractarian movement. I never for a moment seriously contemplated joining the Anglican communion, and, regarded in itself, Puseyism had no attractions for me. It was far better to go at once to Rome than to Oxford. But I looked upon the movement as one of great importance. It was a promising sign of the times, as indicating a tendency on the part of a large portion of the Protestant world to return to Church principles. It would be a great mistake to suppose that the Oxford movement was confined to the bosom of the Anglican communion. An analogous movement was perceptible in the bosom of every sect. Even in the Roman Catholic communion, there was a return towards higher and more living Church principles than those contended for in the eighteenth century, when a Bergier combats the Encyclopedists and defends Catholicity on principles borrowed from an infidel philosophy. In every Protestant sect there was in 1842 a movement party, at war with the fundamental principle of Protestantism, and demanding Church union and Church authority. It seemed that Protestantism had culminated, that the work of disintegration and destruction had gone so far that it could go no farther, and that a reaction in earnest, and not likely to be suspended, had commenced through the whole Christian world against the Protestant Reformation. The letters, which I was constantly receiving from prominent Protestant ministers of the more important and influential sects, denouncing the Reformation as a blunder, asserting the necessity of reuniting the Protestant world with the Catholic, was to me a proof of it. The secret history of my own country for several years prior to 1844, would reveal a Catholic reaction in the more serious portion of the Protestant sects, that would surprise those who look only on the surface of things. I was aware of this reaction, and I hoped from it the union of Christendom. The thing to be done was to encourage this reaction, to strengthen it, and by bringing out, each one from his own stand-point, true Church principles, to Catholicize the several Protestant sects, and prepare them for reunion with the Catholic Church in a body.

With this view I greeted Puseyism as the most important movement of the times, and was from my stand-point as a Congregational Unitarian, prepared to coöperate with it, as well as with analogous movements elsewhere, and in the bosom of other communions. In order to do this, having for the year 1843 discontinued my Review, I started another Quarterly, which I still continue. I started it under my own name, and as the organ of my own views, but with the real aim of contributing my share towards effecting the reunion of Christendom by expounding and defending the Catholicity to which my doctrine of life or communion had conducted me. I was then forty years of age, in the full vigor of mind and body, and had won for myself a respectable position in the American literary world, as the list of names voluntarily sent in as subscribers to the new Review immediately on the appearance of the first number fully proved. I was warmly greeted in quarters where I had hitherto been only denounced or not recognized, and I felt that, for the first time in my life, I had the sentiments of the better portion of the community with me. But I soon found it difficult to maintain my independent position, or to defend the theory on which I was acting. The Roman Catholics looked on, but said little; several of their clergy, as I have since learned, said Mass for my conversion, and many, I have no doubt, in their prayers recommended me to Our Lady. The Puseyites thought I leaned too much to Rome, and was encouraging her in her pretensions. My Unitarian friends thought I was too Orthodox, too strenuous for authority, and that I allowed too little scope to individual reason; and, what was more to the purpose, I was dissatisfied with myself. My position, asserting the Church and the necessity of communion with her as the condition of living the life of Christ, and yet really standing aloof from all communions, belonging in fact to no church, struck me the moment I began to consider it, as anomalous, nay, as untenable. Was I living the Christian life myself? If so, what was the value of my reasoning in behalf of the reunion of Christendom, and of communion with the body of Christ? If not, if I was not living that life myself, what was in fact my own personal condition and my future prospects? Suppose I die before I have effected the reunion of Christendom—what will become of my own soul? I am engaged in a good work, but what if I become myself a castaway? Here is matter for serious thought.

CHAPTER XVIII.

THE work of conversion is, of course, the work of grace, and without grace no man can come into the Church any more than he can enter heaven. No merely human process does or can suffice for it, and I am far enough from pretending that I became a Catholic by my own unassisted efforts. Without the grace divinely bestowed, and bestowed without any merit of mine, all my labors would have been in vain. It was divine grace that conducted me, rolled back the darkness before me, and inclined my heart to believe. But grace does not exclude reason, or voluntary coöperation ; and conversion itself, though a work of free grace, includes, inasmuch as it is the conversion of a rational subject, a rational process, though not always distinctly noted by the convert. All I am doing is to detail the rational process by which, not without but with divine grace, I came into the Church, and that not for those who are within, but for those who are without. Those who are within have no need in their own case of the process, for they have the life, and the life evidences itself, and they know in whom they believe, and are certain. But this sort of evidence they who are without have not, and we cannot allege it as evidence to them. They could take it only on our word, and they have no more reason to take our word than they have to take that of Evangelicals, who pretend to the same sort of evidence in their favor. It is necessary, therefore, to show them that there is a rational process included in the case, and to show them as clearly as may be what that process is.

The process I have detailed, or life by communion, did not, as I have said, bring me into the Church, but, taken in connection with the admitted historical facts in the case, it did remove all my *a-priori* objections, and bring me to the recognition of the Church as authoritative, by virtue of the Divine-human life it lived, for natural reason. This was not all that I needed, but it was much, and required me to go farther and submit myself to her, and take her own explanation of herself and of her dogmas. I saw this clear enough, but my reluctance to become a Roman Catholic prevented me from doing so at once. Yet, even from the first, even from the moment I came to the recognition of the Church as authoritative, I felt, though I refused personally to change my position, that I must take what had evidently been her positive teaching for my guide, and in no instance contradict it.

It was evident, without any special instruction, that the Church, that the whole Christian world, proposed a very different end as the true end of life, from the one I had proposed to myself, and for which, during nearly twenty years, in my feeble way, I had been laboring. As a practical fact, the Church, no doubt, really does aid the progress of society, and tend to give us a heaven even on earth, but this is not the end she proposes, or what she directly aims to effect. The end she proposes is not attainable in this world, and the heaven she points to is a reward to be received only after this life. There could be no doubt that she taught endless beatitude as the reward of the good, and endless misery as the punishment of the wicked. The good are they who in this world live the life of Christ, the wicked are they who live it not, and even refuse to live it. There needs no church or priest to tell me that I am not living that life, and that, if I die as I am, I shall assuredly go to hell. Now as I have no wish to go to hell, something must be done, and done without delay.

It is all very well, no doubt, to follow the example of the weeping Isis, and seek to gather up the fragments of the torn body of our Lord, and restore it to its unity and integrity ; but what will it avail me if I remain severed from that body, and refuse to do what the Church commands ? How can I consistently ask the obedience of others while I refuse my own ? Rewards and punishments are personal, and meted out to men as individuals, not as collective bodies. There is, then, but one rational course for me to take, that of going to the Church, and begging her to take charge of me, and do with me what she judges proper. As the Roman Catholic

Church is clearly the Church of history, the only Church that can have the slightest historical claim to be regarded as the body of Christ, it is to her I must go, and her teachings, as given through her pastors, that I must accept as authoritative for natural reason.   It was, no doubt, unpleasant to take such a step, but to be eternally damned would, after all, be a great deal unpleasanter.   Accordingly, with fear and trembling, and yet with firmness of purpose, in the last week of May, 1844, I sought an interview with the late Right Reverend Benedict Joseph Fenwick, the learned Bishop of Boston, and in the following week visited him again, avowed my wish to become a Catholic, and begged him to be so kind as to introduce me to some one who would take the trouble to instruct me, and prepare me for reception, if found worthy, into the communion of the Church.   He immediately introduced me to his coadjutor, who has succeeded him, the Right Reverend John Bernard Fitzpatrick, D. D.   Of Bishop Fenwick, who died in the peace of the Lord, August 12, 1846, and who has left a memory precious to the American Church, I have given, in my Review for the following October, a sketch to which I can add nothing, and from which I have nothing to abate.   He was a native of Maryland, descended from an old Catholic family that came over with the first settlers of the colony, and to whom the American Church is indebted for some of her brightest ornaments.   He was a great and good man, a man of various and solid learning, a tender heart, unaffected piety, and

untiring zeal in his ministry. Delicacy and his own
retiring character prevent me from speaking of his
successor, the present Bishop of Boston, in the
terms which naturally present themselves. He was
my instructor, my confessor, my spiritual director,
and my personal friend, for eleven years; my intercourse with him was intimate, cordial, and affection-
ate, and I owe him more than it is possible for me
to owe to any other man. I have met men of more
various erudition and higher scientific attainments;
I have met men of bolder fancy and more creative
imaginations; but I have never met a man of a
clearer head, a firmer intellectual grasp, a sounder
judgment, or a warmer heart. He taught me my
catechism and my theology; and, though I have
found men who made a far greater display of theological erudition, I have never met an abler or sounder
theologian. However for a moment I may have
been attracted by one or another theological school,
I have invariably found myself obliged to come back
at last to the views he taught me. If my Review
has any theological merit, if it has earned any reputation as a stanch and uncompromising defender of
the Catholic faith, that merit is principally due,
under God, to him, to his instructions, to his advice,
to his encouragement, and his uniform support. Its
faults, its shortcomings, or its demerits, are my own.
I know that, in saying this, I offend his modesty, his
unaffected Christian humility; but less I could not
say without violence to my own feelings, the deep
reverence, the warm love, and profound gratitude

with which I always recall, and trust I always shall recall, his name and his services to me.

Bishop Fitzpatrick received me with civility, but with a certain degree of distrust. He had been a little prejudiced against me, and doubted the motives which led so proud and so conceited a man, as he regarded me, to seek admission into the Communion of the Church. It was two or three months before we could come to a mutual understanding. There was a difficulty in the way that I did not dare explain to him, and he instinctively detected in me a want of entire frankness and unreserve. I had been led to the Church by the application I had made of my doctrine of life by communion, and I will own that I thought that I found in it a method of leading others to the Church which Catholics had overlooked or neglected to use. I really thought that I had made some philosophical discoveries which would be of value even to Catholic theologians in convincing and converting unbelievers, and I dreaded to have them rejected by the Catholic Bishop. But I perceived almost instantly that he either was ignorant of my doctrine of life, or placed no confidence in it; and I felt that he was far more likely, bred as he had been in a different philosophical school from myself, to oppose than to accept it. I had indeed, however highly I esteemed the doctrine, no special attachment to it for its own sake, and could, so far as it was concerned, give it up at a word, without a single regret; but, if I rejected or waived it, what reason had I for regarding the

Church as authoritative for natural reason, or for recognizing any authority in the Bishop himself to teach me ? Here was the difficulty.

This difficulty remained a good while. I dared not state it, lest the Catholic Bishop himself should deprive me of all reason for becoming a Catholic, and send me back into the world utterly naked and destitute. I had made up my mind that the Church was my last plank of safety, that it was communion with the Church or death. I must be a Catholic, and yet could not and would not be one blindly. I had gone it blind once, and had lost all, and would not do so again. My trouble was great, and the Bishop could not relieve me, for I dared not disclose to him its source. But Providence did not desert me ; and I soon discovered that there was another method, by which, even waiving the one which I had thus far followed, I could arrive at the authority of the Church, and prove, even in a clearer and more direct manner, her Divine commission to teach all men and nations in all things pertaining to eternal salvation. This new process or method I found was as satisfactory to reason as my own. I adopted it, and henceforth used it as the rational basis of my argument for the Church. So, in point of fact, I was not received into the Church on the strength of the philosophical doctrine I had embraced, but on the strength of another, and, perhaps, a more convincing process.

It is not necessary to develop this new process here, for it is the ordinary process adopted by Catholic theologians, and may be found drawn out at length in almost every modern Course of Theology. It may, also, be found developed under some of its aspects in almost any article I have since written in my Review, but more especially in an article entitled *The Church against No-Church*, published April, 1845. I found it principally in Billuart's Treatises *de Deo, de Fide, de Regulis Fidei,* and *de Ecclesia ;* and an excellent summary and lucid statement of it, or what are usually called "motives of credibility," may be found in Pointer's *Evidences of Christianity,* and also in the *Evidences of Catholicity,* by Dr Spalding, the present able and learned Bishop of Louisville, Kentucky. Though I accepted this method and was satisfied by it before I entered the Church, yet it was not that by which I was brought from unbelief to the Church ; and it only served to justify and confirm by another process the convictions to which I had been brought by my application to history and the traditions of the race, of the doctrine of life obtained from the simple analysis of thought as a fact of consciousness. What would have been its practical effect on my mind, had I encountered it before I had in fact become a believer, and in reality had no need of it for my personal conviction, I am unable to say, though I suspect it would never have brought me to the Church,—not because it is not logical, not because it is not objectively complete and conclusive, but because I wanted the internal or subjective disposition to understand and receive it. It would not have found, if I may so say, the needed subjective response, and would have failed to remove to my understanding the *a-priori* objections I entertained to a supernatural authoritative revelation itself. It would, I think, have struck me as crushing instead of enlightening, silencing instead of convincing, my reason. Certainly, I have never found the method effectual in the case of any non-Catholic not already disposed to become a Catholic, or actually, in his belief, on the way to the Church.

The argument of our theologians is scholastic, severe, and conclusive for the pure intellect that is in the condition to listen to it; but it seems to me better adapted, practically, to confirm believers and guard them against the specious objections of their enemies, than to convince unbelievers. Man is not pure intellect; he is body as well as soul, and full of prejudices and passions. His subjective objections are more weighty than his objective objections, and the main difficulties of the unbeliever lie, in our times, farther back than the ordinary motives of credibility reach. It strikes me that my method, though it can by no means supersede theirs, might be advantageously used as a preparation for theirs; not as an Evangelical Preparation, but as a preparation for the usual Evangelical Preparation presented by theologians, especially in this age when the objections are drawn from philosophy rather than from history, from feeling rather than from logic.

Having, however, found the other method of justifying my recognition of the Church as authority for reason, I dropped for the time the doctrine of life, and soon came, without any discussion of its merits or demerits, to a good understanding with the Bishop, who, after a few weeks of further instruction, heard my confession, which included the whole period of my life from the time of my joining the Presbyterians, received my abjuration, administered to me conditional Baptism, and the Sacrament of Confirmation, on Sunday, October 20, 1844, when I had just entered the forty-second year of my age, and just twenty-two years after I had joined the Presbyterians. The next morning at early Mass I received Holy Communion from the hands of Rev. Nicholas A. O'Brien, then Pastor of the Church in East Boston. The great step had been taken, and I had entered upon a new life, subdued indeed, but full of a sweet and calm joy. No difficulties with regard to the particular doctrines of the Church had at any time arisen, for, satisfied that Almighty God had commissioned the Church to teach, and that the Holy Ghost was ever present by his supernatural aid to assist her to teach, I knew that she could never teach anything but truth. The fact that she taught a doctrine was a sufficient reason for accepting it, and I had only to be assured of her teaching it, in order to believe it.

As I did not make use in the last moment of my doctrine of communion, and as I had no occasion for it afterwards for my own mind, I made no further use of it; and when I addressed the public again, proceeded to defend my Catholic faith by the method ordinarily adopted by Catholic writers. I did this, because, seeing the Catholic Church and her dogmas to be infinitely more than that doctrine had enabled me to conceive, I attached for the moment no great importance to it. It certainly was not all I had supposed it, and it might prove to be nothing at all. It had served as a scaffolding, but now the temple was completed, it might serve only to obscure its beauty and fair proportions. At any rate, that and all other philosophical theories which I had formed while yet unacquainted with the Church, should be suffered to sleep, till I had time and opportunity to reëxamine them in the light of Catholic faith and theology. It did not comport with the modesty and humility of a recent convert to be intruding theories of his own upon the Catholic public, or to insist on methods of defending Catholic doctrine, adopted while he was a non-Catholic, and not recognized by Catholic theologians. Was it likely I had discovered anything of value that had escaped the great theologians and doctors of the Church?

But this suppression of my own philosophic theory,—a suppression under every point of view commendable and even necessary at the time, became the occasion of my being placed in a false position towards my non-Catholic friends. Many had read me, seen well enough whither I was tending, and were not surprised to find me professing myself a Catholic. The doctrine I brought out, and which they had followed, appeared to them, as it did to me, to authorize me to do so, and perhaps not a few of them were making up their minds to follow me ; but they were thrown all aback the first time they heard me speaking as a Catholic, by finding me defending my conversion on grounds of which I had given no public intimation, and which seemed to them wholly unconnected with those I had published. Unable to perceive any logical or intellectual connection between my last utterances before entering the Church and my first utterances afterwards, they looked upon my conversion, after all, as a sudden caprice, or rash act taken from a momentary impulse or in a fit of intellectual despair, for which I had in reality no good reason to offer. So they turned away in disgust, and refused to trouble themselves any longer with the reasonings of one on whom so little reliance could be placed, and who could act without any rational motive for his action.

Evidently this was unpleasant, but I could not set the matter right at the time, by showing that there really had been a continuity in my intellectual life, and that I had not broken with my former self so abruptly or so completely as they supposed. Till I had had time to review my past writings in the light of my new faith, the matter was uncertain in my own mind, and it was my duty, so far as the public was concerned, to let the doctrine sleep, and to write and publish nothing but what I had a warrant for in the approved writers of the Church. I acted prudently, as it was proper I should act, and I should continue to do so still, and not have written the present book and taken up the connecting link, had not nearly thirteen years of Catholic experience and study enabled me to perceive that the doctrine of life I asserted is in no way incompatible with any Catholic principle or doctrine I have become acquainted with, and that it did legitimately lead me to the Catholic Church. I do not mean that, as a doctrine of philosophy, it bridges over the gulf between the natural and supernatural, for that no philosophy can do, since philosophy is only the expression of natural reason; but I honestly believe, as I believed in 1844, that it does, better than any other philosophical doctrine, show the harmony between the natural and the supernatural, and remove those obstacles to the reception of the Church, and her doctrines on her authority, which all intelligent and thinking men brought up outside of the Church in our day do really encounter. I believe I am not only clearing myself of an unfounded suspicion of having acted capriciously, from mental instability, or mental despair, in joining the Church, which were a small affair, but also a real service to a large class of minds who still remember me, by recalling it and showing them that in substance I still hold and cherish it.

My Catholic friends cannot look upon my doing so, after years of probation, as indicative of any departure from the diffidence and humility which at first restrained me from putting it forth. The doctrine is new only in form, not in substance, and is only a development and application of principles which every Catholic theologian does and must hold. The fact that it was first developed and applied by one outside of the Church, and served to bring him to the Church, since it is not repugnant to any principle of Catholic faith or theology, is rather in its favor, for it creates a presumption that it really contains something fitted to reach a certain class of minds at least, and to remove the obstacles they experience in yielding assent to the claims of the Church. Non-Catholics do not, indeed, know Catholicity as well as Catholics know it, but they know better their own objections to it, and what is necessary to remove them. If, in investigating questions before them, in attempting to establish a system of their own, with no thought of seeking either to believe Catholicity, or to find an answer to the objections they feel to the Church, they find these objections suddenly answered, and themselves forced, by principles which they have adopted, to recognize the Church as authority for reason, it is good evidence that these principles, and the methods of reasoning they authorize, are well adapted to the purpose of the defenders of the faith, and not unworthy of the attention of Catholic controversialists, when, as in my case, they neither supersede nor interfere with the ordinary methods of theologians.

Motives of credibility or methods of proof should be adapted to the peculiar character and wants of the age, or class of persons addressed. Philosophy could never have attained to Christian revelation, or the sacred mysteries of our holy religion; but now that the revelation is made, that the mysteries are revealed, we know that all sound philosophy does and

must accord with them—must, as far as it goes, prepare the mind to receive them ; and taken in connection with the historical facts in the case, must demand them as its own complement. Now, if I am
not mistaken, a philosophy of this sort has become
indispensable. The age is skeptical, I grant, but its
skepticism relates rather to the prevailing philosophy
than to reason, of which that philosophy professes to
be the exponent. It distrusts reasoning rather than
reason. It has no confidence in the refinements and
subtilties of schoolmen, and, though often sophistical,
it is in constant dread of being cheated out of its
wits by the sophistry of the practised logician. Conclusions in matters of religion, which are arrived at
only by virtue of a long train of reasoning, even when
it perceives no defects in the premises and no flaw in
the reasoning, do not command its assent, for it fears
there may still be something wrong either in the
reasoning or the premises, which escapes its sagacity.
The ordinary motives of credibility do not move non-
Catholics to believe, because these motives start from
principles which they do not accept, or accept with
so much vagueness and uncertainty, that they do
not serve to warrant assent even to strictly logical
conclusions drawn from them. Moreover, they do
not reach their peculiar difficulties, do not touch
their real objections; and though they seem over-
whelming to Catholics, they leave all their objections
remaining in full force, and their inability to believe
undiminished.

The reason is in the fact that the philosophy

which prevails, and after which the modern mind is, in some sense, moulded, is opposed to Christian revelation, and does not recognize as fundamental the principles or premises which warrant the conclusions drawn in favor of Christianity. The prevalent philosophy with very nearly the whole scientific culture of the age, is not only un-Christian, but anti Christian, and, if accepted, renders the Christian faith an impossibility for a logical mind. There is always lurking in the mind a suspicion of the antecedent improbability of the whole Evangelical doctrine. Apologists may say, and say truly, that there is and can be no contradiction between philosophy and faith; but, unhappily, the philosophy between which and faith there is no contradiction, is not generally recognized. Between the official and prevalent philosophy of the day, between the principles which have passed from that philosophy into the general mind, and Catholic faith, there is a contradiction; and not a few Catholics even retain their faith only in spite of their philosophy. The remedy is in revising our philosophy, and in placing it in harmony with the great principles of Catholic faith. I will not say with Bonetty that the method of the Scholastics leads to rationalism and infidelity, for that is not true; but I will say that that method, as developed and applied in the moder world, especially the non-Catholic world, does not serve as a preamble to faith, and does place the mind of the unbeliever in a state unfitted to give to the ordinary motives of credibility their due weight, or any weight at all.

Modern philosophy is mainly a method, and develops a method of reasoning instead of presenting principles to intellectual contemplation. It takes up the question of method before that of principles, and seeks by the method to determine the principles, instead of leaving the principles to determine the method. Hence it becomes simply a doctrine of science, *Wissenschaftslehre*, a doctrine of abstractions, or pure mental conceptions, instead of being, as it should be, a doctrine of reality, of things divine and human. It is cold, lifeless, and offers only dead forms, which satisfy neither the intellect nor the heart. It does not, and cannot move the mind towards life and reality. It obscures first principles, and impairs the native force and truthfulness of the intellect. The evil can be remedied only by returning from this philosophy of abstractions—from modern psychology, or subjectivism, to the philosophy of reality, the philosophy of life, which presents to the mind the first principles of all life and of all knowledge as identical.

Herein is the value of the process by which I arrived at the Church. I repeat, again and again, that philosophy did not conduct me into the Church, but, just in proportion as I advanced towards a sound philosophy, I did advance towards the Church. As I gained a real philosophy, a philosophy which takes its principles from the order of being, from life, from things as they are or exist, instead of the abstractions of the schools, faith flowed in, and I seized with joy and gladness the Christian Church and her dogmas.

The non-Catholic world is far less in love with heresy or infidelity than is commonly supposed, and our arguments, clear and conclusive as they are to us, fail because they fail to meet their objections, and convince their reason. They are not addressed to reason as it is developed in them, and answer not their objections as they themselves apprehend them. The non-Catholic world is not deficient in logical force or mental acuteness, but it expresses itself in broad generalizations, rather than in precise and exact statements. Its objections are inductions from particulars, vaguely apprehended and loosely expressed, are more subjective than objective, and rarely admit of a rigid scientific statement or definition. To define them after the manner of the schools, and to reduce them to a strictly logical formula, is, in most cases, to refute them; but the non-Catholic is not thus convinced that they are untenable, for he feels them still remaining in his mind. He attributes their apparent refutation to some logical sleight-of-hand, or dialectic jugglery, which escapes his detection. He remains unconvinced, because his objection has been met by a refutation which has given no new light to his understanding, or made him see any higher or broader principles than he was before ir possession of.

An external refutation of the unbeliever's objections effects nothing, because the real objection is internal, and the refutation leaves the internal as it was before. The secret of convincing is not to put error out of the mind, but truth into it. There is little use in arguing against the objections of non-Catholics, or in laboring directly for their refutation. We can effectually remove them only by correcting the premises from which the unbeliever reasons. and giving him first principles, which really enlighten his reason, and, as they become operative, expel his error by their own light and force. This can be done only by bringing the age back, or up to a philosophy which conforms the order of knowledge to the order of being, the logical order to the order of reality, and gives the first principles of things as the first principles of science. If Catholicity be from God, it does and must conform to the first principles of things, to the order of reality, to the laws of life or intelligence; and hence, a philosophy which conforms to the same order will conform to Catholicity, and supply all the rational elements of Catholic theology. Such a philosophy is the desideratum of the age, and we must have it, not as a substitute for faith, but as its preamble, as its handmaid, or we cannot recall the non-believing world to the Church of God; because it is only by such a philosophy that we can really enlighten the mind of the unbeliever, and really and effectually remove his objections, or show that it is in fact true that there is no contradiction between Catholicity and philosophy

The greatest and most serious difficulty in the way of the unbeliever is his inability to reconcile faith and reason, that is, the Divine plan in the order of grace with the Divine plan evident in the order of nature. The Christian order appears to him as an after-thought, as an anomaly, if not a contradictioıo, to the general plan of Divine Providence, incompatible with the perfections of God, which we must admit, if we admit a God at all. It strikes him as unforeseen, and not contemplated by the Divine Mind in the original intention to create, and as brought in to remedy the defects of creation, or to make amends for an unexpected and deplorable failure. The two orders, again, seem to stand apart, and to imply a dualism, in fact, an antagonism, which it is impossible to reconcile with the unity and perfections of God. If God is infinite in all his attributes, in wisdom, power, and goodness, why did he not make nature perfect, or all he desired it, in the beginning, so as to have no need to interfere, to repair, or to amend it, or to create a new order in its place, or even to preserve it, and avert its total ruin ? It is of no use to decry such thoughts and questions as irreverent, as impious, as blasphemous; for they arise spontaneously in the unbelieving mind, and denunciation will not suppress them. It will serve no purpose to bring in here the ordinary motives of credibility, drawn from the wants of nature, the insufficiency of reason, prophecies, miracles, and historical monuments, for these only create new and equally grave difficulties. What is wanted is not argument, but instruction and explanation. It is necessary to show, not merely assert, that the two orders are not mutually antagonistic; that one and the same principle of life runs through them both ; that they correspond one to the other, and really constitute but two parts of one comprehensive whole, and are equally embraced in the original plan and purpose of God in creating. God could have created man, had he chosen, in a state of pure nature; but in point of fact he did not, and nature has never for a single instant existed as pure nature. It has, from the first moment of its existence, been under a supernatural Providence; and even if man had not sinned, there would still have been a sufficient reason for the Incarnation, to raise human nature to union with God, to make it the nature of God, and to enable us, through its elevation, to enjoy endless beatitude in heaven.

The doctrine that all dependent life is life by communion of the subject with the object, shows that this is possible, shows the common principle of the two orders, and thus prepares the mind to receive and yield to the arguments drawn from the wants of nature, the insufficiency of reason, prophecies, miracles and historical monuments; for it shows these to be in accordance with the original intent of the Creator, and that these wants and this insufficiency are wants and insufficiency, not in relation to the purely natural order, but in relation to the supernatural. Natural reason is sufficient for natural reason, but it is not sufficient for man; for man was intended from the beginning to live simultaneously in two orders, the one natural and the other supernatural.

Taking into consideration the fact that the skepticism of our age lies further back than the ordinary

motives of credibility extend—further back than did
the skepticism our ancestors had to meet, and shows
itself under a different form, I believe the process
by which I was conducted towards the Church is not
only a legitimate proccss in itself, but one which, in
these times, in abler hands than mine, may be adopted
with no little advantage.   The present non-Catholic
mind has as much difficulty in admitting the motives
of credibility, as usually urged, as it has in accepting
Christianity without them.   Prior to adducing them,
we must, it seems to me, prepare the way for them,
by rectifying our philosophy, and giving to our youth
a philosophical doctrine which reproduces the order
of things, of reality, of life ; not merely an order of
dead abstractions.   Such a philosophy, I think, will
be found in that which underlies the process I have
detailed; and I hope it is no presumption or lack of
modesty on my part, to recommend it to the attention of the schools, as well as to the consideration of
all whose office or vocation it is to combat the unbelief of the age and country.

CHAPTER XIX.

BELIEF ON AUTHORITY.

If I have made myself understood by the reader who has had the patience or the courtesy to follow me thus far, he will perceive that my submission to authority on becoming a Catholic was very different from that which I yielded when I became a Presbyterian. In becoming a Presbyterian, I abandoned the use of reason; in becoming a Catholic, I used my reason. In the one case, I submitted because I despaired of reason; in the other, because I confided in it. The act of submitting to Presbyterianism was a rash act, an irrational act, an act of folly; because no man either can or should divest himself of reason, the essential and characteristic element of his nature; and because I neither had nor asked any proof that the Presbyterian Church had been instituted by our Lord, and commissioned by him to teach me. All the objections usually urged against believing on authority, were valid against my act of submission to Presbyterianism. But my act of submission to the Catholic Church was an intelligent, a reasonable act; an act of reason, though indeed of reason assisted by grace, because I had full evidence of the fact that she is God's Church, founded and sustained by him, and endowed with the authority and the ability to teach me in all things pertaining to salvation. I had proof satisfactory to reason, that God had himself instituted her as the medium of communion between him and men. To Presbyterianism I submitted blindly, without a sufficient reason; to the Catholic Church, with my eyes open, with full light, because I had ample reason to believe that the authority I submitted to could not err, and because her authority, while it obliges, convinces.

To all the Presbyterian doctrines my reason was opposed, and, in following it, I should not only not have believed them, but should have positively disbelieved them. To the Catholic doctrines I had no *a-priori* objections, and reason, if unable of herself alone to accept them, had nothing to oppose to them. Presbyterianism contradicted reason; Catholicity was above reason indeed, but still in accordance with it, and, therefore, credible without violence to reason or nature. In becoming a Presbyterian, I had to surrender common-sense, and give up my natural beliefs and convictions; in becoming a Catholic, I had very little to reject of what I had previously held. I have found, on reviewing my past life, hardly a single positive conviction I ever held that I do not still hold, hardly a denial I ever made that I would not still make, if divested of my Catholic faith. I fell short of Catholicity, but in no instance, where I faithfully followed reason, did I run counter to it. The change I underwent was in taking on, rather than in casting off; and my Catholic faith was, under the grace of God, the slow and gradual accumulation of twenty-five years of intense mental activity, and incessant struggle for light, and a religion on which I could rely.

Belief on the authority of the Church, supposing that authority adequately proved or provable to reason to be from God, and really his authority, is the most reasonable thing in the world. All belief, as distinguishable from science, is mediate assent on authority or testimony; and to complain of the Catholic faith that it is assent on authority or testimony, is to complain that it is faith and not knowledge. No reasonable man will do that. The objection usually urged by non-Catholics is founded on a misapprehension of what Catholics really mean by believing on authority. Authority in the sense of law, in the sense that it simply obliges without convincing, cannot be a reasonable ground of belief. The State may enact a creed and command me to believe it, but I cannot, even if I would, believe it for that reason. There is no necessary or logical connection between the enactment, or the command of the State, and the truth of the creed enjoined; and therefore it is and can be no reason why I should believe it. The command does and can throw no light on the truth of the creed; does and can produce, or aid in producing, no interior conviction, without which there is and can be no belief. The authority of the Church taken in this sense is, indeed, no reason for believing, that is, in so far as belief is an act of the understanding; for, in this sense, authority can merely move the will, and no man can believe by simply willing to believe.

In Christian faith, subjectively considered, there is an act of the will and an act of the understanding. In so far as faith is an act of the will, we yield it, because commanded to do so by our sovereign; and hence faith becomes an act of obedience, and is treated by theologians as a virtue. But in so far as it is simply a belief or an act of the understanding, or a purely intellectual act, it is not and cannot be yielded as an act of obedience to authority, be that authority what it may. In this respect, I was right when I refused to believe because commanded; and, in this respect, Rationalists and all non-Catholics are right, when they object to believing on authority. Nothing is or can be authority for faith, whether human or divine, in so far as faith is an intellectual act, and distinguished from volition, or determination of the will, that does not, at the same time that it commands the will, enlighten and convince the understanding. Authority is authority for the understanding, therefore for that intellectual assent which is called belief, only in that it enlightens and convinces reason, or is itself a full and satisfactory reason for believing,—a real light to the understanding. Nothing is more reasonable than to believe God at his word, but we cannot believe even him by reason that his word is a command; we do so only by reason that his word is the word of eternal, immutable, and absolute Truth. It is overlooking this distinction, and taking authority in the sense that it commands, and not in the sense that it enlightens and convinces, that has excited the hostility to belief on authority we so frequently encounter.

All men, whatever their speculations, admit the authority of reason, and that what is really reasonable is really true and just. But reason is light and worthy of trust, only because God creates it, and is himself its immediate object and light. It is the participation of reason in the Divinity, by virtue of the communion of our reason with the Divine reason as its object, that renders reason itself authoritative, makes it reason, or intellectual light, at all. We see and know things even in the natural order, only because God immediately affirms himself as the intelligible, and, by the light of his own being illuminating them, renders them visible or intelligible to us. The principle, or a parallel principle, holds in the Church. Her authority, though in a higher order, is of a nature parallel with the authority of reason. Reason is created, constituted by the act of God communicating to it the light and truth of his own being in the natural order, and its authority is the authority of the Divine light and truth communicated; the Church is created, constituted by the act of God communicating to it the light and love of his own essence in the supernatural order, and its authority is the authority of his own essential light and love. The ground of the authority, and the principle of inward assent or conviction, is the same in both cases; and no reason can be assigned or conceived why intellectual submission to the teaching of the Church should be less easy than submission to the dictates of reason; or why the one should be more or less derogatory from the rights and freedom of the mind than the other. The whole value of natural reason is derived from the presence of God in and to it, creating and illuminating it: this is the sole ground of its existence and authority. The sole value of the teaching of the Church, the sole ground of her existence and authority, is in the super-natural presence of the Incarnate God in her and to her, creating and illuminating her.

The commission to the Church of which Catholics so often speak, is not merely an external commission, given externally to a person foreign to the Divine Person of our Lord. The Church exists and lives by direct and immediate communion with the Incarnate God; nay, is his body, and, as it were, the outward, or visible, or sensible continuation or representation on earth of the Incarnation. Like our Lord himself, she is at once Divine and human. She is the union of the two natures with the two natures of Christ in one Divine person. Her authority thus derives, not from an external commission, which is only its external sign or symbol, but from the reality of this union, from God himself dwelling in her, from the Paraclete or Spirit of Truth who inhabits her, and operates in her, as in the natural order he inhabits natural reason, and operates in and through it. There is nothing formal or forensic in the case; all is internal, real, living, and the Church is rendered through the indwelling Holy Ghost, in relation to the intellect, the supernatural light and reason of God, which is all the most hesitating human reason can demand for its illumination and assent to what she teaches.

An external commission may suffice for obedience to an external command. I obey the powers that be, when they do not require me to disobey God, although I have no belief in their infallibility, or in the intrinsic wisdom or expediency of their policy, because God commands me to do it; so I obey, in the government and administration of external ecclesiastical affairs, the officers of the Church, although I do not believe them always wise or prudent, because they have been commissioned by Him who has the Sovereign right to command me, and I obey them for his sake. But when it comes to matters of belief, this external commission does not suffice. It must be internal as well as external, and carry with it the internal light and ability that connects the authority indissolubly with the truth of what it teaches; that is, the authority of the Church, to serve the demands of the intellect, though expressed through human organs, must be really the authority of God himself, in his infinite light and truth. Neither Popes nor Councils in their mere humanity, in th ir own nature, wisdom, sagacity, or virtue as men, do or can suffice as authority for believing a single Catholic dogma. No Pope, no member of a Council, is in himself either infallible or impeccable; and no aggregation of fallibles can make an infallible. No elevation of a man to an official station of itself renders him infallible, or adds anything to his wisdom or knowledge. The Pope, if we look only to his external commission, as successor of St. Peter, would and could have only an official, only a reputed infallibility—be infallible only in the sense of being the court of last resort, from which there lies no appeal,—the only sense in which the illustrious Count de Maistre seems to have recognized either the Pope or the Church as infallible. The commission, if it communicates authority for reason, must communicate the ability which teaches the truth, the whole truth, and nothing but the truth. It is the Holy Ghost supernaturally assisting the Pope, and preserving, permanently or for the time being, his judgment from error, that constitutes his definitions authoritative in matters of faith. The same is to be said of Councils. The authority, strictly speaking, is not in them as their own virtue or right, but in the Holy Ghost who is present in them, and whose organs they are. The authority of the Church in matters of faith, therefore, enlightens as well as commands, convinces as well as obliges, because it is intrinsically the light and authority of absolute Truth; and consequently belief on her authority is no blind belief, no blind submission to mere will or power, but an enlightened and reasonable belief, as much so as is or can be any belief on competent and credible testimony.

Of course, the authority, which in this case means the inward infallibility of the Church in teaching, must be established to the full satisfaction of reason, before we can reasonably believe anything because she teaches it. But, this done, belief on her authority is not a mere submission to power, or a command, but a true surrender to the highest reason, and, therefore, a true, real, inward conviction, because her authority is intimately and necessarily connected with the truth of the things taught. That God can found such a Church, and endow her with the inward authority, without violating the principles of the natural order, or in strict accordance with the principles and nature of natural reason, is shown by the doctrine of life by the communion of the object and subject, which I have already explained. Communion between God and man is possible, although only like communes with like, because man has in his own nature a likeness to God. Human reason is the likeness in man of the Divine reason, and hence, nothing hinders intercommunion between the reason of God and the reason of man. Though Divine reason, as the object, is independent of the human, and does not, as Leroux maintained, live by communion with it, yet the human reason lives only by communion with the Divine, as, in all cases, the subject lives only by communion with the object, and not reciprocally, the object by communion with the subject. By this communion, the subject partakes of the object, the human reason of the Divine reason, which is infinite, absolute truth. The Divine Being, in this communion established by himself, communicates the life of his own reason to the life of the subject, so that our reason lives in and by his reason.   This is the origin and ground of the truth and authority of natural reason; and this natural reason, thus in communion with the Divine, is the source and ground of the unity of the human race in the natural order, and the formative principle of natural society; that is, in so far as natural society is the society of men, and distinguishable from mere animal gregariousness.

God does not exhaust his light in natural reason, any more than he does his creative power in natural creation.   In affirming himself in natural reason as the Intelligible, our reason itself bears witness that there is in him, above what it apprehends, the infinite super-intelligible; that there are infinite depths in his being not intuitively affirmed to reason.   Hence, nothing hinders God, if he chooses, from creating, in correspondence with the natural,—as in his own being the super-intelligible is in correspondence with the intelligible,—a super-intelligible or a supernatural order, or from supernaturally elevating reason, and affirming himself to it as supernatural.   In such case, there would be established between human reason and the Divine reason a supernatural communion, whence would result, by the law of all communion, a supernaturalized life, constituting a new, supernaturalized or regenerated humanity; that is to say, the Church, or society, with a supernatural principle of unity and life, as distinguished from natural society. Suppose we become members of this supernatural society by the election of grace, as we become members of natural society by natural generation, and we have not an adequate conception of the Church indeed, but, nevertheless, a conception of the Church as a society above natural reason, and living by communion with the Divine reason, in a sense higher than that in which the natural human race commune with it, and therefore in a sense in which it is authority for natural reason.

This removes all the antecedent improbability of Catholicity, all the *a-priori* objections to an authoritative church, and renders the fact of such a church as probable as any other historical fact. Take, now, the well-known traditions of the race, in all ages and nations, the authentic historical facts and monuments bearing on the question, together with the fact of the continued existence of such a society, under different forms, or in different states, from the first, and which can no more be disputed than the existence of natural society, its identity with the Patriarchs, with the Jewish Synagogue, and, since the accomplishment of the Incarnation, previously foretold, promised, and expected, with the Roman Catholic Apostolic Church, becomes evident and undeniable; for, if anything can be regarded as certain, it is that the Church in communion with the See of Rome is the successor of the Synagogue, the inheritor of the traditions of the race, the depositary of the revelations of God, and the living body of Christ on earth; the real regenerated human society. Come thus far— and thus far philosophy and history, faithfully studied and rightly applied, do bring us—the rest is easy;

for then we may take the Church herself as authority for her own character and doctrine.

This is the process by which I found my way to the Catholic Church as the body of our Lord living his Divine-human life, informed with his reason, having its personality in his Divine Person, and teaching with authority, because teaching with the light and truth of his Divinity. Evidently, then, the authority of the Church in relation to the understanding is the inherent light and truth she lives by virtue of her supernatural communion with the Divine Incarnate Reason or Word, who is one with God, nay, is God, as we are told in the proem of St. John's Gospel. In submitting to her, I yielded to the highest reason; and my submission was intelligent, not an act discarding reason, but an act of reason itself in the full possession and free exercise of her highest powers. No act of belief is, or can be more reasonable; and, in performing it, I kept faithfully the resolution I made on leaving Presbyterianism, that henceforth I would be true to my own reason, and maintain the rights and dignity of my own manhood. No man can accuse me of not having done it. I never performed a more reasonable, a more manly act, or one more in accordance with the rights and dignity of human nature, though not done save by Divine grace moving and assisting thereto, than when I kneeled to the Bishop of Boston, and asked him to hear my confession and reconcile me to the Church, or when I read my abjuration, and publicly professed the

Catholic Faith ; for the basis of all true nobility of soul is Christian humility, and nothing is more manly than submission to God, or more reasonable than to believe God's word on his own authority.

To believe what the Church teaches, because she teaches it, is in this, the Catholic view of the question, perfectly reasonable, because her teaching really is authority for reason, testimony to the understanding, as well as a command to the will. Authority for believing is always necessary, and nothing is more unreasonable than to believe without authority. Belief without authority is credulity, is folly, or madness ; not an act of reason, but an act of unreason. The same is true as to the supernatural order, which, though above nature, is not contrary to it, but in its principles and laws in accordance with it. It is as reasonable to believe that on competent and credible testimony, as it is any fact of the natural order on the testimony of men or of monuments. The difficulty men feel on this subject is, that they conceive the supernatural as antinatural, and the authority of the Church as simply power, giving an order or command addressed to the will, and communicating no light to the reason. This objection is valid against Calvinism and all the other forms of so-called Evangelical Protestantism, but does not avail against Catholicity ; because both the assumptions on which it rests are, as to Catholicity, misapprehensions, since Catholicity presents the natural and supernatural in mutual accordance, as two distinct strings of the same harp, and authority as communicating light as well as issuing an order. I obey God's command because he is my sovereign, and has the right to command me; I believe him because he is truth, and can neither deceive nor be deceived. I believe his word, not because it is his word as my sovereign, but because it is his word as the infinite, eternal, and unalterable truth, absolute truth, the truth in itself, for God in relation to the intellect is the True, as in relation to the will he is the Good. In relation to the will his word is imperative, in relation to the intellect it is light and truth, and produces inward conviction.

Taking this view of belief on the authority of the Church as an intellectual act, and advising my Catholic friends that I am not now engaged in treating of faith as a theological virtue, there can be no ground for the feeling so commonly entertained by non-Catholics, that the teachings and definitions of the Church must needs operate as restraints on mental freedom, and bring the Catholic into a degrading intellectual bondage. Certainly her teachings, her dogmas, her definitions, do bind my will, inasmuch as they are authorized by my sovereign Lord and Proprietor, who has an absolute right to my obedience; but inasmuch as they are at the same time light to my reason, and put me in possession of the truth, they can restrain my intellectual freedom only in the sense that all truth possessed restrains it. They satisfy reason by providing it the communion, without which it cannot live. They place the mind in relation with its proper object, and thus save it from error and falsehood, which are its sickness and death. So far as this is to abridge our mental freedom, and reduce us to intellectual bondage. they undoubtedly do it, but no further. Reason can operate and live only by communion with the intelligible, and all error is unintelligible ; and I cannot persuade myself that anything which saves the reason, without violating her own laws, from sickening and dying, is to be deplored. Whoever makes himself acquainted with the definitions of the Church, will find that they all tend to save reason, as well as faith itself. I have never encountered a condemned proposition that was not an error against reason, as well as a sin against faith. For a man who wishes to err, to run off into all manner of intellectual vagaries and extravagances, the Church, certainly, is not his proper place, he will not be able to gratify his insane propensity in her communion ; but he who would not woo darkness, who would not lose himself in doubt and perplexity, who would really open his eyes to the light, who would really exercise his reason according to her own laws, and live in communion with the truth, will find in her communion full freedom, and ample room to grow and expand to the full capacity of his nature without crowding or being crowded.

I have been, during the thirteen years of my Catholic life, constantly engaged in the study of the Church and her doctrines, and especially in their relations to philosophy, or natural reason. I have had occasion to examine and defend Catholicity precisely under those points of view which are the most odious to my non-Catholic countrymen and to the Protestant mind generally; but I have never, in a single instance, found a single article, dogma, proposition, or definition of faith, which embarrassed me as a logician, or which I would, so far as my own reason was concerned, have changed, or modified, or in any respect altered from what I found it, even if I had been free to do so. I have never found my reason struggling against the teachings of the Church, or felt it restrained, or myself reduced to a state of mental slavery. I have, as a Catholic, felt and enjoyed a mental freedom, which I never conceived possible while I was a non-Catholic. This is my experience; and, though not worth much, yet in this matter, whereof I have personal knowledge, it is worth something.

CHAPTER XX.

CONCLUSION.

I have now completed the sketch I proposed to give of my intellectual struggles, failures, and successes, from my earliest childhood till my reception by the Bishop of Boston into the communion of the Catholic Church. I have not written to vindicate my ante-Catholic life, or to apologize for my conversion. I have aimed to record facts, principles, and reasonings, trials and struggles, which have a value independent of the fact that they relate to my personal history. Yet even as the personal history of an earnest soul, working its way, under the grace of God, from darkness to light, from the lowest abyss of unbelief to a firm, unwavering, and not a blind faith in the old religion, so generally rejected and decried by my countrymen, I think my story not wholly worthless, or altogether uninstructive,—especially when taken in connection with the glimpses it incidentally affords of American thought and life during the greater portion of the earlier half of the present century. Whether what I have written proves me to have been intellectually weak, vacillating, constantly changing, all things by turns, and nothing long, or tolerably firm, consistent, and persevering in my search after truth; whether it shows that my seeking admission into the Church for the reasons, and in the way and manner I did, was a sudden caprice, an act of folly, perhaps of despair, or that it was an act of deliberation, wise, judicious, and for a sufficient reason, my readers are free to judge for themselves.

This much only will I add, that, whether I am believed or not, I can say truly that, during the nearly thirteen years of Catholic experience, I have found not the slightest reason to regret the step I took. I have had much to try me, and enough to shake me, if shaken I could be, but I have not had even the slightest temptation to doubt, or the slightest inclination to undo what I had done; and have every day found new and stronger reasons to thank Almighty God for his great mercy in bringing me to the knowledge of his Church, and permitting me to enter and live in her communion. I know all that can be said in disparagement of Catholics. I am well versed, perhaps no man more so, in Catholic scandals, but I have not been deceived; I have found all that was promised me, all I looked for. I have found the Church all that her ministers represented her, all my imagination painted her, and infinitely more than I had conceived it possible for her to be. My experience as a Catholic, so far as the Church, her doctrines, her morals, her discipline, her influences are concerned, has been a continued succession of agreeable surprises.

I do not pretend that I have found the Catholic

population perfect, or that I have found in them or in myself no shortcomings, nothing to be censured or regretted; yet I have found that population superior to what I expected, more intellectual, more cultivated, more moral, more active, living, and energetic. Undoubtedly, our Catholic population, made up in great part of the humbler classes of the Catholic populations of the Old World, for three hundred years subjected to the bigotry, intolerance, persecutions, and oppressions of Protestant or *quasi*-Protestant governments, have traits of character, habits, and manners, which the outside non-Catholic American finds unattractive, and even repulsive. Certainly in our cities and large towns may be found, I am sorry to say, a comparatively numerous population, nominally Catholic, who are no credit to their religion, to the land of their birth, or to that of their adoption. No Catholic will deny that the children of these are to a great extent shamefully neglected, and suffered to grow up without the simplest elementary moral and religious instruction, and to become recruits to our vicious population, our rowdies, and our criminals. This is certainly to be deplored, but can easily be explained without prejudice to the Church, by adverting to the condition to which these individuals were reduced before coming here; to their disappointments and discouragements in a strange land; to their exposure to new and unlooked-for temptations; to the fact that they were by no means the best of Catholics even in their native countries; to their poverty, destitution, ignorance, insufficient culture, and a certain natural shiftlessness and recklessness, and to our great lack of schools, churches, and priests. The proportion, too, that these bear to our whole Catholic population is far less than is commonly supposed; and they are not so habitually depraved as they appear, for they seldom or never consult appearances, and have little skill in concealing their vices. As low and degraded as they are, they never are so low or so vicious as the corresponding class of Protestants in Protestant nations. A Protestant vicious class is always worse than it appears, a Catholic vicious population is less bad. In the worst there is always some germ that with proper care may be nursed into life, that may blossom and bear fruit. In our narrow lanes, blind courts, damp cellars, and unventilated garrets, where our people swarm as bees; in the midst of filth and the most squalid wretchedness, the fumes of intemperance and the shouts and imprecations of blasphemy, in what by the outside world would be regarded as the very dens of vice, and crime, and infamy, we often find individuals who, it may well be presumed, have retained their baptismal innocence, real Fleurs de Marie, who remain pure and unsullied, and who, in their humble sphere, exhibit brillian⁴ examples of the most heroic Christian virtues.

The majority of our Catholic population is made up of the unlettered peasantry, small mechanics, servant-girls, and common laborers, from various European countries; and however worthy in themselves, or useful to the country to which they have migrated, cannot, in a worldly and social point of view at least, be taken as a fair average of the Catholic population in their native lands. The Catholic nobility, gentry, easy classes, and the better specimens of the professional men, have not migrated with them. Two or three millions of the lower, less prosperous, and less cultivated, and sometimes less virtuous class of the European Catholic populations, have in a comparatively brief period been cast upon our shores, with little or no provision made for their intellectual, moral, or religious wants. Yet, if we look at this population as it is, and is every year becoming, we cannot but be struck with its marvellous energy and progress. The mental activity of Catholics, all things considered, is far more remark-able than that of our non-Catholic countrymen, and, in proportion to their numbers and means, they contribute far more than any other class of American citizens to the purposes of education, both common and liberal; for they receive little or nothing from the public treasury, and, in addition to supporting numerous schools of their own, they contribute their quota to the support of those of the State.

I do not pretend that the Catholic population of this country are a highly literary people, or that they are in any adequate sense an intellectually cultivated people. How could they be, when the great mass of them have had to earn their very means of subsistence, and have had as much as they could do to provide for the first wants of religion, and of themselves and families? Yet there is a respectable

Catholic-American literature springing up among us, and Catholics have their representatives among the first scholars and scientific men in the land. In metaphysics, in moral and intellectual philosophy, they take already the lead; in natural history and the physical sciences, they are not far behind; and let once the barrier between them and the non-Catholic public be broken down, and they will soon take the first position in general and polite literature. As yet our own literary public, owing to the causes I have mentioned, I admit is not large enough to give adequate encouragement to authors, and the general public makes it a point not to recognize our literary labors. But this will not last, for it is against the interest and the genius of liberal scholarship, and Catholic authors will soon find a public adequate to their wants. Non-Catholics do themselves great wrong in acting on the principle, No good can come out of Nazareth; for we have already in what we ourselves write, in what we reprint from our brethren in the British Empire, and in what we translate from French, German, Spanish, and Italian Catholics, a literature far richer and more important, even under a literary and scientific point of view, than they suspect.

I have known long and well the Protestant clergy of the United States, and I am by no means disposed to underrate their native abilities or their learning and science, and, although I think the present generation of ministers falls far below its predecessor, I esteem highly the contributions they have made and are making to the literature and science of our common country; but our Catholic clergy, below in many respects what for various reasons they should be, can compare more than favorably with them, except those among them whose mother tongue was foreign from ours, in the correct and classical use of the English language. They surpass them as a body in logical training, in theological science, and in the accuracy, and not unfrequently in the variety and extent of their erudition. Indeed, I have found among Catholics a higher tone of thought, morals, manners, and society, than I have ever found, with fair opportunities, among my non-Catholic countrymen; and taking the Catholic population of the country, even as it actually is, under all its disadvantages, there is nothing in it that need make the most cultivated and refined man of letters or of society blush to avow himself a Catholic.

Certainly, I have found cause to complain of Catholics at home and abroad, not indeed as falling below non-Catholic populations, but as falling below their own Catholic standard. I find among them, not indeed as universal—far from it—but as too prevalent, habits of thought and modes of action, a lack of manly courage, energy, and directness, which seem tc me as unwise as they are offensive to the better class of English and American minds. In matters not of faith, there is less unanimity, and less liberality, less courtesy, and less forbearance, in regard to allowable differences of opinion, than might be expected. But I have recollected that I am not myself infallible, and may complain where I should not. Many things may seem to me wrong, only because I am not accustomed to them. Something must be set down to peculiarity of national temperament and development; and even what cannot be justified or excused on either ground, can in all cases be traced to causes unconnected with religion. The habits and peculiarities which I find it most difficult to like, are evidently due to the fact that the Catholics of this country have migrated for the most part from foreign Catholic populations, that have either been oppressed by non-Catholic governments directing their policy to crush and extinguish Catholicity, or by political despotisms which sprang up in Europe after the disastrous Protestant revolt in the sixteenth century, and which recognized in the common people no rights, and allowed them no equality with the ruling class. Under the despotic governments of some Catholic countries, and the bigotry and intollerance of Protestant states, they could hardly fail to acquire habits not in accordance with the habits of those who have never been persecuted, and have never been forced, in order to live, to study to evade tyrannical laws or the caprices of despotism. Men who are subjected to tyranny, who have to deal with tyrants, and who feel that power is against them, and that they can never carry their points by main force, naturally study diplomacy, and supply by art what they lack in strength. This art may degenerate into craft. That it occasionally does so with individuals here and elsewhere, it were useless to

deny; but the cause is not in the Church or anything she teaches or approves. In fact, many things
which Englishmen and Americans complain of in
Catholics and the populations of Southern Europe,
have been inherited from the craft and refinement
of the old Græco-Roman civilization, and transmitted
from generation to generation in spite of the Church.

As yet our Catholic population, whether foreign-
born or native-born, hardly dare feel themselves
freemen in this land of freedom. They have so long
been an oppressed people, that their freedom here
seems hardly real. They have never become recon-
ciled to the old Puritan Commonwealth of England,
and they retain with their Catholicity too many
reminiscences of the passions and politics of the
Bourbons and the Stuarts. They are very generally
attached to the republican institutions of the country,
no class of our citizens more so, and would defend
them at the sacrifice of their lives, but their interior
life has not as yet been moulded into entire harmony
with them; and they have a tendency, in seeking to
follow out American democracy, to run into extreme
radicalism, or, when seeking to preserve law and
order, to run into extreme conservatism. They do
not always hit the exact medium. But this need not
surprise us, for no one can hit that medium unless
his interior life and habits have been formed to it.
Non-Catholic foreigners are less able than Catholic
foreigners to do it, if we except the English, who
have been trained under a system in many respects
analogous to our own; and no small portion of our

own countrymen, "to the manner born," make even more fatal mistakes than are made by any portion of our Catholic population,—chiefly, however, because they adopt a European instead of an American interpretation of our political and social order. Other things being equal, Catholic foreigners far more readily adjust themselves to our institutions than any other class of foreigners; and among Catholics, it must be observed that they succeed best who best understand and best practise their religion. They who are least truly American, and yield most to the demagogues, are those who have very little of Catholicity except the accident of being born of Catholic parents, who had them baptized in infancy. These are they who bring reproach on the whole body.

Undoubtedly there is in Catholic, as well as in non-Catholic states, much that no wise man, no good man, can defend, or fail to deplore. I have not travelled abroad, but I have listened to those who have, and I claim to know a little of the languages and literatures of Southern Europe. From the best information I can get, I do not believe that things are so bad in Spain, Portugal, and Italy, as Protestant travellers tell us; nor that the political and social condition of the people in those states is so beautiful or so happy as now and then a Catholic, who imagines that he must eulogize whatever he finds in a Catholic state, or done by men who call themselves Catholic, in his pious fervor pretends. Yet, be the political and social condition of the people in these

countries as bad as it may be, it does not disturb my
Catholic faith, or damp my Catholic ardor.   All the
modern Catholic states of Europe grew up under
Catholicity, and were more Catholic than they are
now at the period of their greatest prosperity and
power.   The decline which is alleged, and which I
have no disposition to deny, in the Italian and
Spanish Peninsulas, is fairly traceable to political,
economical, commercial, and other causes, independent in their operation of Catholicity, or of religion
of any sort.   Moreover, as a Catholic, I am under
no obligation to defend the policy or the administration of so-called Catholic governments, not even the
policy and administration of the temporal government
of the Papal States.   The Pope, as Supreme Doctor
and Judge of the Deposit of faith, in teaching and
defining the faith of the Church, I hold is, by the
supernatural assistance of the Holy Ghost promised
to his office, infallible, and I accept his definitions,
ex animo, the moment they reach me in an authentic
shape; but I am aware of no law of the Church, of
no principle of Catholicity, that requires me to
believe him infallible in matters of simple administration, which our Lord has left to human prudence·
In these matters, so far as they are directly or
indirectly ecclesiastical, I obey him as the Supreme
Governor of the Church, as I obey the constitution
and laws of my country, not because it is impossible
for him to err, but because he is my divinely-
appointed ruler.   Much less am I bound to believe
in the infallibility or impeccability of nominally

Catholic sovereigns and states. I am as free to criticise, to blame the acts of the Catholic as I am non-Catholic governments, and as free to dispute the political doctrines of Catholics, whether monarchical, aristocratical, or democratical, as I am the political doctrines of non-Catholics. The Church prescribes and proscribes no particular form of government; she simply asserts that power, in whose hands soever lodged, or however constituted, is a trust, and to be administered for the common good on pain of forfeiture.

As a matter of fact, no doubt that much of what is objectionable or deplorable in Catholic Europe is due to the character of the governments which have existed and governed the Catholic populations since the epoch of the Protestant revolt; and the chief obstacle to the revival and progress of Catholic civilization in Catholic states, as well as the recovery to the Church of the mass of European Liberals, now bitterly hostile to Catholicity, there is just as little doubt, is to be found in the habits and manners generated by political and civil despotism. Catholicity leaves to every people its own nationality, and to every state its independence; and it ameliorates the political and social order only by infusing into the hearts of the people and their rulers the principles of justice and love, and a sense of accountability to God. The action of the Church in political and social matters is indirect, not direct, and in strict accordance with the free-will of individuals and the autonomy of states. Individuals may hold very erroneous

...otions on government, and sustain their rulers in a very unwise and disastrous policy, without necessarily impeaching their Catholic faith or piety. To be a good Catholic and save his soul, it is not necessary that a man should be a wise and profound statesman.

The Protestant movement, directed chiefly against the Papacy, and involving as it did a hundred years of so-called religious wars, gave the princes who took the side of the Church an opportunity, of which they were not slow to avail themselves, to extend and consolidate their power over their Catholic subjects, and to establish in their dominions monarchical absolutism, or what I choose to call modern Cæsarism. They extended, under plea of serving religion, their power over matters which had hitherto either been left free or subjected only to the jurisdiction of the spiritual authority. They were defenders of the faith against armed heretics, and to restrict their power, they pretended, would be to embarrass them in their defence of the Church. A habit of depending on them as the external defenders of religion and her altars, the freedom of conscience, and Catholic civilization itself, was generated; the king took the place in the thoughts and affections of the people due to the Sovereign Pontiff, and by giving the direction to the schools and universities in all things not absolutely of faith, they gradually became the lords of men's minds as well as bodies. In France, Spain, Portugal, and a large part of Italy, all through the seventeenth century, the youth were trained in the maxim, The Prince is the state, and his pleasure is law. Bossuet, in his politics, did only faithfully express the political sentiments and convictions of his age, shared by the great body of Catholics as well as of non-Catholics. Rational liberty had few defenders, and they were exiled, like Fénelon, from the court. The politics of Philip II. of Spain, of Richelieu, Mazarin, and Louis XIV. in France, which were the politics of Catholic Europe, hardly opposed except by the Popes, through the greater part of the sixteenth and the whole of the seventeenth century, tended directly to enslave the people, and to restrict the freedom and efficiency of the Church. Had either Philip, or after him Louis, succeeded, by linking the Catholic cause to his personal ambition, in realizing his dream of universal monarchy, Europe would most likely have been plunged into a political and social condition as unenviable as that into which old Asia has been plunged for these four hundred years; and it may well be believed that it was Providence that raised and directed the tempest that scattered the Grand Armada, and that gave victory to the arms of Eugene and Marlborough.

Trained under despotic influences, by the skilful hand of despotism, extending to all matters not absolutely of the sanctuary, and sometimes daring with sacrilegious foot to invade the sanctuary itself, the people were gradually formed, interiorly as well as exteriorly, to the purposes of the despot. They grew up with the habits and beliefs which Cæsarism, when not resisted, is sure to generate. The clergy sympathizing, as is the case with every national clergy, with the sentiments of their age and nation in all not strictly of faith, had little disposition to labor to keep alive the spirit of freedom in the heart of the people, and would not have been permitted to do it, even if they had been so disposed. Schools were sustained, but, affected by the prevailing despotism, education declined, free thought was prohibited, and it is hard to find a literature tamer, less original, and living than that of Catholic Europe all through the eighteenth century, down almost to our own times.

As the Catholic religion was professedly patronized by the sovereigns, the Church, in superficial minds, seemed to sanction the prevailing Cæsarism. The clergy, because they preached peace, and sought to fulfil their mission without disturbing the state, came, for the first time in history, to be regarded as the chief supporters of the despot. They who retained some reminiscences of the liberties once enjoyed by Catholic Europe, and the noble principles of freedom asserted in the Middle Ages by the monks in their cells, and the most eminent doctors of the Church from their chairs, became alienated from Catholicity, in proportion as they cherished the spirit of resistance, and unhappily imbibed the fatal conviction that, to overthrow the absolute throne, they must break down the altar. Rightly interpreted, the old French Revolution, although bitterly anti-Catholic and infidel, was not so much hatred of religion and impatience of her salutary restraints,

as tne indignant uprising of a misgoverned people
against a civil despotism that affected injuriously all
orders, ranks, and conditions of society. The
sovereigns had taken good care that an attack on
them should involve an attack on religion, and
to have it deeply impressed on their subjects that
resistance to them was rebellion against God. The
priest who should have labored publicly to correct
the issue made up by the sovereigns in accord with
unbelievers, would have promoted sedition, and done
more harm than good; besides, he would have been at
once reduced to silence, in some one of the many
ways despotism has usually at its command.

The horrors of the French Revolution; the universal breaking up of society it involved; the perse-
cution of the Church and of her clergy and her religious it shamelessly introduced in the name of
liberty; the ruthless war it waged upon religion, virtue, all that wise and good men hold sacred, not un-
naturally, to say the least, tended to create in the
minds of the clergy and the people who remained
firm in their faith, and justly regarded religion as
the first want of man and society, a deeper distrust
of the praticability of liberty, and a deeper horror
of all movements attempted in its name. This,
again, as naturally tended to alienate the party
clamoring for political and social reform still more
from Catholicity; which in its turn has reacted with
new force on the Catholic party, and made them still
more determined in their anti-Liberal convictions
and efforts. These tendencies on both sides have

been aggravated by the recent European revolutions and repressions, till now almost everywhere the lines are well defined, and the so-called Liberals are, almost to a man, bitterly anti-Catholic, and the sovereigns seem to have succeeded in forcing the issue: The Church and Cæsarism, or Liberty and Infidelity.

Certainly, as religion is of the highest necessity to man and society, infinitely more important than political freedom and social well-being, I am unable to conceive how the Catholic party, under the circumstances, could well have acted differently. Their error was in their want of vigilance and sagacity in the beginning, in suffering the political Cæsarism to revive and consolidate itself in the state, or the sovereigns in the outset to force upon the Catholic world so false an issue, or to place them in so unnatural and so embarrassing a position. How they will extricate themselves in the Old World from that position, I am unable to foresee, for every movement on either side only makes the matter worse. Yet the internal peace and tranquillity of Catholic states cannot be restored, and the Liberals brought back to the Church in any human way that I can see, unless the Catholic party abate something of their opposition, exert themselves to change the issue the sovereigns have forced upon them, and take themselves the lead in introducing, in a legal and orderly way, such changes in the present political order as will give the body of the nation an effective voice in the management of public affairs. Rebellions, when they break out, must of course be put down; but, at the same time, every effort should be made to disconnect religion from the cause of despotism, and to remove every legitimate source of discontent. All attempts to remedy the existing evil by decrying liberty, by sneers or elaborate essays against parliamentary governments and their advocates, by permanently strengthening the hands of power, by muzzling the press, abridging the freedom of thought and speech, or by resorting to a merely repressive policy, which silences without convincing, and irritates without healing, are short-sighted and unstatesmanlike. They can at best be only momentary palliatives which leave the disease, uneradicated, to spread in the system, and to break out anew with increased virulence and force. The truth is, the Catholic party, yielding to the sovereigns, lost to some extent, for the eighteenth century, the control of the mind of the age, and failed to lead its intelligence. They must now recover their rightful leadership, and be first and foremost in every department of human thought and activity; and to be so, they must yield in matters not of faith, not essential to sound doctrine, or to the free and full operation of the Church in all her native rights, integrity, and force; but, in political and social matters subjected to human prudence, they must, I say, yield something to the changes and demands of the times.

That the struggles in Europe have an influence on Catholic thought in this country is very true, and sometimes an unfavorable influence, cannot be denied.

A portion of our foreign-born Catholics, subjected at home to the restraints imposed by despotism, feel on coming here that they are loosed from all restraints, and forgetting the obedience they owe to their pastors, to the prelates whom the Holy Ghost has placed over them, become insurbordinate, and live more as Protestants than as Catholics; another portion, deeply alarmed at the revolutionary spirit and the evils that it has produced in the Old World, distrust the independence and personal dignity the American always preserves in the presence of authority, and are half disposed to look upon every American as a rebel at heart, if not an unbeliever. They do not precisely understand the American dis . position that bows to the law, but never to persons, and is always careful to distinguish between the man and the office; and they are disposed to look upon it as incompatible with the true principle of obedience demanded by the Gospel. But I think these and their conservative brethren in Europe mistake the real American character. There is not in Christendom a more loyal or a more law-abiding people than the genuine people of the United States. I think European Catholics of the conservative party have an unfounded suspicion of our loyalty, for I think it a higher and truer loyalty than that which they seem to inculcate. I have wholly mistaken the spirit of the Church, if an enlightened obedience, —an obedience that knows wherefore it obeys, and is yielded from principle, from conviction, from free will, and from a sense of obligation, is not more grateful to her maternal heart than the blind, unreasoning, and cringing submission of those who are strangers to freedom. Servile fear does not rank very high with Catholic theologians ; and the Church seeks to govern men as freemen, as Almighty God governs them, that is, in accordance with the nature with which he has created them, as beings endowed with reason and free-will. God adapts his government to our rational and voluntary faculties, and governs us without violence to either, and by really satisfying both. The Church does the same, and resorts to coercive measures only to repress disorders in the public body. Hence our ecclesiastical rulers are called shepherds, not lords, and shepherds of their Master's flock, not of their own, and are to feed, tend, protect the flock, and take care of its increase for him, with sole reference to his will, and his honor and glory. We must love and reverence them for his sake, for the great trust he has confided to them, not for their own sakes, as if they owned the flock, and governed it in their own name and right, for their own pleasure and profit. This idea of power whether in Church or State, as a delegated power or trust, is inseparable from the American mind; and hence the American feels always in its presence his native equality as a man, and asserts, even in the most perfect and entire submission, his own personal independence and dignity, knowing that he bows only to the law or to the will of a common Master. His submission he yields, because he knows that it is due, but without servility or pusillanimity.

But though I entertain these views of what have been for a long time the policy of so-called Catholic governments, and, so to speak, the politics of European Catholics, I find in them nothing that reflects on the truth or efficiency of the Church; for she has no responsibility in the matter, since, as I have said, she governs men, discharges her mission with a scrupulous regard to the free-will of individuals and the autonomy of states. She proffers to all every assistance necessary for the attainment of the most heroic sanctity, but she forces no man to accept that assistance. In her view, men owe all they have and are to God, but they are neither slaves nor machines.

In speaking of Catholic nations and comparing them with the Catholic standard, I find, I confess, much to regret, to deplore, and even to blame; but in comparing them with non-Catholic nations, the case is quite different, and I cannot concede that the Catholic population of any country is inferior to any Protestant population, even in those very qualities in respect to which Catholics are usually supposed to be the most deficient. In no Catholic population will you find the flunkyism which Carlyle so unmercifully ridicules in the middling classes of Great Britain; or that respect to mere wealth, that worship of the money-bag, or that base servility to the mob or to public opinion, so common and so ruinous to public and private virtue in the United States. I do not claim any very high merit for our Catholic press—it lacks, with some exceptions, dignity, grasp of thought, and breadth of view, and seems intended for an unlettered community ; but it has an earnestness, a sincerity, a freedom, an independence, which will be looked for in vain in our non-Catholic press, whether religious or secular. The Catholic population of this country, too, taken as a body, have a personal freedom, an independence, a self-respect, a conscientiousness, a love of truth, and a devotion to principle, not to be found in any other class of American citizens. Their moral tone, as well as their moral standard, is higher, and they act more uniformly under a sense of deep responsibility to God and to their country. Owing to various circumstances as well as national peculiarities, a certain number of them fall easily under the influence of demagogues ; but as a body, they are far less demagogical, and far less under the influence of demagogues, than are non-Catholic Americans. He who knows both classes equally well, will not pretend to the contrary. The Catholics of this country, by no means a fair average of the Catholic populations of old Catholic countries, do, as to the great majority, act from honest principle, from sincere and earnest conviction, and are prepared to die sooner than, in any grave matters, swerve from what they regard as truth and justice. They have the principle and the firmness to stand by what they believe true and just, in good report and evil report, whether the world be with them or be against them. They can, also, be convinced by arguments addressed to their reason, and moved by appeals to conscience, to the 'ear of God, and the love of justice. The non-Catholic has no conception of the treasure the Union possesses in these two or three millions of Catholics, humble in their outward circumstances as the majority of them are. I have never shown any disposition to palliate or disguise their faults; but, knowing them and my non-Catholic countrymen as I do, I am willing to risk the assertion that, with all their faults and shortcomings, they are the salt of the American community, and the really conservative element in the American population.

I have found valid, after thirteen years of experience, none of those objections to entering the Catholic communion which I enumerated in a previous chapter, and which made me for a time hesitate to follow the convictions of my own understanding. To err is human, and I do not pretend that I have found Catholics in matters of human prudence, in what belongs to them and not the Church, all that I could wish. I have found much I do not like, much I do not believe reasonable or prudent; but it is all easily explained without any reflection on the truth or efficiency of the Church, or the general wisdom and prudence of her prelates and clergy. Undoubtedly our Catholic population, made up in great part of emigrants from every nation of Europe, with every variety of national temper, character, taste, habit, and usage, not yet moulded, save in religion, into one homogeneous body, may present features more or less repulsive to the American wedded to his own peculiar nationality, and but recently converted to the Catholic faith; but the very readiness with which these heterogeneous elements amalgamate, and the rapidity with which the Catholic body assumes a common character, falls into the current of American life, and takes, in all not adverse to religion, the tone and features of the country, proves the force of Catholicity, and its vast importance in forming a true and noble national character, and in generating and sustaining a true, generous, and lofty patriotism. In a few years they will be the Americans of the Americans, and on them will rest the performance of the glorious work of sustaining American civilization, and realizing the hopes of the founders of our great and growing Republic.

Such are the views, feelings, convictions, and hopes of the Convert. But he would be unjust to himself and to his religion, if he did not say that, not for these reasons, or any like them, is he a Catholic. He loves his country, loves her institutions, he loves her freedom, but he is a Catholic, because he believes the Catholic Church the Church of God, because he believes her the medium through which God dispenses his grace to man, and through which alone we can hope for heaven. He is a Catholic, because he would believe, love, possess, and obey the truth; because he would know and do God's will; because he would escape hell and gain heaven. Considerations drawn from this world are of minor importance, for man's home is not here, his bliss is not here, his reward is not here, he is made for God, for endless beatitude with him, hereafter;

and, let him turn as he will, his supreme good, as well as duty, lies in seeking "the kingdom of God and his justice." That the Church serves the cause of patriotism; that, if embraced, it is sure to give us a high-toned and chivalric national character; that it enlists conscience in the support of our free institutions and the preservation of our republican freedom as the established order of the country, is a good reason why the American people should not oppose her, and why they should wish her growth and prosperity in our country; but the real reason why we should become Catholics and remain such, is, because she is the new creation, regenerated Humanity, and without communion with her, we can never see God as he is, or become united to him as our Supreme Good in the supernatural order.

FINIS.